British Light Dragoon

Book 3 in the Napoleonic Horseman Series
By
Griff Hosker

Published by Sword Books Ltd 2014
Copyright © Griff Hosker First Edition

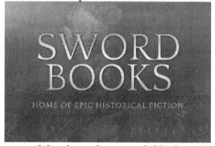

A CIP catalogue record for this title is available from the British Library.
The cover courtesy of Wikipedia – published before 1923 and public domain in
the US

CONVERSATION across the WATER

Maps courtesy of Wikipedia (William Robert Shepherd) *This image (or other media file) is in the* **public domain** *because its copyright has* **expired**. *This applies to Australia, the European Union and those countries with a copyright term of* **life of the author plus 70 years**.

Chapter 1

The road to Canterbury
December 1802

My name is Robbie Macgregor and I am a wanted man both in England and in France. I dare say that I cannot return to Egypt either. I fled the French Army after I killed an officer in a duel and I am wanted in London for the deaths of some cutpurses. I do not regret any of the deaths; all of the men I killed deserved to die. All of them were trying to kill me. I regret the effect the deaths had on my life. I was forced to change my name to Matthews to avoid detection and capture and I had to change my appearance. The moustache I had grown as a chasseur and my pigtails had had to go. That was the most inconsequential of the effects. I would now, however, be constantly looking over my shoulder and I would be able to trust no one. My new master, for I was, in all but name a slave, was Colonel Selkirk. He worked in a shady area of the War Department and I was to be his spy in France. Of course, I had to be an officer in a cavalry regiment as well. Colonel Selkirk was a Scotsman and liked to get value for money. The fact that I was born, illegitimately of a French aristocrat and a Scottish lady meant I was fluent in both languages. I had even learned to speak Italian quite well and I could understand some German. All of these would aid me in my life as a spy. He was building on the experiences I had when working for Napoleon Bonaparte. He was now Consul of France; the ruler in all but name.

Colonel Selkirk had obtained for me a captaincy in the 11th Light Dragoons. It had been his brother's commission so I suspect he had not lost any money. I had been a captain in the 17th Chasseur a Cheval when I served Napoleon Bonaparte. He was the main reason I was in England. His cold-blooded attitude had caused the death of almost all of my friends and comrades when we had served with him in Egypt. Now that he was running France I felt that I owed it to my dead father, who had been an aristocrat guillotined in Paris, to fight Napoleon until France was returned to its people.

I did have family. The Alpini family who lived in Sicily were my distant cousins and they had taken me in when I had landed on their shores after fleeing Egypt. I had a home there should I want it. Ironically the island was under the rule of Bonaparte too, which gave me another reason to hate him. The family had helped to make me well off. I had money in a bank in London and shares in a ship which brought the Alpini goods to London. The money meant nothing and could not make my life better. It enabled me to buy objects which made my life bearable.

As I rode along the road to Canterbury, where my new regiment was based, I felt lonelier than when my mother died and I was left alone in the world. All my friends from that time, Jean, Albert, Tiny, Charles and Jean-Michael were all dead. Only the crippled, irascible Pierre still lived close to where I had been brought up in France. Nor was I looking forward to joining this new regiment. I had been happy in the 17th Chasseurs. I had risen through the ranks from trooper to captain. I knew all the men and felt safe. I would know no-one in the 11th. Colonel Selkirk had explained to me that the British Army did not work the same way as in France. In England, the officers were all from wealthy backgrounds and shared similar education. I did not think I would fit in. I was just grateful that, now that we were at peace, the officers were on half-pay and the majority would not be in the barracks. I could find my feet and then leave for the mission Colonel Selkirk had planned for me. I had two months of army life to endure and then I would return to my homeland, this time as a spy.

I had known nothing but a life in the army for the last nine or ten years. The difference was that when I had been a soldier in France I had been amongst friends. Now I would be amongst, not only strangers but the same men I had fought in the Low Countries when I was a young trooper. I had never known a peaceful life in a barracks and I was not sure I would enjoy the tedium. During the quiet times in the 17th, Napoleon Bonaparte had used me and my friends as his tools. We had travelled in Italy to spy for him and to Austria to guard his envoy. We had even scouted out Malta before that island had been captured. I was used to an active life and the next couple of months promised me nothing.

I have never been one to dwell on misfortune and I decided to make the best of my new life. I was alive unlike most of the people I had served with.

The day was pleasantly cold yet dry and my horse, Badger, enjoyed the opportunity to ride beyond the confines of Hyde Park. I had sent my trunk with my uniforms and weapons, by cart, to the barracks directly. It would not arrive until the following day and so I had decided to find an inn close to the barracks and enjoy a night there. One advantage of having a little money was that I could afford one or two luxuries. I had slept in enough fields to appreciate a good bed and a cooked meal.

I saw a sign telling me that Canterbury was only two miles away and I spied a small village. I reined in outside the 'George and Dragon'. It was a typical Kentish inn. I could see that coaches used it as it had an inner courtyard. That usually meant better food but, more importantly, a good stable for my horse. The ostler came running out when he heard Badger's hooves clattering on the cobbles.

Badger began to drink greedily from the horse trough and the grey-haired and a rather thin man said, "Yes sir?"

"I need a room for the night and a stall for my horse."

He grinned cheerfully as he nuzzled Badger's nose. "We have both, sir. If you would like to come with me."

I dismounted and he led me through the gate into the courtyard. The stables were ahead of me. "Do you mind if I see where you put Badger?"

"Of course not sir." He gave me a curious look. "You are a horseman then."

It was a statement and not a question. "Let us say I appreciate a good horse and I wish mine to be as comfortable as I hope to be."

He seemed satisfied, "I wish more young gentlemen were like you. I love horses, sir but the condition of some of the mounts who come in here." He shook his grey head in wonder. "Their sides are scored with the rowel marks of spurs and they are lathered to the point of exhaustion." He took off my saddlebags and laid them on the ground and then began to take off Badger's saddle. "You wonder why they joined the cavalry at all."

"Do you get many young men like that? I would have thought this quiet inn just had the carriage trade from London."

He put a nose bag on Badger and hefted my bags on his shoulder. "Aye, sir. There is a barracks just a mile away from here and they like to come here at night. Thank the lord there is peace at the moment and many of them are still on leave. It fair upsets me to see horses mistreated like that. Still, the master likes the money they bring."

I could understand that. Times were hard and a man had to earn his crust any way that he could.

I ducked beneath the low lintel and we entered the inn. "Customer, Master Popwell."

The inn had a roaring and welcoming fire blazing away. The room was empty allowing me to get a better view of the interior. The tables and chairs were rough and simple and showed the evidence of much wear. I had learned, in my time in England, that this would be what they called the bar area. This was where the ordinary folk would eat and drink. I looked around and saw there were rooms leading off. These would be the private areas used by those with more money, power and status. I looked at my fine clothes and knew that the landlord would treat me and charge me accordingly. I would be paying the highest rate but I would get good service.

The owner popped his head up from behind the long oak bar. Mr Popwell was a rotund and cheerful fellow. He was not a tall man and only came up to my chest. He reminded me of one of those children's toys which always right themselves whenever they are knocked over. He had a clay pipe sticking out of his mouth. I learned that he rarely took it out, save to refill it.

"Good afternoon sir. A room?"

"Yes please, just for the night and stabling for my horse."

He looked up at the ceiling as though that was where the list of empty rooms was written. "Just take the gentleman's bags up to room two, Harry."

The ostler knuckled his head, "Yes sir."

"Here Harry," I slipped Harry a sixpence.

He seemed genuinely surprised and delighted. "Thank you, sir."

Mr Popwell's cheerful face darkened. "It doesn't do to tip them, sir. It gives them ideas above their station." I shook my head. It was worse than the days in France before the Revolution. Even this little innkeeper wanted to look down on another. He took out a ledger, "And your name sir?"

"Matthews, from London."

He carefully wrote it out and asked, "Will you sign, sir?"

I suddenly realised this would be the first time I would be signing my new name and it felt strange. I would have to get used to this.

That done he looked up and said, "We have fine food here sir. Mrs Popwell is a good cook. Will you eat now or later?"

"I think I will clean up first."

"Good. I will keep you a table."

I was surprised; I had seen no other horses. "Why, will it be busy?"

"It depends how many of the young men from the barracks come but don't you worry sir. You shall have a table and a comfortable one at that."

The bedroom was simple but comfortable. I smiled to myself. I had slept in the royal residences of Austria. I couldn't expect that now that I was merely Captain Matthews of the 11th Light Dragoons. I had no military clothes with me and only my stiletto as a weapon. I had acquired the blade when attacked by bandits in Italy and it had served me well in the years since. My four pistols and my Austrian sword were all in my trunks. Colonel Selkirk had made it quite clear that I had to be as anonymous as possible.

At our last meeting, in Whitehall, he had wagged his finger at me. "Do not speak French or Italian. Remember the British Army is not the French one. We do things differently. They will expect you to be raw and not know what to do." He had ruefully laughed, "The British Army is led by amateurs who think they are on a fox hunt."

I had much to learn I knew that. I changed out of my riding clothes and gave myself a body wash using the bowl of cold water which was on the dresser. I like horses but their smell tended to linger longer than one would like. I had good civilian clothes; a fine silk shirt and tailored trousers, waistcoat and jacket. When I crossed to France in two months I would need to be taken for a gentleman. After I had shaved I dressed myself. I looked in the mirror. I missed the pigtails and queue I had had as a chasseur but I knew that they marked me out as a Frenchman and a French horseman at that. Colonel Selkirk had also made me shave off my moustache. It was hard to see it go it had taken years to achieve the effect I desired. I remember how my friend Pierre had brought me oils and waxes from Paris to make me look dashing but the English did not trust men with moustaches; at least not in the regiment, I would be joining. It had changed my appearance radically and I was not sure that anyone would recognise me. Certainly, my clothes now matched my station as an officer and a gentleman.

When I was quite ready I descended the stairs. At the bottom, I turned left to go to the stables. I would see that Badger was happy in his new environment. There were four new horses there and Harry shook his head, "Do you see what I mean, Mr Matthews?"He pointed at the lathered horses which stood forlornly sweating and shaking in their stalls contrasting sharply with the calm and sleek Badger. "And they have only ridden a couple of miles. How can you get a horse in that condition after such a short ride?" he shook his head, "And they call themselves cavalrymen! Wouldn't have happened in my time."

"Soldiers from the barracks?"

"Yes, sir." He pointed to the number shaved into the rump, 11th; my new regiment. He patted Badger. "This is a good 'un though sir. How big is he?"

"Almost sixteen hands."

He nodded approvingly, "He'll keep going all day if you ride him steady." He pointed to the other horses all of which looked to be about fourteen and a half hands. "They couldn't handle a horse like this one." He saw me stroking Badger's nose. "Don't worry sir, I sleep above the stalls. I'll keep my eye on him."

"Thank you Harry." I paused, "Were you in the cavalry?"

He stood proudly, "Yes sir. The 14th Light Dragoons. They were a fine regiment."

As I left him I reflected that he was, at least, able to continue his life in the world of horses. There were many old soldiers who were crippled and discarded after a lifetime serving their country.

I heard the noise and smelled the smoke as soon as I walked into the inn proper. It was as though a flock of seagulls had landed; a cacophony of noise and smells assaulted both my ears and my nose. It was in marked contrast to the serenely peaceful place I left a couple of hours earlier. There was barely enough space to move through. The bar area looked to be filled with the troopers of my new regiment. They were all dressed in their overalls with forage caps. They seemed a lively and raucous group of men save for one solitary figure who appeared to be trying to disappear into the bar. Had he been in France I would have marked him as a spy trying to remain unobserved. He was an unhappy-looking trooper and he was squeezed between a wall and the bar. His comrades did not appear to even notice him.

Mr Popwell was busy serving a couple of soldiers and so I stood to watch these men with whom I would soon be serving. There were none above the rank of corporal which I found interesting. One of the corporals looked like a huge brute of a man and he was very loud. It was obvious to me that some of the men were afraid of him; I recognised the looks that they shared. It was one of fear. This man-made them cower. I had seen his type before. The other corporal looked oblivious to it all and smoked his pipe whilst watching the flickering flames of the fire.

I heard Mr Popwell shout, above the noise, "Be with you in a moment, Mr Matthews. Sorry about the delay."

I waved an airy hand to show I was not concerned. My movement attracted the attention of the soldiers but they soon forgot me when they saw that I was not wearing a uniform. The loud corporal, however, had noticed the soldier at the bar.

"If it isn't butter fingered Sharp! Hey landlord, you had better watch out; that dozy bugger drops everything. He'll break all your tankards."

The rest of the men dutifully laughed but the other corporal said, "Leave him alone Jem, he looks miserable enough as it is."

The loud corporal became angry quite suddenly and he stood. "Well if he was a better soldier we wouldn't have had to clean out the stables for Mr DeVere so he will have to take it for a while longer eh?" He approached the man called Sharp. "Drink up and then sod off!"

The man looked thoroughly miserable and complied. He swallowed the beer quickly. I had always hated bullies and I stepped close to the corporal and said quietly, "Why don't you leave the man alone and let him enjoy his drink in peace?"

The young trooper gave a frightened little smile, "It's all right sir; I had finished anyway."

The corporal saw another target and he turned aggressively to me, "What's it got to do with you, Mr Fancy Pants?" His breath reeked of beer and tobacco whilst his personal odour left much to be desired. He stood as close to me as he could get without actually touching me. I had seen this tactic before and it did not worry me. I was almost a head taller than the corporal and I stood my ground.

"I hate bullies and you, Corporal, are a bully."

His eyes widened and he reddened, "I have a good mind to…"

Suddenly Mr Popwell appeared next to me. "Sit down or get out. Do not abuse my customers Jem Green."

Despite his portly frame, the landlord must have handled people like Corporal Green before. The corporal suddenly smiled but there was no smile in his eyes. "Of course, anything for a peaceful life. Besides the useless bugger has left. He's a coward as well." He gave an ironic bow, "Enjoy your meal eh?"

I saw that Trooper Sharp had left. Mr Popwell took my arm, "Sorry about that, sir. I have your dining room all ready."

He took me to one of the chambers off the main room. It was the second one along. In the first one we passed, a much larger room, I could see four officers from the 11th in their undress uniforms; their cocked hats stacked untidily behind them. They glanced in my direction and then went back to their drinking and gambling. My dining chamber only seated two people. It had a curtain which could be drawn across the entrance which indicated to me that it would be the perfect place for a romantic tryst.

The landlord smiled apologetically, "A little cramped I know but I didn't know this lot would be in. It's a good job we have had no coaches today." His eyes went heavenward. "It brings in money but the regulars stay away when this lot are in."

I nodded to the room on my left. "Why don't you have a word with their officers?"

"They are just as bad. I normally have young girls waiting on the tables but they refuse to work when these are in. It will be just me and the missus tonight." He must have thought I was worried about the service for he added, quickly, "Oh don't worry sir, I won't neglect you."

"I am not worried. Just bring me a bottle of wine and whatever you think will be good tonight."

"The wife has made a nice beef and oyster pie but the wine won't be the best sir. Since the trade with France was stopped we don't get much in."

I suddenly had a thought, "Have you thought about buying Italian wine?"

"Italian? I can't say that I have ever tried it." His face and voice showed his surprise.

"I have contacts in Sicily. I'll tell you what I will do for you, next time I am in London I will have a bottle or two sent to you to try."

He looked genuinely surprised. "That is most kind of you, sir." He sniffed and added loudly, "It's good to have a real gentleman in here for a change."

He was right about the wine. I had used better wine as vinegar on my food but the steak and oyster pie more than made up for it. I was able to listen to the conversation in the next room. From it, I discerned that Colonel Fenton and Major Hyde-Smith were not in the barracks and it was being run by the senior captain. The other three officers appeared to be sycophantic lieutenants. None of them could hold their liquor and they became rowdier and rowdier.

I was about to leave when one of them burst through the curtain and then giggled, "Oh sorry, wrong room." He slipped a little and when he righted himself, said, "Good job you didn't have a doxy in here eh what?"

I helped him to his feet and, as he staggered back into his room, I stood to leave. The minute I stepped into the bar area I saw every eye was on me. Even the quiet corporal with the pipe watched me. I suspect I had been the subject of their conversation. I smiled and nodded in their direction. One or two smiled back but the loud corporal gave me a surly stare. He was in for a shock in the morning.

The bar itself was empty and I approached Mr and Mrs Popwell who were standing behind it. "The pie was delicious. I have not eaten so well in a long time."

Mrs Popwell positively glowed and I saw the appreciative nod from her husband. "Sorry about the wine sir."

I gave a dismissive wave of my hand, "Don't worry about that and when you have tasted the Italian wine from my family's estate, you will know what a good wine tastes like. I will retire now."

"Goodnight sir. And I'll get them to keep the noise down."

I shook my head. I knew how belligerent some drunks became. "I can sleep through anything. Pray, don't bother yourself on my account."

As I walked up the stairs I heard Mrs Popwell say to her husband, "Estates in Italy! That's the kind of customer we want. Not these noisy soldiers."

Chapter 2

It was fortunate that I was a sound sleeper for when I went to pay my bill the following morning Mr Popwell was most upset. "I am sorry Mr Matthews. I tried to keep them quiet but they were all drunk…"

I held my hand up. "They did not wake me, sir. Rest easy." I smiled as I handed over the coins. "Hopefully it will be quieter from now on."

He shook his head, sadly. "Not until the war begins again. Do you think it is mean spirited of me to wish for war again so that we can have a peaceful life once more?"

"No, Mr Popwell, but you should expect more from these soldiers. After all, they are paid for by the likes of you and the other taxpayers."

The thought had obviously not crossed his mind. He brightened. "Yes, I shall remember that. Thank you, Mr Matthews, and if you are ever travelling in this part of the world again…"

"I shall be sure to stay here."

Harry was happy with the tip and he had obviously spoiled Badger. His coat gleamed. He had been curried and combed. His tail had been trimmed and his hooves given a polish and blacked. Harry seemed embarrassed by my thanks. "It was a privilege, sir. A fine horse and a fine gentleman."

My mood, as I headed towards the barracks, was much better than it had been the previous day. I had met some good people and been treated well. I had put the thoughts of the troopers and the officers behind me. Once I donned my uniform then I would deal with them in my own way.

When I reached the guardhouse I was given a bored look by the troopers on duty. I could see that to them I was just another smartly dressed gentleman. I had, in my pocket, the letter from Colonel Sinclair as well as my orders. I would be damned if I would show them to two troopers and so I dismounted and walked up to them.

"Can we help you, sir?"

"You lost?"

As I walked up to their small hut I noticed, with some irritation, my trunks. They had been left there. My name and rank were clearly marked for all to see. "I am Captain Matthews and I have been given a commission in the 11th Light Dragoons." Although they did not salute, after all, I was not in uniform, they did at least stand to attention. "Those are my trunks behind you."

They both exchanged a guilty look and said, hurriedly, "Captain DeVere, he was duty officer, he said he had never heard of you sir, so we was to leave them there."

There was just the hint of a smirk on the man's face. I would remember these two. "And where is Captain DeVere now?"

"He's gone up to London for a few days."

This got better and better. "Very well. One of you, take me to the regimental office. I will send someone for my bags." They looked as though they were going to object until I said quietly but with plenty of threat in my tone, "It would not do to annoy me, gentlemen, would it?"

They shrugged and one of them said, "Follow me, sir." The sir was forced from his lips. I suppose it was my fault. I should have arrived in uniform. I was now pleased I had not worn it; it had given me an insight into the way the regiment was run.

The sentry at the door gave me a curious look until my escort said, "New officer, Captain Matthews." His job done he gave a curt bob with his head and trotted back across the square.

The sentry knocked on the door and then opened it. "Lieutenant Wolfe is the duty officer sir; the last office on the left."

I noticed another office on the left and it was ajar. I tapped on it and a voice roared, "Come!"

I peered in and saw the Regimental Sergeant Major. I almost spoke in French for he was the double of my old friend Albert who had also been a Sergeant Major. He gave me a look which suggested I had better have a good reason for intruding. "Can I help you?"

"I'm sorry Sergeant Major; I am the new officer, Captain Matthews."

He gave, what I suppose passed for a smile and said, "Ah yes sir, 7th Troop, D Squadron. They'll need a firm hand. I hope you have one." He hesitated. "Sorry if I have offended you, sir."

He was testing me and my mettle to see if he could intimidate me. "No offence taken, Sergeant Major. Give me a month and then we'll have a little talk eh?"

He smiled, "Yes sir."

I knocked on the door of the last office and a drawling voice said, "Come!"

It was the giggling officer from the previous night. He looked a little worse for wear. I did not give him the chance to take the initiative. I took out my orders. "Captain Matthews reporting, as ordered."

I could see his confusion. He hurriedly fastened his buttons and then opened the orders. "Er, Captain DeVere should be here but…"

"But he has gone to London and left you in charge, lieutenant."

"Er, yes."

I narrowed my eyes. If this was the Chasseurs I would have ignored the breach of discipline but I knew I had to establish myself quickly."Yes, sir."

"Sorry sir, yes sir. Er, you are to be in command of 7th Troop, D Squadron. "

"And what are they like lieutenant?"

"Oh, they are a good bunch of troopers. You'll like them."

I was pleased I had spoken with the Sergeant Major. Lieutenant Wolfe was a liar. Good, it confirmed my opinion of him. My trunks are in the guard post. If you could direct me to my quarters and arrange for my trunk…"

I got no further. There was a knock on the partly opened door and the Sergeant Major was there. "Begging your pardon sir but I took the liberty of having your trunks sent over. If you like I will take you to your rooms."

"Thank you very much, Sergeant Major…?"

"Jones, sir, Jack Jones."

As we walked across the square he gestured to Badger. "Your horse sir?"

"Yes Sergeant Major."

"A fine animal. I can see he is looked after and I bet he takes some riding."

I smiled, "He is a spirited beast but we understand each other."

He glanced at the way I walked. "You march like a soldier sir. Have you served before?"

I smiled benignly, "I have never served in a regiment of Light Dragoons. I am looking forward to it."

"I can see you are going to be an interesting officer sir." He directed me down a small alley between two buildings. "Do you mind me asking sir, where is your servant?"

For the first time that day I was taken aback. "My servant? I don't have one why?"

He smiled, "Well that shows you have never been in a cavalry regiment anyway, sir. All of the officers have their own servant. They normally serve in the troop but look after the officer."

"I see. Well, I don't have one."

"Not a problem sir. We will find a trooper for you."

"Do you mind if I find my own trooper, Sergeant Major?"

"Of course not sir. If you are as good a judge of men as horseflesh he will be a good one. Here we are, sir."

The officer's quarters were much grander than those in the French Army. I had two rooms complete with a wardrobe. There were two troopers unpacking my things. The Sergeant Major looked curiously at my weapons. He gestured to the sword. "Do you mind sir?"

"Be my guest. I will just change into my uniform." I grinned at him impishly, "Feel free to examine all the weapons."

When I came out the two troopers had finished and all my clothes were either hung up or in the drawers. The Sergeant Major lifted the sword as I came in. "This is a magnificent weapon, sir. Austrian?"

"Yes Sergeant Major. Two of the pistols are French and the other two are British army issue."

"I recognise them. " He looked at me shrewdly. "Something tells me, sir, you have seen a little bit of action." Before I could deny it he held his hands up. "I don't need to know sir but I am happy if you have because, between the two of us, apart from the colonel and the major the officers here are green as grass."

"Let's just say that I can handle those weapons well and ride as well as most men." I smiled, "Although I expect I will have to prove that to some people."

He nodded sagely, "You have been around, sir. If you would like to come with me I'll give you the tour. There aren't many officers at the moment and we have the men working on their sword drills. Very keen on swords is the colonel."

"Do you use musketoons much?"

He frowned, "Never used them, sir. We have carbines but I can't remember anyone actually using them."

I just nodded and said, "I see." I remembered when we had fought the English in the Low Countries. They had an over-reliance on swords even then. I put on my cocked hat; it felt strange.

The Sergeant Major smiled. "If you will allow me, sir." He tilted it and turned it slightly. "That's better."

As we strode to the barracks block I was pleased that there was at least one friendly face. He pointed out various buildings as we went. "The stables are over there. When we meet your troop we will send one to get your horse." He saw a trooper walking along and his top four buttons were undone. "Rawlinson! Fasten up those buttons or you will be shovelling shit for the next week." As the man complied Sergeant Major Jones shook his head. "The lads need some action, sir. All this shilly-shallying around the barracks does no one any good."

That was the difference between the two armies. My Chasseurs would have been quite happy to practise their sword and gun skills. This seemed not to be the case here in England.

We arrived at the practice ground where the troopers were on horseback and waving their swords at each other. This was not practice the way that I understood it. The Sergeant Major seemed to be of the same opinion. "The problem is, sir, that Quartermaster Grant is on compassionate leave. His mother is dying. The other two senior sergeants, White and Dale argue all the time. They just don't get on and the corporals take advantage of them. They need an officer with a firm hand sir. 8th Troop is not nearly half so bad.

They have a young lieutenant, keen as mustard. He will have those lads off somewhere else. He doesn't want them tainted."

We halted to watch them. "I'm sorry Sergeant Major. Am I missing something? Surely there should be two captains and two lieutenants for this squadron."

"There should be sir. You are right but there is just you and two lieutenants."

"Then what about the other lieutenant?"

He looked seriously at me and spoke slowly. "The other lieutenant is the senior captain's brother. Lieutenant DeVere is off with his brother in London and he does not spend a great deal of time with the troop." He spread his arms apologetically. "Sorry, sir. The good news is that the two troops are the smallest in the regiment and you have a full complement of non commissioned officers."

"Actually, Sergeant Major, that is bad news because they should have more discipline if they have more NCO's. In my experience, they can more than make up for a poor officer."

He nodded and then took in the import of my words. He gave me a wry smile. "You'll do sir. And now shall we introduce them to you?"

"If you please."

As we strode across I saw the two sergeants who were arguing. I also saw some of the men from the inn. There was the loud corporal and the quiet corporal. I saw, almost by himself, the young trooper who had been bullied. I was even more pleased that I had stayed in the inn. I now had an insight which even the Sergeant Major could not have given me.

"Attention!! The voice carried across the ground and everyone stopped. "Officer's inspection. Stand by your mounts."

What should have been an easy and slick procedure took forever and looked dreadful. The Sergeant Major shook his head. When the shambles eventually attained some sort of order he roared. "That was the worst drill I have ever seen in my life. This," he pointed to me, "is your new officer, Captain Matthews." He stepped back.

As I stepped forward I saw the expressions on the faces of the men whom I had seen the night before. The loud corporal looked as though he was ready to be sick.

"I agree with the Sergeant Major. That was dreadful. However, I understand that you have not had an officer nor have you had a senior sergeant for some time." I saw the two sergeants look guiltily at each other. "That said we start afresh, this morning."

I walked down the line of troopers. I noticed but did not comment on all the minor infractions of dress and stance. That would come later on. I did, however, notice the poor state of the horses. I stopped next to the young trooper from the bar. He and his horse were perfectly presented. "Well done. You are the only soldier properly turned out and your horse is a credit to you."

He lowered his head in embarrassment and said, "Thank you, sir."

"It's Trooper Sharp isn't it?"

He looked up in surprise as though I was a mind reader. "Yes, sir."

I said nothing but moved on. The loud corporal was two men down and I halted in front of him. He had buttons undone and was not at attention. He had an insolent look on his face and I knew I could have him flogged for that alone. However, it would be a bad start if I flogged the first man who upset me. I had been a sergeant and I knew how to roar when needed. Now was such a time. "Stand to attention, you slovenly excuse for a soldier." I was so

loud that the men nearby started. The result was that every man
stood crisply to attention. "Now do up your buttons." The insolent
look gone he complied. "Now I see that you are a corporal. If that
is the case then it must be so easy to be promoted in this regiment I
am surprised that the troopers don't have to salute horses." A few
of the men dutifully laughed and the corporal's look changed to
one of anger. I could see him clenching his fists. "What is your
name?"

"Corporal James Green, sir!"

"And they call you Jem?"

Light dawned in his eyes as he remembered the previous night.
"Yes, sir."

"Well a word of advice, Corporal, watch how you look at me
and how you speak to me. I take offence easily and I will have the
stripes from your arm and replace them with some on your back.
Clear?"

"Sir."

When I had finished my inspection I returned to the front of the
men. I saw Sergeant Major Jones nodding appreciatively. "This
has not been a good opening, gentlemen. You now know that I
have high standards. You will meet those standards." I stared at the
two senior sergeants. "And that goes for everyone. You all have
one hour to groom your horses and yourselves and then present
yourself back here with sword, carbine and pistols. I will see all of
the sergeants in the troop office now!" They all began to move and
I shouted, "Trooper Sharp, a word if you please."

Sergeant-Major Jones walked over to me and said, "That's a
good start, sir. Anything else I can help you with?"

"Could I have a copy of the standing orders please?"

For the first time he looked surprised, "Certainly but why?"

"I have a feeling that some of the things I want to do might upset some of my colleagues and I would like to know where I stand."

"A sensible idea sir."

"And you had better let me have a regulation sabre. Otherwise, they might think I have an unfair advantage."

"Yes, sir."

Trooper Sharp stood looking a little self-conscious before me holding the reins of his horse. "At ease Sharp. Are you happy in this regiment, Sharp?"

The question appeared to take him by surprise. "I joined sir, because I love horses and my father was a cavalryman." I gave him a sympathetic look to encourage more information. "He died in the colonies."

"I see. And your mother?"

"She died soon after my dad; I think it was a broken heart."

"And you had no brothers and sisters either eh?"

"Can you read minds, sir? Yes, sir."

"How long have you been with the regiment?"

"Just four weeks sir."

"But it seems longer eh?"He nodded miserably. "Well, look, I like the way you look after your horse and I need a trooper to be my servant. How do you feel about that?" He hesitated. "There will be more pay."

"It's not that sir. I get enough stick as it is off the other lads. They would make my life in the barracks hell."

I nodded, "Well the post of officer's servant also moves you out of the barracks and into the servant's quarters."

"At that, his face lit up in a smile. "Then, in that case, I am your man."

"Good. Well, your first task is to bring my horse around from the guardhouse. His name is Badger."

"Sir!"

My mood was lightened already but I knew that I had a depressing meeting looming large. The four sergeants all stood in the office as far apart from each other as it was possible to get. This did not bode well. I sat on the chair and faced them.

I looked at every face and held the stare until each sergeant looked down at the ground. "I realise that Quartermaster Grant is not here and that leaves a void to be filled and, until today you had no officer. However, I cannot understand why you allowed the troop to become the shambles that it is. Have you no pride in the regiment?"

Those words stung them and they stared at me with anger written all over their face. "Good. I can see that I have provoked a reaction at last. Now you don't need to like each other but you have to work together and not against each other. Is that clear?"

One by one they nodded. "I intend to make changes to this troop and squadron. I hope that you will be part of it and that we can be proud of this troop and this regiment."

They all smiled. One of them looked at the others and said, "Sir, permission to speak candidly?"

"Within bounds yes sergeant…?"

"Sergeant Thomas sir. We did try to drill the men but all that Lieutenant DeVere wants to do is have the men charging at each other and fighting."

"Oh, I see."

"Yes sir and that means that the horses get hurt as do the men and they don't practise the skills they need like fencing and riding"

"Thank you sergeant.?"

"Emerson sir, Jacob Emerson."

"Well, that explains much. I am pleased that we have cleared the air. Leave the lieutenant to me. I want all of you to work with your own men. Forget the rest. If each of us works on our own part of this troop then it will be better. I want your corporals to be of the same mind. Who is the sergeant of Corporal Green?"

Sergeant Emerson raised his hand, "Me sir."

"I meant what I said on parade. He either improves or I have his stripes."

"Yes sir but like Sergeant Thomas said the lieutenant plays favourites and the corporal is one of his."

I nodded but refrained from comment. "This afternoon I want to practise moving from column to line and firing carbines. That will entail using horse holders." I saw the looks of horror on their faces. "I take it they have never practised this?"

"No, sir."

"Then we will all learn a most valuable lesson this afternoon. When you reach your men assign the horse holders then. How many troopers do we have?"

"Fifty-six sir. The 8th troop has slightly less."

If they expected me to be disappointed then they were wrong. I was delighted. We would have more control over the men once they were trained. "Excellent. I take it the other troops are largely at full strength?"

"A Squadron is but the rest are a few men short."

The Sergeant Major was correct. My squadron was the dumping ground for the rest of the regiment. I just couldn't work out why Captain DeVere had his brother as the lieutenant in this barrel of poor apples. I would have to discover that later.

When we left the office they were surprised to see Trooper Sharp there with my horse. "He is a magnificent horse, sir. He must be the biggest in the regiment."

I saw the looks on their faces and I said, "Oh sorry, I forgot to say that I have appointed Trooper Sharp as my servant. That doesn't cause anyone a problem does it?"

The relieved looks on their faces told me that I had solved a problem. Would that all the problems I faced could be solved as easily.

Chapter 3

The afternoon went better than I could have hoped. The men did at least try and seven of my non-commissioned officers threw themselves into the spirit of it. Corporal Green was the exception and I decided to give him a week to improve and then he would be demoted with subsequent loss of pay. I was not certain how that worked in the British Army but I was sure that the redoubtable Sergeant Major Jones would know of a way.

"Sharp, when you have looked after Badger, report to my rooms. I would like to show you where everything is and you will need to bring your equipment and uniform to your new room.

The Sergeant Major found me as I headed across. "I hear it went better this afternoon."

"You must have good ears, Sergeant Major."

He smiled, "Nothing gets past me. I put the standing orders and the sabre on your bed sir. I had a word with the other servants. Trooper Sharp should have an easier time of it than he did in the barracks."

We stopped as we were approaching the officer's mess. "You knew then?"

"Yes, sir. As I said there is little that goes on in this regiment that I don't know about. Doing something about it is sometimes above my rank." He shrugged. "Trooper Sharp's dad and I served together. He was my corporal when I was a trooper. He was a good soldier and so is his son. The trouble is young Alan doesn't stand up for himself and he allows the others to put on him. I appreciate what you are doing for the lad sir."

"No, Sergeant Major, I am doing it for me. I need a servant and I need someone who is good with horses. Sharp is both." I suddenly felt nervous. When I had become an officer in France I had known the officers I was joining well. Here I knew no-one. There was nobody to guide me through the protocols and customs. "Are all the officers here tonight?"

I think he knew my worries for he came closer and spoke quietly. "Lieutenant Austen and Lieutenant Hargreaves are good sorts. They keep to themselves. Captain Stafford is a gentleman. Captain Platt is hard to read and keeps himself to himself."

His silence about the other officers was pure eloquence. "Thank you for that. I appreciate it."

"Don't worry sir, when the colonel and the major get back it will improve." He became serious and spoke in a quiet, almost reverential tone. "I heard that Sergeant Grant's mother died yesterday and he will be back within a week. He is the salt of the earth and he will appreciate what you are doing too."

I turned right at the officer's mess to head to my rooms and to change. I didn't know if we changed for dinner or not but better to be overdressed rather than underdressed. As I passed the open window I could hear the raucous banter of the few officers who were still on the post. It would be an ordeal but I would have to deal with it.

The standing orders were mercifully few in number and I put it on the bedside table for a little night reading. The sabre on the bed was the one issued to all troopers. It would suffice. I took off my overalls and began to wash the smell of horse away. There was a tap on the door and Sharp stood there looking nervous. I suspect the sight of me with just my breeches on had alarmed him.

I smiled, "Get used to it, Sharp. You will be seeing much more of me, quite literally." I laughed and was relieved to see him smile.

"Badger's all seen to sir."

I dried myself and said, "Good. Come in. I won't keep you long. I know you need to get yourself squared away too." I pointed to the door. "Just shut the door eh? There's a good fellow." He did so. "Now, I have never had a servant before. I will be finding out what I need you to do for me as I go along."

"Me too sir."

"Good. Now I expect you will lay out my clothes each morning." I pointed to the wardrobe, "They are there. I will use this sabre unless we are in action and then I will use this one." I pointed to my Austrian sword.

"That's a really good blade sir. I'll keep it really sharp for you. Like my dad said '*a blunt sword is about as much good as a lump of iron*'." He suddenly smiled at his own joke. We would get on.

"There are four pistols there. If we are in action then I am happy for you to have one as a spare. I have two on my saddle and one in my belt." He nodded. "Now I would like you to do one thing for me first thing in the morning. I am going to write a letter to go to London. I will do this frequently. As with everything to do with what you learn of me this will be our secret. Understand?"

He suddenly looked serious, "I know sir. It's what Uncle Jimmy told me."

"Uncle Jimmy?"

"Sergeant Major Jones."

"Ah, of course. You will need to take the letters and post them in the town." I smiled at his serious face. "This first one is not so dramatic. I just want a couple of cases of wine."

He looked surprised. "You don't look like a drinker sir."

"I'm not but I assume it will make me more friends amongst the officers and I would like to give a case to Mr Popwell."

Understanding dawned on his face and he said, "Yes sir. You can leave all of this with me. I will not let you down."

After I had dressed I walked back to the officer's mess. I felt as though I was going to the guillotine and I would have done anything but face that sea of faces when I walked through the doors. In the end, it was, as with most things, worse in the expectation rather than the reality.

There were just four officers in the mess when I arrived. The dirty dishes told me the story of the others; they had gone already. They all looked at me and I took the initiative again. "Good evening gentlemen. I am the new officer. Captain Robbie Matthews."

One of the captains stood and extended his hand, "Captain Stafford 5th Troop. This is Platt, the 6th Troop." The dour soldier merely waved a hand and went back to his food. "Captain Platt is a bit of a trencherman. You'll get nothing out of him until the tureens are all empty."

"I'm Lieutenant Hargreaves, also 6th Troop."

I turned to the last lieutenant, "Then I am guessing that you must be Lieutenant Austen. Pleased to meet the other officer in D Squadron." Percy Austen had a very young and serious face but I like his handshake. It oozed sincerity.

Captain Stafford gestured with his hand. "Do sit down and eat before Old Platty wolfs the lot down. Orderly, another plate for Captain Matthews."

The orderly brought me a plate and then hovered. "Don't worry orderly, I can serve myself."

I had been worried that they would give me a barrage of questions. Instead, they seemed quite happy to gossip about the other officers who were not present. I pretended that I was too polite to speak whilst eating and they chatted on merrily. Of course, Captain Platt continued to eat and drink but he did glance in my direction occasionally. I soon gathered that Captain DeVere was the informal leader of the officers and what he said was law. The rest of the officers were always following in his lead. The reason there were just the five of us was that they had all gone to the inn for a drinking session. Although Captain DeVere was not on the post it had been his habit and they were creatures of habit.

I had just finished a mouthful of food and I said, "But surely they could drink here and far more economically."

Lieutenant Austen had become more open since the conversation had begun. "No women, do you see? They want women and then gambling."

I was desperate to ask why these four did not join the others but I kept my silence and continued to eat. I learned that the two lieutenants came from relatively poor middle-class families. It had cost them almost a thousand pounds to buy the commission and so they had to live from their pay. It transpired the others did not.

I looked questioningly at Captain Stafford who grinned cheerfully, "My people are high up in the Church of England. My father is a Bishop up in Ripon. It wouldn't do for me to be drunk as a lord now would it?"

"And who is duty officer tonight?"

They squirmed uncomfortably at that. "Should be Captain DeVere but it seems he had a party to go to in London and his little brother went with him."

I finished my meal and the orderly took the plates away. Captain Platt, seeing the food depart, joined it with a waved grunt. Flashing wit and repartee were not part of his arsenal. Captain Stafford poured me a glass of port. "A present from Pater. It's been open a couple of days so we ought to finish it. Cheers Captain Matthews and welcome to the 11th!"

We all toasted each other. The crusted port slipped down beautifully. "I am intrigued as to why Lieutenant DeVere is not in A Squadron."

They all looked at each other and then Captain Stafford said, "Come on then, David. We have much to do tomorrow. Let's leave the officers of D Squadron to get to know each other."

I was beginning to see that this was a divided mess. At least there were three officers with whom I could talk. The lieutenant said, "Sorry about that." He held out his hand, "The name's Percy by the by."

"Robbie."

He looked around to see that we weren't being overheard and then gestured me closer. He smelled heavily of alcohol. He had drunk more than was good for his tongue. "The thing is the two of them thought Lieutenant DeVere would be able to be captain of D Squadron. Captain Sinclair didn't last very long. Lieutenant DeVere had only been here a week when your predecessor died." He drank some more of the port. "Captain DeVere sees it as a way to control the regiment. With his brother in command of D Squadron and his friends in command of the others then he controls the regiment. He has desires to be colonel." He sat back in his chair. "That's why I keep the 8th Troop away from the 7th, no offence, but Aubrey has let them get away with murder."

I nodded, "That stops now and tomorrow the whole squadron will work together. I intend to make changes."

"But you don't know the De Veres. They are well connected."

I shook my head. "He can be the Prince of Wales for all I care. I run my squadron my way using the standing orders as my guidelines." I smiled, "What is your Quartermaster Sergeant like?"

"Sergeant Sinclair? A good man. He gets the job done and does not suffer fools gladly."

"I think I will use him for the whole squadron until Grant returns."

"He will enjoy that, sir. He hates the thought of troopers getting away with anything. I'll speak with him first thing in the morning."

"Good. I appreciate that. Tell me, has either of the DeVeres ever fought in a battle or a skirmish." He shook his head, "Seen any action at all?"

He giggled, "Just in the upstairs bedrooms of the inn."

"I thought not. Well, Percy, thank you for your honesty. I will not divulge a word of what you said."

That was the moment when he realised he had been indiscreet. "Oh thank you, sir. I knew you were a good egg the moment I laid eyes on you."

The next morning my clothes were already laid out for me when I awoke. Sharp stood by the door smiling. He held a mug of something steaming in his hand. "I wasn't sure if you liked coffee or tea in the morning, sir. This is coffee but…"

"That will do fine. Good man." I took a mouthful of the strong black coffee. It began to wake me immediately. "Sharp, today Quartermaster Sergeant Sinclair will be in charge of the troop; what do you think the men will make of that?"

He smiled, "Some of them will hate it but most of the boys are good lads. They like order and Sergeant Sinclair will give them that."

"Excellent. The letters are on my desk. If you take them now you can be back before we begin the new training regime. Have you eaten?"

"First thing sir. Uncle Jimmy told me how to get food from the mess before it was open."

There was just Captain Stafford in the mess hall when I arrived. He waved his arm around the empty room. "Captain Platt likes to eat when the others are here and young Percy was in and out bright and early. I take it you had a word with him?"

"He seems like a good officer. I like him. Yes, we came to an understanding. We are working as a squadron for a while until 7th Troop are more disciplined."

"Excellent and until your other lieutenant arrives you will find it all plain sailing."

"And afterwards?"

He smiled impishly, "Let's just say I always enjoy a good firework display." I had been warned.

The new sabre felt just that, new, as it dangled from my belt. It was a much better sabre than the French used but it seemed different and it would take some getting used to. I would try it out and see how it fared. I strode over to the squadron office where the sergeants were gathered. I saw a Quartermaster Sergeant there. "You must be Sinclair."

He appeared to have been carved from a single piece of oak. He had the weathered look of someone who likes to be outdoors. He clapped his heels together and shouted, "Sar!" He stared straight ahead.

"I take it Mr Austen has had a word?"

He nodded, "Sar!"

I smiled, "Quartermaster Sergeant Sinclair, I am not on parade and we are in the office. You can loosen up a little." It was marginal but the face vaguely cracked a little and the shoulders drooped ever so slightly. I suspected that, for Sinclair, this was relaxed. "How do you feel about that?"

"George Grant is a good friend of mine sir and it is a shame the way his troop has suffered when he has had such trouble. I am glad I have the chance to make them a little more like his troop before he returns."

"We have a week I understand."

"Yes, sir. I'll be pleased to see him again."

"Good. I want to get the men disciplined first. None of this charging around nonsense. We both know that the Light Dragoons don't charge that often."

It looked as though I had surprised him. "You are the first officer who has said that sir."

"You served in the colonies. Did you charge much?"

He finally grinned, "No sir. Vedettes and skirmishing."

"Exactly. We will drill them in the changes of formation and pace today. I want them in perfect lines. This afternoon we will practise skirmishing; from horseback and on foot," I paused, "with carbines."

His eyes widened and, as he looked at my four sergeants they all nodded. "Well sir, this will be an interesting day. Shall I send for your horse?"

"No thank you. Trooper Sharp is delivering some letters for me so I shall get my own horse." If I had surprised them before then I positively shocked them with the statement that I would not expect a trooper to fetch my mount.

The squadron were all waiting for me in straight lines, each man standing next to his horse. I had deliberately taken my time as I was sure that Sinclair would have had a word with them. Lieutenant Austen was mounted and facing them. The bugler stood behind him.

"Morning Austen."

"Morning sir." He gestured behind me to the bugler, "This is Trooper Jones.

I looked at the trooper who looked small enough to be a jockey. "Morning, Jones. Stick close to me today; we shall be trying out a great number of manoeuvres and they all depend on you. I hope you know all the calls."

He had a sing song Welsh voice, "Good sir, and yes I do. I get bored playing the same call. The charge is a little boring when it is the only call you make."

Even the men knew that they had been doing the wrong drills. After half an hour I could see that Percy had been right, Sinclair was a good sergeant. By the end of the morning, the squadron began to look as though they were cavalry. They rode straighter and actually appeared to enjoy what they were doing. As the men led the horses away to the stables I saw Quartermaster Sinclair and Sergeant White with Corporal Green. Sharp was returning my horse to the stables and so I wandered over. I heard the arguments as I approached them.

"I'm just saying sarge..."

"Quartermaster Sergeant if you please!"

I'm just saying Quartermaster Sergeant Sinclair that Mr DeVere won't be happy when he comes back and finds us just drilling like this. Me and the lads …"

Sinclair thrust his face into Green's. "You and the lads? That sounds like sedition and mutiny to me, Corporal Green."

"No, of course not Quartermaster Sergeant, but they come to me as their corporal with their grievances."

Sergeant White almost exploded, "You lying little toad! You are the one who stirs them up."

They all stood to attention as I arrived. "I think I have heard enough." I stood in front of the corporal and said, "Corporal Green, you have three days to improve. That means your work rate and your attitude. If you fail then you will be demoted."

"You can't do…"

"Shut up! How dare you speak back to an officer. Three days in charge of the stable detail." Quartermaster Sergeant Sinclair looked shocked and said, "Sorry sir. We will make sure he improves, won't we Bill?"

"We will that."

As I strode away I reflected that all that the troop had needed was a good non commissioned officer to take charge and Sinclair had done that. This was not the same, truculent Sergeant White I had seen the first day. When I was passing the regimental office Sergeant Major Jones stuck his head out of the door and said, "Sorry to report sir but Captain and Lieutenant DeVere won't be returning for a couple of days more." He was grinning when he said, "I hope that doesn't cause too much of a problem for you, sir."

"No, Sergeant Major, I think that I can manage."

After two days there was a visible improvement in all save Green. He had become even worse and had had to be reprimanded for striking one of his men. The man said it was in fun and no charges were laid but I knew that it was inevitable that I would have to demote him.

I had got into the habit of strolling across to the stables each night to take a carrot or an apple to Badger. I had just left him when I sensed a movement in the stables. It was not a horse for it came from the loft above the stables. It had been a long time since I had been in danger and my reflexes were slow. The pitchfork which was thrown at me almost pierced my eye before I could deflect it with my arm. As it was it scored my face and I felt the blood spurt. Suddenly a horse reared up with a rider upon it. I rolled to my right and just missed having my head crushed beneath its hooves. By the time I got to my feet, the horse and rider were gone.

I ran to the guardhouse. One of the guards was lying on the floor having been struck by the fleeing horse and rider. The other sentry looked shocked. When he saw my face he jumped back. There was more blood than he was used to. "Sir, you are injured."

"I know. I will be fine. Go and fetch the surgeon. But before you go who was that?"

"Corporal Green."

Chapter 3

The view of most of the sergeants agreed with the judgement of Sergeant-Major Jones, "Good riddance. The regiment and the squadron will all be better off without him."

The departure of the corrupt corporal seemed to lighten the mood and marked a change in the fortunes of the regiment. Quartermaster Grant arrived the next day. He was a grey-haired soldier and he bore the scars which were testament to combat and service. We hit it off directly, mainly, I suspect because he met Sergeant Major Jones first.

"Pleased to meet you Sergeant and sorry for your loss."

"She was old sir but she suffered at the end. If she had been a horse we would have put her out of her misery but we make humans hang on don't we?" It did not require an answer and I gave a sympathetic nod. He nodded too and rubbed his hands together. "Right sir, I'll get back into it straight away with your permission." He turned to go and then said, "Thank you, sir, for what you have done for the troop. Jimmy Sinclair is a good lad. It should have been done earlier and I knew that Jem Green was a bad 'un." He hesitated, "I opposed his promotion. Still, now you are here, things might change for the better eh?"

He strode off whistling. He was quite a remarkable man. The next two days saw the squadron become the most efficient on the post. It was strange but I had still to meet the other officers. It seems they started work later than me and finished well before. The inns and taverns seemed to draw them like moths to a flame. It did not worry me as I just spent every waking minute, thinking of ways to improve my squadron.

The colonel and the major arrived together. I saw them glance in my direction as I paraded my men. An hour later I was summoned to the office. I took with them the two documents: the letter from Colonel Sinclair and my orders.

Colonel Fenton was a very upright gentleman and he was not young. He looked as though he lived and breathed cavalry. He had a white moustache and the face of someone who has lived well. Major Hyde-Smith, by contrast, was barely older than I was. He had sharp quick eyes with the features and the mind to accompany them. He was incredibly clever and reminded me of Bessières, Napoleon Bonaparte's general.

I handed over my orders. The colonel gave them a cursory glance and then handed them to the major who scrutinised the document closely. "It seems you have made a real difference to D Squadron. Well done Captain Matthews. Have you served before?"

"I have never served in the British Army, sir."

The major looked up and examined my face for a lie. "From what we have been told, you are a most accomplished soldier and horseman. The NCO's are most impressed by you and young Austen positively hero worships you." He stopped speaking and waited for an answer.

I remained silent and the colonel asked, "What made you choose to buy a commission in the 11th Captain Matthews?"

"That was the idea of Colonel Selkirk from Horse Guards. He said his brother had had a commission but had died."

"Ah, young Selkirk, tragic accident that."

There was something about the look they exchanged which made me want to learn more but this was not the time for that. I took out Colonel Selkirk's letter and handed it to the colonel. "This is from Colonel Selkirk, sir. It may shed a little more light on my commission."

This time he read the letter slowly and I saw his eyebrows raised. He handed the letter, silently, to Major Hyde-Smith. When he had read it I held out my hand for the letter. The major frowned. "I'm sorry sir but if that letter says what I think it says then it would compromise me if it fell into the wrong hands."

Enlightenment dawned on the major and he smiled and said, "Quite."

The colonel said, "This leaves us with a bit of a quandary then. You see the regiment has been ordered to the Cape of Good Hope in the next couple of weeks but the letter says that you are needed by Colonel Selkirk later this month."

I knew not what to say but Major Hyde-Smith smiled as he said, "I think it will work out perfectly sir. We have to leave a squadron here as replacements. D Squadron is the smallest and young Austen can run things when Captain Matthews here is away doing his derring-do. The Sergeant Major is more than capable of helping him and now that Captain Matthews has rid us of the rotten apple…"

"One of the rotten apples." They both exchanged another secretive look.

"Quite, sir, one of the rotten apples, then we should have a good source for replacements. So, Matthews, if you would work closely with young Austen, then I think the colonel will be able to accommodate you." He leaned over to me. "Will there be much of this sort of thing?"

"I don't know sir. Colonel Selkirk needs my somewhat special abilities to do particular tasks which others cannot do."

The colonel beamed, "By God sir but you have me intrigued. Have you done this sort of thing before?"

I nodded, "A few times sir but you will appreciate I cannot talk of them."

The major had been watching me while I spoke. "The Sergeant Major tells me that you advocate the use of firearms. Can you tell me why?" He held up a hand in apology, "I am merely interested, I do not judge." He glanced at the frowning face of the colonel as he did so.

"Well sir, the heavy cavalry are the ones the generals use for charges and they are equipped well for such tasks. They wear armour, or at least those on the continent do, and they, generally, ride bigger horses."

"You have a big horse Captain Matthews."

"I have indeed sir." When I did not elucidate further he waved me to carry on. "Light cavalry are generally used for skirmishing and outpost duty. A firearm is of more use in those situations. You have a particularly fine carbine in the Paget model. It seems to me to be a reliable weapon."

"And I understand you have four pistols!" The colonel sounded incredulous, making the major smile.

"Yes, sir. I suppose if you are outnumbered it is an effective weapon and four of them give me a little more protection."

The major asked, "Why not five?"

"Where would I keep the fifth, sir?"

They both laughed. "You are dismissed, Captain Matthews. Oh, by the way, keep that bit about Africa to yourself eh? I expect you are used to keeping secrets."

As I left the thought flickered through my mind, 'If you only knew.'

When I returned to my quarters Sharp was laying out my evening dress. I gave him a questioning look, "Now that the colonel is back it is all very formal, sir. He is a bit of a stickler for such things and we all have to eat at the same time." There was the hint of criticism in his voice.

"So you are telling me to get from drills quicker?"

He smiled, "Unless you want the wrath of the colonel upon you, yes sir."

"Thank you; I don't know what I would do without you." It suddenly struck me that he needed some more information than the others. "In two weeks time I shall be away for about a month or two and you will be here at the barracks." I wondered why I had said it like that and I added, lamely, "Just thought you ought to know."

He looked disappointed, "Oh, I'm sorry. I thought I had done a good job."

I was puzzled, "You have! You have performed in an exemplary fashion. Why do you say that?"

"I thought I would have been with you as your servant sir. That's the way it works in this regiment."

"Oh, then I apologise. I did not know." I decided that he deserved a little more information. "The thing of it is I may be travelling abroad and it may be dangerous."

He nodded, "Right sir."

"And I would not be in uniform. I could not risk you coming to harm."

He shrugged, "I have no family sir. This regiment is my family and I would do anything for this country. My father drilled in to me that we were British and should be proud of that. He could never understand the traitors who rebelled against us in the colonies. I hope you reconsider, sir."

"I will think about it."

As I dressed for dinner I wondered if I could embroil the young man in Selkirk's machinations. I remembered the times when one of my comrades had come to my aid when serving Napoleon and wondered if Trooper Sharp might fulfil the same function. I was due in London the following week and I would ask Colonel Sinclair for his opinion.

I made sure I was in the mess hall promptly and saw that Sharp had been correct. Everyone was dressed in his best. The other officers had also returned and the only ones who were missing were the DeVere brothers. It was a very formal affair and I saw that not only were there more orderlies but they too were well turned out. We had the regimental silver out and the best wines. After Grace and the loyal toast, we ate.

Captain Stafford sat on one side of me and Percy on the other. We found that we all got on very well. To be fair to the other officers I had seen little of them but it felt comfortable to sit and chat with these two.

After the wine was poured Captain Stafford said, "You will find that the wine will be added to you mess bill."

He looked at me as though I might object, "That is not a problem Captain Stafford." I smiled, "I have an income."

"Call me William, and that is a fortunate thing."

"I wish I had one. The only way I can get promotion is on the battlefield and that seems unlikely now."

I laughed, "Don't worry Percy; I am sure Bonaparte will try something again soon."

The lieutenant brightened at that, "Do you really think so. I thought after we drubbed him in Egypt he would have stayed in France."

"I am not a gambling man but I will bet each of you ten guineas that we will be at war within a couple of years at the most." I tapped my nose, "Bonaparte is a very ambitious man."

David sipped his wine and pulled a face, "About time we had some decent wine in the mess." He put the glass down with a distasteful look on his face, "You seem to know the man well."

"No, but I have been around, and I know the type."

Percy said innocently, "Yes I noticed your tanned face. I just thought you liked the outdoors."

"Well I do but I have travelled abroad. Italy, Austria, that sort of thing." I was deliberately vague. They couldn't know of my true background.

Just then there was a commotion outside and two officers burst through the doors, dishevelled and a little drunk. I whispered to David, "I take it they are the DeVere brothers."

"Oh yes. And making their usual entrance. The old man will not like this."

Before I could reply the major, as chairman of the mess stood and said quietly. "Gentlemen your dress and manner are both unacceptable. Go and change and return to the mess when you have dressed appropriately."

Captain DeVere, I recognised his rank, waved an airy hand, "Don't bother old chap. We'll get something from the inn."

At that, the colonel stood and actually raised his voice, "Captain DeVere, you will not. I order you to dress and return here. You have disobeyed enough orders of late."

The two of them tried to stand to attention and then they left. "Why does the colonel tolerate them? The elder gave his duty to a junior lieutenant the other day. Isn't that a court-martial offence?"

"It can be but the DeVere's father used to serve in the regiment and is a close friend of the colonel. He also has an uncle who has a great deal of influence at Horse Guards."

I saw it all now and I remembered similar examples in the French Army. It explained how they got away with so much.

We were on to the main course when they returned. It was a beef stew with a rich sauce. Some of the food I had eaten in the mess was poor but this was as good as Mrs Popwell's beef and oyster pie. They both bowed to the chairman of the mess and then sought a seat. To their obvious chagrin, the only seats available were opposite David and me. We both nodded as they sat down.

They both held up their glasses for the orderly to fill them. The colonel frowned. They looked at me and then Captain DeVere said to his brother, "I didn't know we had any Indian officers here. Things must be pretty desperate."

The major heard it and stood. "Captain DeVere you will apologise for that remark."

I was confused. Percy whispered from behind his hand, "Sir, he is insulting you. Officers who do not have much money can buy a commission in an Indian regiment. Then they can transfer to a regular regiment. It is the colour of your skin you see. He thinks you served in India."

Captain DeVere stared at me, "Apologise? Well, the fellow obviously served in India so how am I insulting him?"

Before the major could answer I stood, "I am sorry sir, and we haven't been introduced. My name is Captain Matthews and I have never served in a British regiment either here or in India. It seems you are confused by my tanned complexion. I apologise if it offends you but you see I have the funds to travel and I did so before joining this fine regiment."

As I sat down I saw both the colonel and the major nodding. Many of the other officers banged the table and said, "Well said. Hear, hear."

The look on Captain DeVere's face told me that I had made an enemy. He gave me the false smile the Egyptians associated with the crocodile. "I do apologise sir. You are correct; I took your colouring for the effect of India. Matthews? I don't know the family. Which school did you attend? Eton? Harrow?"

"I was educated by a tutor, abroad."

"Oh, I see. And your family?"

I was now aware that I was in danger of giving away too much information. "The Matthews."

He looked irritated and thought I was mocking him, "Yes I know but where is your property?"

"We have a little in London but most of it is in Italy where the estate is."

"So how do you get your money then eh? The Frogs have Italy all sewn up."

David said, "I believe you are overstepping the mark here DeVere."

He shrugged and nodded to me before turning to his brother and saying, just loud enough for me to hear. "Trade. That explains everything."

I knew he was insulting me but the last thing I needed was another duel. I merely smiled a thin smile and stared at him until he was forced to look away. I was not afraid of him and I was letting him know it.

The meal was both long and formal. The chairman told us when we could loosen our collars and when we could smoke. We had port and brandy to finish and I felt fuller than I had felt in a long time.

Sharp was waiting for me at my quarters. He looked red-faced and embarrassed. "Come in Sharp, what is the problem." He shook his head slightly. I said quietly, "Tell me."

"When Lieutenant DeVere came in he asked me why I was skulking around here when I should be in the barracks. I explained I was your servant and he said I was too incompetent to be a servant to a decent officer so either I was lying or you were a fool, sir."

I nodded, "Don't let that bother you. I have met their type before. Put them from your mind they are not worth bothering about."

The next morning the whole regiment was ordered on parade. I noticed that Lieutenant DeVere tried assiduously to avoid looking at me. I could see that it galled him to have to serve under me and I wondered how he would react to learn that he was being separated from his brother.

The colonel addressed the whole regiment his voice carrying across the parade ground as clearly as Sergeant Major Jones'. "Men of the 11th Light Dragoons; our wait for action is at an end. We will be sailing at the end of next week for the Cape of Good Hope. "

There was some murmuring until Sergeant Major Jones roared, "Silence on parade!"

"As you know we have to leave one squadron at the depot to provide replacements. As D Squadron is the smallest then they will remain here under the command of Captain Matthews. Upon dismissal of the parade all officers will join me in the mess so that I can give more information."

As he rode off Sergeant Major Jones rode forwards. "All sergeants to report any equipment which needs replacing. Dismiss!"

Once in the mess, everyone was busy chattering. I felt guilty for I had known in advance. Percy looked thoroughly depressed. "My only chance to get promoted and I have to stay here at the depot."

"Don't worry, Percy. As far as I know there is little action over there anyway."

David sat next to me. "This is a bit of luck eh? Not too far for the horses and a damned sight warmer than here in January."

I noticed that both the colonel and the DeVere brothers were missing. The major arrived and unrolled a map which he had an orderly pin to the wall. I also noticed that one of their cronies, Lieutenant Jackson looked as though he had a toothache.

When the colonel eventually arrived he began by announcing. "Lieutenant DeVere will be taking over Lieutenant Jackson's duties in A Troop. Lieutenant Jackson has requested that he stay in England for family reasons."

I looked at David who said, "And that my friend, is a lie. It looks like Captain DeVere put pressure on the young lad."

"What is he like? He will be serving with me."

"A bit wet if you ask me but this might be the making of him. He is a bit of a mummy's boy. DeVere gambles as does Jackson." He looked at me, "Jackson loses."

The next hour was spent going over the logistics of transporting men and material to the Cape. Lieutenant St.John the adjutant lieutenant went through the majority of the instructions. He would be remaining in England with our squadron. Major Hyde-Smith then stood. "The new grey uniforms we will be wearing in Africa and Tarleton Helmets will arrive this afternoon." He smiled in my direction, "Captain Matthews will be pleased to know that his squadron will not require the uniforms."

Captain DeVere shot an irritated glance in my direction and then said, in a slow drawl, "I take it we can leave the carbines and pistols at home eh sir? Don't need to carry that excess baggage all the way to Africa and it will be too damned hot anyway."

The major smiled, "You weren't in Egypt, Captain DeVere but I was. Those pistols and carbines come in very handy. When we fought the French Chasseurs they cut us up pretty badly with their muskets let me tell you. And those weapons were only half as good as the Paget. We will take the firearms with us."

I thought how ironic it was that I had fought the 11th just a year or so back and here I was fighting for them.

"Typical Froggies, too afraid to use a sword. So they hide behind a pall of smoke. Give me a good sword any day."

I suppose it was the slur on my dead comrades which did it or perhaps I just didn't like Captain DeVere. I stood. "In my view, a man with a carbine and a brace of pistols will beat a man armed with a sword any day of the week."

Captain DeVere stood, "And would you back that statement with a wager sir."

Major Hyde-White stood. "Gentlemen."

The officers in the room were divided. There were the supporters of DeVere and those who disliked him. Surprisingly the colonel held up his hand and said, "Do not be so hasty, major. Let us hear what Captain DeVere proposes."

The captain gave me a smug smile, "Well I doubt that Captain Matthews will agree to it but I propose we test this on the drill ground this afternoon."

Major Hyde-White exploded, "Impossible. Someone could get hurt."

Percy's small voice broke the silence, "There is a way sir. If Captain DeVere charges a practice dummy and we have four moving targets for Captain Matthews then when Captain DeVere begins his charge Captain Matthews could try to hit the four targets all of which would be progressively closer. If Captain Matthews failed to hit the targets before Captain DeVere struck the dummy then he would have lost."

I liked it and I could see Captain DeVere looking for the trick. Of course, there was none and he suddenly beamed, "Capital. And the wager. Could you afford fifty guineas?"

There was a gasp from some of the junior officers. I smiled, "I was thinking more of a hundred guineas but fifty is fine by me."

His face became angry as he snapped, "A hundred guineas it is then."

The colonel smiled which I found strange. "And we will have the regiment present to watch the exhibition. It might well be educational."

As I left David and Percy both joined me. "Are you sure you can afford the money, sir?"

"Don't worry, Percy, if I couldn't afford it I wouldn't have bet. Besides, I do not intend to lose."

"But Robbie, that's a moving target!"

"I will not fire my carbine until he is a hundred paces from me."

"But how will you draw your pistols quickly enough to fire again?"

I laughed, "You do not even know your own equipment do you, David?" He looked blankly at me. "On your swivel belt is a little clip for your carbine; you drop the carbine and draw your primed pistol."

He smiled, "You might just do this. If no one mentions it to the aged parents then I might have a little flutter myself. I think you might just do it. I am looking forward to this."

I was not arrogant enough to think this would be easy. Trooper Sharp and I cleaned and loaded all four pistols and the carbines. We replaced the flints in all of them and chose the most spherical balls we had. "When we have time I will show you how to cast balls. It can make all the difference."

He looked at me in amazement. "You can make musket balls?"

I laughed, "I worked in a smithy when I was young and I can even shoe a horse if needs be although it is a long time since I had to do so."

There was a buzz of excitement in the regiment. A great deal of money had been wagered on the exhibition. I found out later that virtually all of D Squadron had placed money on me. This was partly because they hated Captain DeVere but many had seen me shoot and knew that I could.

The colonel appointed Sergeant Major Jones to see that there was fair play. Captain DeVere's course was marked at three hundred, two hundred, and one hundred and fifty yards respectively. There was a bugler at each mark and they would sound their bugle at each point when he passed. I had asked for targets at one hundred, fifty, twenty and ten yards respectively. Major Hyde-Smith seemed quite concerned. "Are you sure that you can change pistols that quickly?"

I nodded, confidently, "I hope so sir."

The targets were offset so that I could not make a lucky hit. A trooper was assigned to set them swinging when the captain made his charge.

I sat astride Badger. I wanted them to see that this could be done from the back of a horse. Of course, Badger was well trained; not every horse would stand as still as he would. To make it more realistic Lieutenant Austen and Trooper Sharp were on either side of me on their horses. Captain DeVere had his brother and Lieutenant Jackson with him. They would replicate the effect of a cavalry charge.

The Sergeant Major's voice boomed out. "Ready!"

I shouted, "Ready!"

In the distance, I heard Captain DeVere shout, "Ready!"

The Sergeant Major's pistol started the horses and the swinging targets. I rested my left elbow on the pommel of Badger and lined up the carbine on the swinging target. It seemed an age before I heard the first bugle. I waited until I heard the third bugle and I fired then dropped the carbine. I drew my first pistol and rested my elbow again. I heard the last bugle and I fired at the second target. I dropped the pistol. I drew my second and third pistols and repeated the shots at the last target. I heard a cheer behind me as the dummy was decapitated.

Percy looked at me in awe as Sharp recovered my first pistol. "You managed four shots!"

"Yes, but did I hit anything?" I turned and rode towards the major and the colonel who were chatting with Captain DeVere.

"That was impressive shooting Matthews. I thought you might get two shots off but four was amazing."

Captain DeVere sniffed imperiously, "It remains to be seen if you hit anything." He pointed to the headless dummy. "There is my evidence!"

Sergeant Major Jones strode over to us with the paper targets in his hand. His face was impassive. As he approached he put the targets behind his back. Captain DeVere frowned.

The colonel had a half smile on his face. "Well Sergeant Major, what are the results?"

"Well, Captain DeVere I am sorry to say that you and your fellow officers are dead and, probably, your bugler." He flourished the targets like a magician at a fairground. Two of them had a single hole in them while the last had two less than two fingers apart.

The colonel took them and shouted, "Captain Matthews wins the wager!"

Captain DeVere became red and shouted. "That was not fair. You could not have faced charging horses like that. You would have run. You had two pistols in your hands."

The colonel was not happy, "Captain DeVere, I protest. Pay the wager. It is a matter of honour."

I could see that he would not let it lie and so I said, "Captain DeVere, I have won the wager however if you are saying I could not have stood then let us have a separate wager of fifty guineas eh? I will stand where the dummy was and I will hold the pistol and you and your two companions can charge at me and I will stand until you reach me." He smiled, "Of course you and your companions have to be good enough horsemen to avoid striking me and my stationary horse."

The major and colonel tried to hide their smiles. Captain DeVere snarled, "Wager accepted and if any of us touches your horse then I will pay double the wager."

As they rode off the colonel said, "I have learned, today the value of firearms. When we return from the Cape we will start to use your drills with the men."

While I waited I reloaded my pistols. I had a surprise in store for the three horsemen. I calmed Badger and we stood. I held the pistols in my hands and they pointed to the sky. The Sergeant Major's pistol cracked and the three horsemen began galloping towards me. Each leaned forwards in his saddle with his sabre well ahead of the horse's head. In a real battle that was a mistake. You leaned forwards at the last minute to gain the momentum and strike a heavier blow. Time seemed to stand still. I imagined firing at them as they passed the silent buglers. They were riding boot to boot which would cause a problem once they neared me. I saw Captain DeVere pulling ahead of his brother officers in his haste to prove a point and win the wager. I saw the tip of his sabre and it was aimed directly at my head. He had to lean to one side to avoid his horse hitting Badger who stood as placidly as though on parade. As his horse's head flashed by I fired my pistols. The effect was dramatic. Lieutenant DeVere's horse reared up and threw him. Lieutenant Jackson's horse took off across the drill field. Only Captain DeVere was a good enough horseman to control his mount.

The whole regiment exploded in spontaneous applause. As the major and Captain DeVere approached me the major said, "That settles both wagers conclusively and shows us that the two lieutenants need their horses schooling a little better. Agreed Captain DeVere?"

His face was white with anger but he nodded, "I will send my man with the guineas this afternoon."

I nodded too, "Thank you, Captain DeVere, for a most illuminating exercise. I have learned much and I thank you for the lesson."

Sergeant Major Jones strode over to me, "He barely missed you with the sabre. An inch closer and you would have lost an eye. You have some nerve, sir."

"Let's just say I do have a stubborn streak and a dislike of those who would bully others."

I was surrounded by all those officers, not of the DeVere persuasion. It was the first stage to my acceptance in the regiment.

Chapter 4

The new uniforms and helmets arrived in the afternoon. My squadron were equipped first as the others were busy with their new grey uniforms. The Tarleton helmet was leather with a bearskin crest. It looked magnificent but I wondered how it would stand up to and the rigours of campaigning. For D Squadron it was not a problem. We would not need them in the foreseeable future.

I sent for Lieutenant Jackson. There was no one in the Squadron office; I had sent the orderly on an errand.

He stood there like a naughty schoolboy with his head hung down. "Sir, you sent for me."

"I did. Close the door." He did so and looked even more worried. My smile did not seem to help. "Look I know that the decision to join my squadron was not your choice." He looked startled and I held up my hand to calm him. "I take no offence at that but I believe you can become as good an officer as Lieutenant Austen given the right encouragement. What's say we make a new start eh? You give me and your new troop a chance and we'll see how it goes."

He seemed somewhat relieved at that. "Thank you, sir."

I took a deep breath. I had always found that having things in the open helped. "Tell me, Jackson, how much do you owe Captain DeVere?" He looked ready to deny it. "New start eh? Let's begin with honesty."

His shoulders sagged. "Fifty guineas to the captain and ten to his brother."

I counted out sixty guineas from the wager. "Here you are then. Pay off your debts and we will start anew."

He straightened, "No sir, I could not accept a loan…"

"It is not a loan, it is a gift from me to you. There are no strings and no conditions. I do not think that the money will make you like me. That does not concern me but I want an officer I can rely upon. I need an officer who is not worried about paying off a debt." I paused, "Actually there is a condition attached; I want you to foreswear gambling."

His face showed the torment he was feeling inside. Eventually, good sense got the better of him. He held out his hand for the money. "Thank you, sir and I think if I am not in their company then I will be able to give up gambling."

"Good. Look to Percy, he is a good officer and a good model for you."

I was summoned to the regimental office. "Sir, there is a case of wine here for you from Fortnum and Mason's in London."

"Excellent. Have it sent over to the officer's mess."

Later in the afternoon, I sought out the mess sergeant. "Sergeant Mann, I sent over a dozen bottles of wine today. Be so good as to open a couple tonight would you." I smiled, "Compliments of D Squadron."

He grinned back at me, "In the way of a celebration eh? I won a couple of bob today backing you sir."

It seemed that all of D Squadron and many of C Squadron had benefitted from my display. The winners were obvious from their good humour while the losers looked as miserable as sin.

That evening DeVere and his associates were subdued. I was inundated with questions about my pistols and carbine. Many of the officers could not believe how quickly it was possible to fire the weapons. "You need to have them primed and in good holsters. I have a spare pair of holsters which allow me to have an extra two pistols if I wish."

Major Hyde-Smith stood, "Gentlemen, be upstanding. I would like to propose a toast to Captain Matthews. Firstly for his skilful display of shooting and secondly for this wonderful wine he has generously shared with us."

"Captain Matthews."

After jackets were loosened and cigars lit Major Hyde-Smith came over and took me to one side. "The wine; is it from your family's estate?"

"It is."

"Fortnum and Mason's?"

"They are the sole supplier, sir."

"Good. I shall order a couple of cases so that when we return from the Cape we shall celebrate with a decent bottle of something." It required no answer and so I nodded. "You know you are a deep one. When I first laid my eyes on you I thought that you were a chicken ready to be plucked. I shall watch you, sir, for I think that you will be good for the regiment."

"Thank you, sir, for your confidence."

He leaned in, "And by the way that was an extremely honourable thing you did for young Jackson. It might be the making of him."

I assumed an innocent look. "I don't know what you are talking about sir."

He smiled, "Well keep your secrets but everyone is putting two and two together. Jackson suddenly pays off a debt and the coins are the same ones used to pay off the wager. But I respect your modesty. You are a gentleman."

The next day I asked the colonel's permission to ride up to London to speak with Colonel Selkirk. I was in his good books and so he gave me permission. I took Trooper Sharp with me. As we were passing the 'George and Dragon' I called in. Mr Popwell was effusive in his thanks. "The wine you sent sir, it has gone down very well. Thank you." He hesitated, "How much do I owe you?"

"Let us call it a gift and besides I assume you will be buying more and so my family will benefit."

He bobbed his head up and down in gratitude and then seemed to notice not only my uniform but Trooper Sharp too. "You didn't say you were a soldier."

"No, I didn't and I apologise for that. I didn't want a fuss with the other officers. You may find it quiet for a while."

"The last few days have been better sir and my regulars have begun to return." He gestured me over, "Mind you there has been a highwayman hereabouts. Haven't had one for nigh on thirty years and now we have a pair of them. They have robbed a couple of travellers. It seems they are a ruthless pair. One man had his head laid open. You take care. Two mail coaches have been robbed and one poor passenger was shot."

"Thank you for the warning. We will take care."

It was six hours to London along the main road and I hoped we would reach it before dark. I needed to be briefed by Colonel Selkirk and then return before the regiment sailed. The journey was dreadful. The late January rains drove into our faces and I felt sorry for our horses. It also made conversation impossible. I had hoped to get to know my young servant a little better on the road. That would have to wait.

I headed for the part of London I knew best, close to the river. "It's too late to go to Horse Guards. We will find rooms."

Trooper Sharp looked nervous, "I've never been to London before sir."

"Don't worry. It's no worse than the George when the 11th are getting drunk."

He laughed. "You have travelled sir."

"Yes I have but it was only last year when I visited London for the first time."

I rode towards the 'Coal Hole Tavern'. It was rough and it was ready but the landlord was honest, the beds were clean and the beer was good. Badger enjoyed staying here. I hoped I would see my old friend, Geordie.

The landlord, thankfully, remembered me. I suspect the fact that I had paid promptly in cash had helped. "Two rooms sir. That will be fine. We have servant rooms if you wish."

"The two rooms will be the same quality please, landlord."

I was pleased I had done that for Trooper Sharp looked grateful. "How many nights?"

"Just the one and stabling for two horses." He wrote it down in the ledger and I handed him the payment. "Is Geordie in port?"

"Aye, he sails on the morning tide. He will be in soon enough. He is just checking the manifest at the agent's office."

"Good. Send our bags up to our rooms and we will have some food and some of your fine beer."

We headed for the table by the roaring fire. The steam from our damp clothes began to rise the moment we sat down. The beer came first.

"Cheers, trooper."

"Cheers sir. Thank you for this."

"For this?"

"Yes sir, for treating me like a person. My dad warned me that some officers see the men as little more than horses that talked. There are some like that in Canterbury but you and Mr Austen, you are gentlemen."

"You are welcome. Every man deserves respect, regardless of rank, until he does something to lose that respect."

I saw Geordie enter the inn. He shook his mane like a wet dog. I had to smile. Geordie was larger than life. I stepped towards him and his face lit up in recognition. "Why if it isn't Robbie M…"

"Matthews. That's right. Good to see you again Geordie. How are Betty and the children?"

"Oh, they're canny." He had questions written all over his face but he knew me well enough to say nothing.

"Would you like to join me? We are having a bite to eat."

"Well aye, that'd be grand."

Trooper Sharp stood, terror written all over his face. "Trooper Sharp this is Captain Geordie a good friend of mine."

He stood and shook Geordie's outstretched hand.

"Geordie, this is Trooper Sharp. One of the soldiers from my regiment."

As they shook hands I saw the gratitude in Sharp's eyes that I had not called him a servant.

"Well I sail tomorrow Robbie so we don't have long."

"I know the landlord told me and I return to the barracks tomorrow too."

"Ye look fine in your best bib and tucker. How do you like the army life then?"

"It's a good life. And is the sea treating you well?"

"I canna complain."

It was a delightful evening. I think Trooper Sharp was mesmerised by the apparition that was Geordie. He regaled us with tales of the sea and corrupt officials. He spoke of life in Newcastle and the money he was losing because of the peace. The whole evening was a delight. It made me realise that you cannot put a value on a real friend.

The next day we headed towards the west end of London. Before I met with Colonel Selkirk I wished to speak with my banker, Mr Hudson and then Mr Fortnum. I left Trooper Sharp outside with the horses while I went inside to see the banker. My meeting was brief. I wished to know how my finances were doing and was pleased that I had almost doubled my money in the last four months. The peace was not good for Geordie but my half share in a boat and my income from the Alpini estate were paying dividends.

"Now I may be travelling in Europe soon. Have you any arrangements with banks so that I can access some funds over there?"

He frowned slightly, "The situation is still volatile. How much would you require?"

"Enough for emergencies."

He seemed relieved. "I will write a draft for you and give you a list of banks that will facilitate your request. I am afraid they are all in the major cities."

"That is not a problem. I have to see Mr Fortnum. I will return in an hour and pick up the documents and some cash for the journey."

He nodded and then said, "I take it you will not be travelling in uniform, Captain...er Matthews?"

"No, Mr Hudson. I think that would be a little unwise."

Poor Sharp had to be left with the horses again outside Fortnum and Mason's but he seemed quite happy to watch all the colourful ladies and their beaus who frequented this fashionable part of London.

Mr Fortnum was delighted to see me again. "The peace has done wonders for our trade and your family's wine is the most popular item we have."

"Excellent. Thank you for the wine you supplied me with."

"You are welcome. I suspect that I may be receiving further orders once those customers taste it so you have done me a favour too."

"Now the reason I came here is because I will be travelling abroad soon and I need some things."

He glanced at the uniform. "With the regiment?"

"Er, no. This will be a private visit. I need sturdy, functional luggage for two please."

"That will not be a problem. Shall I send them to the barracks?"

"If you please and take the payment from my account."

"Of course, Captain Matthews."

We crossed London to get to Horse Guards in Whitehall. It still intimidated me for I had only been there once. It was different this time for I was in uniform. Once again Trooper Sharp was left with the horses. "Keep your eyes and ears open, Sharp. We may learn something here." I knew from my time serving Napoleon that the gossip from headquarters was usually reliable.

I attracted fewer stares, this time, as I walked the corridors. I was in uniform. Colonel Selkirk's office was nondescript and tucked away from the busier areas. I think it suited his secretive nature.

I knocked on the door and his gruff Scottish voice barked, "Come!" He smiled when he saw me. "Well you look splendid in a British uniform. How are you settling in?"

"Fine." I was tempted to ask him about his brother's death. It did not seem as clear cut now that I had been with the regiment. This did not seem an appropriate time besides which I still had to get to the bottom of it.

"Good. Let's get down to business. Take a seat. Now, as you know I do not trust Boney. Nor, I think, do you." I nodded. "We need to take advantage of this peace. I am convinced he is up to something but we have no diplomats in Paris at the moment and the news from the ships which trade with France is a little vague. I need you to have a wander around Paris and the north of France. Two weeks should suffice."

That sounded more than a little vague to me. "What do I do there?"

"Use your eyes and your brain. You know the important men who surround Bonaparte. Find them and see what they are doing. Is he conscripting more men? If he is and they are just intended for the east and Austria that is useful information but if they are gathering in the west of France then we need to know."

"When I did missions for Napoleon I had a specific task and I knew what I was doing."

"Well," he added bluntly, "now you work for me and I expect you to use your initiative. You are a captain in the Light Dragoons. You serve Britain now."

I saw now that the commission was not a prize but a halter. I sighed, "Well, sir, I have a request to make."

He looked at me sharply. "A request or an ultimatum?"

"A request. I will be travelling through France as a gentleman." He nodded. "Then it would seem appropriate if I had a servant."

He closed his eyes briefly and then nodded. "It makes sense and shows that you are using your mind but I do not see where this is going."

"I have a trooper servant and he would make a perfect cover for me."

"He doesn't know what you do then?"

"No, but when I said I might be travelling to my family's estate in Italy then he told me he would like to accompany me."

"Does he speak French?"

"I do not think so, but I thought he could play a mute. People tend to think if someone cannot speak they cannot hear and they can be indiscreet."

"Yes, I see that. Very well you have my permission but you must impress upon him the need for secrecy. Your life depends on it. If you are captured then we will deny all knowledge of you."

"I realise that." It seems that both sides of the Channel had a low regard for the men who served them.

He handed me a sack of coins. "Some gold Louis. The French might not like their Royal Family but they like their coins. Some clerk will want you to hand in a record of where you spent this so try to keep receipts." He took out two documents from his desk and he wrote on one and then asked, "What is this fellow's name?"

"Alan Sharp."

He wrote on the second document and then blotted them. He folded them and handed them to me. "Here are your passports." I put them into my tunic pocket. "How you get to and from Paris is your own business but you should be back here in two weeks. All I need you to do is to sniff around. You will be going back but your regiment won't need you for a while."

It suddenly struck me that the fortuitous posting of the 11th might not have been that. "You arranged for them to go to Cape?"

"Let us just say that they needed a regiment of cavalry there and it fitted in with my plans. Good luck Robbie."

With that, he went back to his documents and I was summarily dismissed. I pocketed the coins and went to search out Sharp. I would give him the chance to reconsider once we were on the road but I now liked the idea of having a companion. I would not be alone.

As we headed down the Dover road I asked him if he had learned anything of value. "No, sir. The sentries were just saying how quiet it has been lately. Lots of officers have taken the opportunity to go back to their estates." He shook his head, "It must be nice to have the option."

He was, of course, right. "Well Trooper Sharp, if you still wish to travel with me then you can but I have to tell you that it may be dangerous. Your life could be at risk."

He seemed to consider this and did not speak for a few moments. "Would we be serving our country, sir?"

"Yes."

"Then I am your man."

I was relieved and I think it showed in my smile for he smiled back at me. "We will be going to France. I take it you cannot speak French?"

"Some would say my English isn't that good but I have no French."

"I thought not. It does not matter although I will teach you some words. You will play a mute so that you do not have to speak. That will be hard, I know but you are a diligent lad and you will manage it. As soon as we get back we need to pack civilian clothes. Have you some?"

"Yes, sir, but no bag."

"Don't worry. There will be luggage awaiting us at the barracks. We leave tomorrow. We will buy horses once we are in France. We shall take the coach from Canterbury."

He suddenly seemed animated. "I have never travelled in a mail coach before sir."

"Neither have I. It will be a new experience for both of us."

The next few miles were spent in a pleasant discussion about the differences between France and Britain. I thought it important that he understand the new world he would be entering. We were a few miles east of Gillingham when the black rain clouds, which had been threatening us for some time, finally decided to drop their entire contents upon us. There was little point in trying to fight it and we took shelter in a dilapidated barn by the side of the road. Fortunately, it still had part of its roof and we were protected from the deluge which descended.

"Look, sir, there is the mail coach."

We saw the London to Dover mail coach splashing through the rain. I felt sorry for the driver and guard. Despite their rain coats, they would be soaked to the skin. They did not have the luxury of being able to shelter in a barn. The rain was torrential but, as with all such storms, it soon blew itself out and after half an hour we were able to continue our journey.

The road was awash with puddles and debris. "I expect we will soon catch up with the coach. It would not be able to make good speed on a road in this condition."

The road had a few dips and crests on it and we saw the coach when reached the top of one such rise. It was stopped. "That is strange."

"Why sir? You said it would have trouble negotiating the road in this condition."

"I expected it to be going slowly but not to stop. Remember what Mr Popwell said about highwaymen?" Trooper Sharp suddenly became alert. "Have you your pistols?"

"Yes sir but they are not loaded."

I felt a little irritated. I had impressed on all the men the need to keep your weapons loaded if not primed. Here was my own servant and he was not obeying me. I would speak to him later. "Here take one of mine. It needs priming." I could see that he was shamefaced about the whole thing.

Our weapons primed we rode cautiously along the road. The fact that the coach had not moved was now even more suspicious.

When I heard the crack of the pistol I knew that caution was now a luxury we could ill afford.

"You take the right and I will take the left."

As I galloped up I saw a body lying next to the front wheel and a masked man holding two pistols. He must have heard Badger for he suddenly turned and fired one of his pistols. It was too hasty a shot and it missed. He threw himself on his horse. I heard the double crack of two pistols. I hoped that Sharp had not wasted his shot. As I galloped past the coach I saw the driver climbing down to see to his wounded guard.

It was futile to try to fire a pistol from the back of a horse at a moving target and so I holstered my gun. I had confidence that Badger would catch the other horse for he was bigger and stronger than the horse we were pursuing. I drew my sword and urged Badger to go faster. Gradually we began to catch up to the horse and rider. The mount was slowing. When I was thirty yards from its rear I saw the 11th stamped on its rump. It was a horse from my regiment.

The rider glanced around and saw my approach. He must have known that I would catch him for he suddenly threw his horse around and drew his sword in one motion. It was an impressive piece of horsemanship. I recognised his sword too. It was a British Light Cavalry sabre. This highwayman was a soldier! I had no more time for speculation for the blade came slicing down towards me. I was not carrying my sabre, it was my longer, Austrian sword and I easily parried the blow. I wheeled Badger around to face my opponent again. His horse was not as nimble and he was slow to turn. I sliced down with my longer blade and he jerked out of the way. The tip of my sword caught the scarf which was concealing the lower portion of his face. It was Jem Green!

"I'm going to pay you back now for what you did to me Mr Bloody Matthews!" He swung his sword at my middle. Had he connected it would have ripped open my stomach. I flicked the sabre away when it was but an inch from gutting me. I turned the blade and jabbed forwards. The long straight blade caught his left hand and he released his reins. His horse stopped and he was almost thrown from its back. He now had a worried look on his face. I stabbed forwards again and he hacked ay my blade. I had a firm grip and the tip pierced his shoulder. In desperation he stood in his stirrups to hack down at me and I sank my sword into his middle. His face had a look of disbelief as he fell from the back of his horse.

Before I had time to dismount and see if he lived or not I heard the sound of the coach behind me. "Are you alright sir?"

I turned and saw Trooper Sharp with the other wounded highwayman on his horse and the coach behind. "Yes thank you Trooper. And you?"

"He was a poor shot and your pistol was a good one."

The driver dismounted and came to shake my hand. "Thank the lord you came when you did. You have saved us and my mate Harry."

"You are welcome. We will escort you the rest of the way. We are going to Canterbury anyway." As Sharp and I lifted the body of the dead highwayman on to the back of his horse Sharp suddenly recognised him. I nodded. "It seems the corporal fell a long way when he deserted."

Chapter 5

We were treated like royalty when we boarded the mail coach the following day. We were the talk of Canterbury. The two highwaymen were notorious and there was a reward for their capture. Despite his protestations, I insisted that Trooper Sharp have it all. He used some of it to buy better clothes before we boarded the coach. Our sudden departure was also mitigated by the return of the horse and the death of the deserter. Percy was delighted to be in command, albeit briefly, although he was curious about where we would be going. I hated having to lie to him. As the regiment was leaving at noon he would soon be embroiled in the running of the depot squadron. It would, hopefully, stop him speculating.

Dover was still the front line port and the defences, despite the peace, were still heavily manned. There were ships which travelled over to Boulogne and Calais to trade and to take passengers. Having sailed on a number of ships I knew the type of vessel I was seeking. The one I eventually settled upon surprised Sharp for it was smaller than the rest.

"Notice the neatly coiled ropes and the uncluttered decks; this ship is well run. I would rather a safe ship than a comfortable one. You stay here with the bags whilst I go and negotiate a price."

The captain was due to sail on the next tide and the sight of the gold Louis persuaded him. Although I had told Sharp that this was a good ship I had no doubt that the captain would do a little smuggling on the side and French coins would make those transactions much easier.

As we left the busy harbour at Dover it hit me that I was now travelling to a country where I was a wanted man. Many people knew my face. I just hoped that my clean shaven looks and my shorter hair might confuse people. I was also travelling in civilian clothes which helped to disguise me.

"Well Sharp, this will be your last chance to talk for some time. Even when we are alone, unless we are well away from anyone else, you cannot speak. I will be speaking French. I will tell whoever we meet that you are an American which would explain why you cannot understand them. If anyone asks then say you come from Winchester in Virginia."

"Why there, sir?"

"I looked at some maps when I was growing up and I remember thinking that there was a place in England with the same name. It stuck. The American Winchester is far from the sea and it is unlikely that we will meet anyone from that town and besides… you cannot speak can you?"

The crossing was cold and it was rough. I remembered the Channel well. It was not one of my favourite places. I preferred the warm Mediterranean. We spent the time huddled in the cabin reserved for passengers; we were the only two. I went through Sharp's French lessons again. He had proved to be a quick learner and could understand many words. The advantage we had was that he would not need to speak it. I had heard enough execrable French massacred by Englishmen to realise that it was a giveaway to their nationality. The English did not speak foreign languages well. Colonel Selkirk was the only man I knew who could master a foreign accent.

I had a sinking feeling in my stomach as Calais hove into view. I would be stepping back into Napoleon's lair. I knew that his National Guard were xenophobic and I hoped that I would be able to pull off this deception. The passports were tucked away in my luggage. If I had to use them in France then all was lost. I had to persuade them that I was French and I had a name and a story which I hoped would fool them.

As the ship edged into the crowded Calais harbour I sought out the captain. "Do you call in here often?"

"While the peace remains we come every couple of days." He smiled and I noticed he had no front teeth which gave him an oddly comic look. "I get the French wine cheap and the French seem to like English lambs. We do a good trade."

"We'll be back here in a couple of weeks." I handed him a guinea. "I hope this secures our berth."

"It certainly does." He pointed to a bar at the corner of the harbour. "We normally drink in there. Sometimes we have to moor further along but we always go in there."

"Thank you, captain. Come along, Sharp. Bring the bags."

The captain said quietly, "The customs officer is at the end to the harbour. They have a small gate." He looked at me, "It is the only way in to Calais."

"Don't worry, captain, I have no worries about getting in to France." I did not need to fill in the gaps.

The two customs officials had two National Guardsmen lounging close by. I hoped that I could bluff my way through them. Officials such as this were full of self-importance. I just had to persuade them that I was even more important. I remembered how Jean Bartiaux had done this when we escaped Paris following my father's execution.

The senior one held out his hand and said, "Papers."

"I do not need papers." I affected a superior tone. I just thought of the way my father, the Count had spoken and copied that.

I could see that I had put him on edge. "Everyone needs papers to enter France."

I leaned in, "Even those who are working on behalf of General Bessières?"

The name of Bonaparte's right-hand man made him sit up straight. "But why have you no papers sir?"

"If I had had papers identifying me as French do you think that the British would have let me travel to America?" I tapped my nose.

Enlightenment lit up his face. "Of course." He nodded to the two national Guardsmen who raised the barrier. The two Customs officers saluted us and we were in France. I was learning that a positive attitude and total confidence could achieve much.

With a mere thirteen days to complete our mission, we could afford no delays. We strode into town with Trooper Sharp carrying both our bags. My only visible weapon was my sword but we had pistols in our bags. I would be happier when we had the horses and our pistols could be closer to hand.

It is strange but the smell of France was different to that of England and I felt at home immediately. I think my French lessons with Trooper Sharp had helped me to get into the French language once again. I slipped into the language as though I had only ever spoken it. Trooper Sharp was just staring at everyone and everything. It was all new to him.

I smelled the stable before I saw it. The owner was sitting outside smoking a pipe and drinking wine from a pichet. He glanced up as we approached and, when he saw my clothes, he jumped to his feet.

"Sir, may I help you?"

I could see him working out how much to overcharge me for the horses. "I require two horses for a few days."

"To buy or rent?"

I smiled, "That depends upon the price and the quality of the horses."

He waved a hand and we entered the dingy stables. There were just five horses and none of them was of the highest quality. The owner spread his arm as though they were Arab thoroughbreds. I sniffed and said, "If this is all that you have." I turned as though I was going to leave.

"No sir, I can see that you know your horseflesh. I will give you a good price for any of them."

"What for? Meat?"

"No sir, they look worse than they are. I will tell you what; if you buy them from me then I will take them off your hands when you return for a quarter of the price." I gave him the look I used to reserve for troopers who had annoyed me. "Let us say half then sir and I will throw in the saddles and feed."

If he had known it he had us over a barrel for we needed horses no matter how poor the quality. I nodded and we agreed on a price. He saddled them for us and Trooper Sharp loaded the bags. Mr Fortnum had provided us with bags which fitted easily over the rump of the horses. We set off with the sad looking beasts. As we passed a market I purchased a few old apples for a handful of copper coins and we gave the horses those as we trotted along the road.

When we were well out of Calais and well out of earshot. Trooper Sharp was able to speak with me. "How long will it take us, sir? To get to Paris I mean."

"We could push it and do it in one day but I think we will stop in an inn for the night. You can sometimes hear more gossip that way."

It was getting towards dark when we reached Beauvais. The weather had been kind to us and it was just cold and windy. We were spared the English rain. I spied a small inn which looked as though it had stables. The horses had done remarkably well considering their condition but I would not have wished to push them further. The ostler nodded to the inn. "There are rooms sir although we have a big party just arrived. I'll see to your horses."

As soon as we entered the inn my heart fell. It was filled with officers of the 47th Infantry regiment. I had seen them in Piedmont when I served there. They all looked around as we entered. It was too late to withdraw without attracting attention.

The landlord saw my fine clothes and raced over to greet me. "Rooms or just food sir?"

I affected my aristocratic drawl, "Both if you have them."

"Yes sir and you are lucky I have one with servant's quarters attached."

"We'll take it." The landlord looked grateful that I had not asked a price. I would be overcharged; I had no doubt of that. "Show my man to the room. He cannot speak and he will not understand you." He looked at Trooper Sharp as though he was a circus freak. "He is American and they don't have much call to speak French."

Understanding dawned and the landlord led Trooper Sharp upstairs with the luggage. Now that I had a chance to look at the room I could see that the dozen or so officers had appeared larger in number because they were all crowded around the bar. There were, however, many empty tables and I selected one which was next to a wall so that I could observe the room and have my back protected.

As I passed a clutch of officers, a major asked me, "I heard you tell the landlord that your servant was American. You are not American are you?"

I shook my head and smiled, "No, I am French but my own servant died whilst I was in America and this chap was available. I have grown somewhat attached to him."

That seemed to satisfy the major. "What is America like? I have heard it is a land of opportunity."

"It is. I was visiting my relatives in the colony there but I had a chance to see their cities. New York is a lively town."

"Ah, so I have heard."

I waved a hand at the officers. "And what of you, major? There are no barracks close by are there?"

He laughed, "In this backwater? I hardly think so. Our camps are closer to the coast. No, sir, we were being briefed by a general from Paris." He shook his head, "You know how full of themselves some of these armchair generals are. Something is in the air." He realised he had been indiscreet, "Of course I can say no more."

"Of course not, nor would I wish you to." I saw the landlord and Trooper Sharp approaching. "I will take my leave, sir. I am hungry although I am not sure of the quality of food here."

The major shrugged as he turned back to his companions. "It is edible and that is all."

The landlord held my chair out for me, "Now then sir, what can I bring you?"

"A bottle of your best red for me and ale for my servant. As for food... do you have chicken?"

"Yes, sir."

"Then bring us that." One advantage of me having a servant who could not speak was that I could watch and observe without being considered suspicious. The major was standing with two captains just a few paces away and I could hear all that they said. There was nothing of major interest save that at least eight

regiments had been represented at the briefing. I gathered that
Bessières had been there too. That was important because it meant
it was initiated by Bonaparte but also that I had to be on my guard;
the general would certainly recognise me.

I had only been to Paris on two occasions; one was to witness
the execution of my father and the second was to meet with
Bonaparte. I wondered if this visit would be as momentous. What I
noticed immediately was the difference between London and Paris.
Apart from the area around Whitehall, I had seen few soldiers.
Here in Paris, it seemed that young men not in uniform were the
exception. Bonaparte had not disbanded his army. The fact that
there were so many here in Paris was also interesting. This was the
hub of the country. It was where Bonaparte himself resided like a
fat spider in the middle of a web. He was not in a passive state of
mind; he was still belligerent.

I took us close to the Conciergerie which had many small hotels
and also afforded me the opportunity to observe the powerful men
of Paris. The hotel I chose had a bunch of grapes outside and was
not far from the Pont Neuf. The owner was happy to take money
from a civilian rather than being forced to have soldiers billeted
there for a tenth of the money he would get from me. He proved to
be garrulous and a mine of information. I discovered that
Bonaparte had taken over the Petit Luxembourg Palace. I would be
able to avoid that easily. The owner also remarked on the number
of soldiers in Paris.

"Of course they will be gone by summer."

"And why is that?"

"They will be campaigning."

"But we are at peace."

He laughed, "Our little leader has, once again, fooled the world.
Every soldier who has stayed with me has commented on the fact

that soon they would be fighting again." He shrugged, "Where? I do not know and, so long as it is not Paris then I care not." He tapped his nose. "Many of them say that the little general wishes to invade England."

I suppose we could have returned to Colonel Selkirk there and then for I had the information he required. However, I liked to do things properly and I wanted to know where Bonaparte planned to attack. We left our horses at the hotel and I took Trooper Sharp over the bridge towards the left bank. I intended to make my way to the military school. There were many bars and eating establishments and I knew that they would be full of officers. If there was the likelihood of some action then they would be full of excitement.

We passed the military hospital, Les Invalides, and wandered down the busy streets towards the military school. It was early afternoon and I guessed that many officers would either still be eating or drinking the afternoon away. I had arranged that Sharp would do a circuit of the school and then wait outside the bar I would choose. I didn't expect him to hear anything but he could recognise the uniforms of senior officers and that would help.

I sat at a small table and ordered a glass of wine. I was the only civilian in the bar and that was a mistake. Two young lieutenants from a cuirassier regiment wandered over, both slightly drunk.

"Why aren't you in uniform? You look healthy enough. Why aren't you defending France from the damned beef eaters?"

I smiled, "I am no longer able to serve."

"I can't see a wound. Stand up and show me."

A captain of infantry walked over, "That is enough. If the man is a veteran then he has served France and you two should be ashamed of yourselves."

"Sorry, sir."

The two of them staggered out and the captain turned to me. "I apologise, sir, for their behaviour. They are typical of the young men who have recently joined up. They have not fought and think it will be easy. Where did you serve sir?"

I glanced at his uniform and realised that his regiment had not been in Egypt. "I was invalided out after the battle of the Pyramids."

He nodded sympathetically, "Ah yes and that was a waste. So many good men died and we have nothing to show for it. Tell me, when you fought the British what did you make of them?"

"Their infantry is like a rock wall. They are able to stand there and take all that we can throw at them. And they can fire much quicker than we can. They are a tougher enemy than the Austrians, that is for sure."

He seemed to see my sword for the first time. "That looks Austrian. May I?" I took it out and gave it to him. "A magnificent weapon."

I could see he wanted more information. "I took it from its previous owner after I had killed him. It was in the campaign at the Texel."

"And you sir. Where do you serve?"

"I serve in Austria and they have now given me a job there." He pointed to the school. "I use my knowledge to help plan. May I sit sir?"

"Of course."

"That is why I asked you about the British. You see we have no-one over there who could tell us how they fight and what they are like as enemies. We know that they are better now than when we fought them eight years ago."

"Yes, but they are now on their island. It is unlikely that we would be fighting them."

"Perhaps that is true now but the Channel is a very narrow stretch of water." He grinned, "It would be quite easy to cross it."

"Ah yes but they have their admiral, what was his name? Ah yes, I remember, Nelson. Surely the navy would have something to say about it."

"True but we have our own men who can defeat this Nelson. Admiral Villeneuve is just such a man." He finished his drink. "Are you sure I can't persuade you to join us in the school?"

"I am afraid that I am a man of business now. I import and export wines."

"Then I envy you. Good day sir."

After he had gone I paid and left. Sharp was outside and he looked agitated. I began to walk back to the river. I waited until the street was quiet and slowed down. "What is it Sharp?"

"You are being watched, sir. There were two men in dark coats outside the bar and they were watching you talking with that captain. They are still behind us sir."

"How do you know?"

He smiled. "They smell different sir. They wear, you know, perfume."

"Well done. We will not head directly back to our hotel. We will walk towards the Sorbonne. Are you armed?"

"Yes, sir. I have my bayonet and a knife."

"That will have to do."

As we turned a corner to head down a side street I turned to view the two men. Trooper Sharp had been correct. There were two men and they were about a hundred paces behind us. They were definitely following us. Dare we try to lose them? The alternative was to do something about them. I knew that Trooper Sharp was a good soldier but I had no idea how he would cope with a deadly fight in an alley. I knew that I had to speak to the two men and find out why they were following us. That meant luring them into somewhere where we could do so without being seen. My knowledge of Paris was not the best but I vaguely remembered an old and gloomy church not far from the Louvre. There was a bridge nearby which would enable us to flee to the island in the middle of the Seine if we had to.

"Right Sharp, I want to begin to slow down and let them catch us. I need some answers. I will be speaking in French so keep your silence. You will know when I want you to do anything."

I heard him take a deep breath and he said, "Sir."

"Don't worry Trooper, you handled the highwayman. This will be easier. They aren't on horses."

The streets became gloomier as we entered the warren of alleys and narrow roads around this old part of town. There were fewer people around and the ones I saw looked to be up to no good themselves. They might pose a problem once we had dealt with these two but I would have to cross that bridge when I came to it.

As we slowed I could hear their feet on the cobbles. I suddenly saw, to my left, a blind alley and I darted quickly down it. As soon as I was around I stopped. Trooper Sharp kept on. I heard the sound of feet running after us. Trooper Sharp stopped when he realised I was no longer close behind him. The two men hurtled around the corner and saw him. I hit one with my fist and he collided with the other wall and fell in a heap. The second man made the mistake of going for a weapon. I grabbed his free arm and pulled him towards me. His head cracked into the wall and he too fell down.

We could have escaped then but I did not want to be pursued by these two. "Grab the first one and disarm him."

I searched my man and found a pistol and a sword. I disarmed him and threw them to one side. He began to come too. "Who are you and why were you following me?"

He had a ferrety face and a squeaky voice. "I am the police and you are in trouble."

I laughed, "In trouble for protecting myself and my servant? You are wrong. It is you who is trouble."

It was his turn to laugh. "I recognised you. You are the bastard son of the aristo. You are wanted for murder and I will claim the reward. As soon as I saw you near to Les Invalides I recognised you. You cannot escape."

At least he did not know where we were staying. I took off his belt and tied his hands behind his back. I whistled and got Sharp's attention. He nodded and did the same to his unconscious man. I took the man's scarf off and gagged him before he could protest more and begin to shout. I think I took him by surprise. Perhaps he thought we would just have fled. I took off his shoes and, as he raised his head, hit him hard on the side of the head. He fell down in an unconscious heap.

"Right. Get their weapons and their shoes and follow me."

He did so without a word. I knew he would be wondering what the problem was but I had no time to explain. When we reached the bridge over the Seine we threw the boots and weapons into the waters and hurried across towards our hotel. As the Conciergerie loomed up I remembered when I had been incarcerated there. If I was caught again, this time there would be no Napoleon Bonaparte to save me.

The owner was surprised to see me. I smiled. "I am sorry sir. I will have to pay and then we must leave. I have had some bad news and I must return south to my home in Provence."

As soon as I said I would pay he relaxed. He did not care where I was going; he could rent out our room and make more money. I led the horses south as I had told him and crossed the Seine. Then we headed along the river and crossed back over the river at Notre Dame. Sharp was in the dark but we had to be out of the city before the police started a hue and cry.

Luckily for us, it was a busy time of day and many people were moving along the streets. We went at the same speed as everyone else. The last thing we needed was to attract attention. The gates to the north of the city were jammed. A wagon bringing in goods had broken its wheel just inside the gates and it was mayhem. The guards were busy shouting at the poor carter and I could see that we could not escape that way.

A baker stood in the doorway of his shop laughing and shaking his head. He saw the two of us and said, "If you go over there," he pointed to his right, "there is a small gate. You'll have to lead your horses but you can get out."

"Thank you, sir. I am indebted to you."

Poor Trooper Sharp had no idea what was going on save that he saw the gesticulations. When I saw that the small postern gate was still open I almost shouted out with joy. We dismounted and left the city. Night was falling quickly along with a light drizzle which promised an uncomfortable journey north. As we left the outskirts of Paris behind us I wondered what to do for the best. I had no doubt that the police would be looking for us. I hoped that they would head south but I could not count on that. I thought of heading for the more familiar country around Breteuil but that was out of the question as they associated me with the death of Mama Tusson and her Russian lover. No, we would have to return the way we had come and that meant risking the soldiers at Beauvais.

My new career as a spy for Colonel Selkirk could be the shortest one yet.

Chapter 6

A few miles from Beauvais I took a side lane on the right of the main road. I had no idea where it went but I reasoned that if we rode along it for some miles and then kept taking a left turn, eventually I would rejoin the main road; hopefully beyond Beauvais. We were like ghosts in the night as we tried to get as far from Paris as we could on our poor mounts.

"Sir, mine won't get us much further. She's about all in."

"We can't stop but let us try leading them for a while."

In the end, it proved a blessing. We kept turning left at each junction and we reached the western outskirts of Beauvais. It was quiet and there were few people around. We were able to slip back along the main road and continue leading our horses. I held my finger to my lips. I did not want our voices to carry. The only sound was the gentle clop of the horse's hooves on the road. I was just about to remount when I heard hooves coming from the direction of Beauvais. I grabbed Sharp's shoulder and pushed him into the hedgerow. Had we been mounted then we would have been seen. As it was we were invisible in the dark.

It was a courier who rode by. I recognised the uniform. He was whipping his horse dangerously fast along the darkened road. I wondered if he carried news of us to Calais. If that was the case then we were in trouble. When his hoof beats had faded I gestured for Sharp to mount and we continued along the road. I knew from our earlier journey that the next part of the road was devoid of houses and habitation which meant we could risk riding again.

Suddenly I heard the distant crack of a pistol. I drew my sword and hurried on. The gunshot might attract someone from Beauvais but I did not want us stumbling into something dangerous whilst unarmed. We turned a bend in the road and saw three men standing over the courier. His horse had wandered off and they were searching his pouch. They were robbers.

"At them, Sharp!" I think the use of English confused them for they stared at us as though we were monsters.

We kicked our horses on and the three men stood looking like startled hares. I barged my horse into one as I slashed down at a second. I saw a pistol from the third man lining up at my head. Sharp's knife flew through the air and transfixed him. The man I had knocked down jumped to his feet and ran towards the courier's horse. He mounted it and scurried off across the fields.

"Search the bandits."

The courier was still alive although death was not far away. I could see that his life was oozing away through the hole in his stomach. "Thank you, sir, although I fear those felons have done for me. I pray you take these despatches to the admiral at Calais. They are most…" Then he died.

"You have done your duty, sir." I closed his eyes and laid him back down. I picked up the pouch. I felt guilty. He had thought I was a friend but I was an enemy. Fortune had favoured me that night. "Right Trooper Sharp, let's go. That bandit may have friends. We will have to risk these animals. We now have urgent information for Colonel Selkirk."

At least the message was not about us. There was a chance, perhaps, that we might be able to reach Calais and escape detection. Our good fortune ended with the storm which battered us as we neared the coast. I could tell that we were not receiving the worst of it although it was bad enough. Any ship caught at sea would be in serious difficulties.

It was mid-morning by the time we reached Calais. The storm was still buffeting the town and the rain sliced down like sabres.

The cold sleet seemed to penetrate every pore. The good news was that it kept people's heads down and we entered the town unobserved. We went directly to the stables where the surprised owner looked at the two nags he had sold us.

"I didn't expect you back so soon." He looked dubiously at the sorry-looking horses. "You have ridden them hard."

"They are horses and are there to be ridden. I believe you owe us some money now." I hated having to be so ruthless but I was playing the part. A businessman would not allow himself to lose money. For my own part, I would happily have returned them to him. Eventually, we agreed on a price. I think he thought he had robbed us but I was satisfied. I was concerned that he did not remember us.

We headed for the bar the captain of the boat had told us he used. As he had only sailed back the previous day I was not hopeful that he would be there and each moment we spent in Calais increased the risk of our capture. The bar was poorly lit and was filled with sailors who had just come ashore along with those seeking employment. It meant that they all left us to our own devices. I bought some drinks and transferred the documents from the courier's pouch to my coat. We would dispose of the pouch when it was convenient.

Suddenly I noticed that the landlord was paying us rather too much attention and he was talking with a stranger who had only just arrived. I dared not risk being trapped in the bar. I whispered to Trooper Sharp, "Drink up."

I had noticed that my companion never panicked and obeyed every order instantly. I had made a wise choice. I did not want to head back down the quayside to the town and so I headed along harbour towards the ships. I was just looking for a vessel which might be heading across the Channel although anywhere out of

France would do. I glanced behind me and saw the landlord and the stranger watching us. This would not do. I scanned ahead to find an escape route. There were only warehouses to the right and I did not wish to enter one only to find that I was trapped.

I noticed that there were far more ships in the harbour than there had been when we had arrived. Many of them looked storm damaged. My hopes of finding the same ship faded. It would probably have taken shelter in Dover.

Trooper Sharp suddenly said, "Those men; they are following us."

I looked over my shoulder and saw that there were now three men following us. Ahead of us, I saw the customs officers and their desk. That meant we were trapped. We could not pass them and we could not go back. I contemplated drawing my sword but that would have done us no good whatsoever. Then I heard a voice I recognised, "Mr Macgregor, what are you doing here?"

I saw Richard, who had been the First Mate on the Witch, Captain Dinsdale's ship. "Thank God, Richard! Where is the Witch?"

I looked down the line of ships and did not see Captain Dinsdale's ship. He laughed and shook his head, "She is in Sicily." He pointed to the ship tied up next to us. It was called 'The Star'. "This is your ship sir and I am the captain."

I felt relief but recognised that we were still in danger. "Sharp, get the bags on board. Richard, we are in danger. I am a wanted man."

Richard was a giant of a man and many people took his size to indicate slowness of mind. They could not have been further from the truth. "Get aboard then sir." He cupped his hand as he shouted to his men, "Hoist the foresail. Cast off forrard."

We raced aboard. His crew might have been shocked at the captain's orders but they obeyed. The wind caught the little foresail and the bow edged away from the harbour as I scrambled aboard with Richard and the gangplank was yanked on board. I saw the Customs officers point at us and the two National Guardsmen aimed their muskets at the ship. The men who had been following us ran towards the last line which held the ship to the shore.

"Cast off aft! Hoist the mainsail."

Thankfully the seaman was able to throw the line ashore. I don't know if we would have been able to carry out the manoeuvre had the wind not been so strong but the ship suddenly leapt away from the land like a spurred horse. The two muskets popped ineffectually at us and we were safe.

Richard came over to me grinning. "You are the most interesting owner I have ever met. You are lucky that I had to call in at Calais last night for repairs." He pointed at the carpenter who was still making a new spar. "We hadn't quite finished. Still, all's well that ends well."

"Don't count any chickens yet, captain." I pointed to the Customs officers who were racing to the guard boat at the end of the harbour."

"You and your man had better get below. We don't want you in the way do we sir?"

I suppose I could have taken offence but I knew that Richard was a good sailor and I would be in the way. "Very well Captain. Come along Trooper Sharp, let's go to the cabin."

The ship was very similar to 'The Witch' and I found the main mess easily. "Best make ourselves comfortable, Sharp. We are being chased."

He laid the bags down and then said, "This is your boat, sir?"

I nodded, "Well half of it is anyway."

"Then why are you a soldier, sir? Couldn't you just live off the profits?"

It was a thought which had flickered through my mind before. "I could but I enjoy the life in the cavalry."

He smiled, "There are rumours in the barracks that you have served before. Even Uncle Jimmy says that. I know you have, sir."

"Well the less you know the better."

"Some of the lads reckon you did something awful in another regiment and have rejoined under a false name."

"Which would be silly as, if that was the case, then I would risk being identified by a former comrade. However, let them think that, Sharp. It will stop their speculation."

I took the opportunity of looking at the documents intended for the admiral in Calais. When I saw the seal and the signature I knew that we had struck gold. It was an order from Bonaparte himself ordering the admiral to prepare to supply Admiral Villeneuve's fleet. They were to capture Haiti and Louisiana. If they did that then France would become far richer. My trip might have been a short one but it had been fruitful; if we could evade the guard boat.

I knew when we had left the harbour for the ship began to pitch and toss alarmingly. Sharp's eyes widened in terror. "Do not worry trooper. The captain is a good seaman."

I could hear orders being shouted and the noise of sails being hoisted. Then I heard the unmistakable pop of small cannon. I waited for the crack which would tell me that they had been lucky and struck us. There was nothing and then we heeled so much that Sharp fell from his seat. He had a shocked look upon his face as though he thought we were sinking. There was another couple of pops but mercifully no hits.

After another half hour or so a messenger came from the captain. "Captain says you can come on deck if you like. The Froggies have given up." He laughed. "Last we saw they were bailing like buggery!"

The deck was slick with water but Richard had rigged ropes as handrails and we made our way aft where the huge skipper was steering the ship himself. He gestured with his head, "The open sea was a bit much for them. The French are not good sailors."

"Thank you, captain." He inclined his head. "Did you see anything of the French Fleet when you were sailing north?"

"Aye, they were just off the Portuguese coast. A big fleet it was too. I must be honest I was a bit nervous." He pointed to the masthead. "Luckily we sail this under the flag of Naples. The French tolerate us."

I heard the sound of Sharp emptying the contents of his stomach over the side and I smiled. I had earned my sea legs the hard way. He would be better the next time we sailed. "Where are you bound?"

"London. Trade has picked up since the peace and Mr Fortnum can't get enough of our wines. This is the new vintage. We had a good summer and we can't get enough of it." He nudged me gently in the ribs. "A tidy profit both ways for you then sir eh? Your family and the ship."

"I suppose you are right."

"Which begs the question, what were you doing in France and being chased?" He held up his hand, "I don't want to know the answer although I have probably closed Calais to my ship now."

"Sorry about that, Richard."

"It is your ship, sir."

We would be back in London quicker than Colonel Selkirk had anticipated. It would save us the long ride from London to

Canterbury too. On the journey up the Thames, I wrote a letter for my relatives in Sicily explaining my position as a Captain in the 11th Light Dragoons. I knew we had peace now but I was not certain that it would last. As I stepped ashore I gave the letter to Richard. "Please have this sent to my family when you are next in Sicily and thank you again, captain."

He smiled, "Thank you, sir. I'll have another tale to tell Captain Dinsdale now won't I?"

I took rooms at the 'Coal Hole' again and left Trooper Sharp there. He still looked a little green around the gills from the crossing and I did not need him for my meeting with the colonel.

To say he was surprised to see me was an understatement. He frowned. "Did ye not go then?"

"I did go sir but I was recognised in Paris and had to flee."

"Bah, a waste of time then." He was like a grumpy bear awoken early from hibernation.

I smiled, "No sir, quite the contrary. I discovered that the French are on a war footing. There are manoeuvres and briefings taking place all over northern France. There must be many camps there and…" I flourished the letters. "I discovered this on a courier who had been attacked by robbers. They are sending the French Fleet to Calais."

His demeanour changed in an instant. He banged the table in excitement, "Are they by God!" he grabbed the documents and began to read them.

As he was reading them I told him what Richard had told me. "The French Fleet is sailing along the Portuguese coast even as we speak."

He jumped up and pumped my hand. "Well done Robbie. I knew you would do well. This is just the sort of thing I hoped that you would discover." He clutched the letters and led me from his office. "I will need you again but not for some little time. I was going to send you to Malta; I know you know the island well but Prime Minister Addington has decided not to hand it over to the French after all. Enjoy yourself and settle down at the regiment."

"But they are in the Cape."

"Oh didn't I tell you, they will be coming back as soon as they arrive. The damned politicians have given the Cape back to the Dutch as part of the peace treaty. So you see you haven't missed anything. They'll be back by early summer." He smacked the letters against his open palm. "And now I will get our little admiral to put the French's nose out of joint."

I shook my head as I left the building. What a waste of time for the regiment. To be on a cramped transport for weeks on end only to find that you had the same journey to endure was a crime. The colonel was right, damned politicians!

Sharp and I took the mail-coach back to the barracks. We caught up on our lost sleep and travelled much faster than had we been on horseback. We reached the barracks by evening and surprised Percy and the Sergeant Major.

"Sorry Percy; I have come back to spoil your fun."

He shrugged, "I had a few days to play at commanding officer. That will suffice."

I nodded to Sergeant Major Jones. "And while I was in Whitehall I heard that the regiment will be coming straight back here. They will arrive by late spring at the earliest, perhaps early summer. You know what that means?"

He sighed, "Yes sir. The horses will be in awful condition. We will need to send out a party to get remounts. We will need more than twenty. We will require an officer to accompany them."

I looked at Percy, "Well Austen, you or Jackson?"

"Well if we have the choice sir then me!"

"Good. You can choose your men and leave tomorrow. Have we had many recruits?"

"No, sir. Only about eight or so."

"Right well I will take out a recruiting party and we will see how many we can drum up."

I suddenly realised how excited I was to be performing relatively mundane tasks. No-one would be shooting at me and I would be leading some fine troopers. Life was becoming good, for a change.

I spent the next two days getting to know Lieutenant Jackson. He seemed to have gained confidence in the last week and I saw the sparks of a decent officer. Talking to him I discovered that his family were not well off and, like Austen, he would need to win a promotion on a battlefield. I could not tell him but I knew that we would be at war sooner rather than later.

His face lit up when I told him that I was leaving him in command when I took out the recruiting party. I took with me Quartermaster Sergeant Grant, Trooper Sharp, Bugler Jones and Corporal Seymour. The corporal had improved as a soldier since Jem Green had deserted. I wanted the opportunity to observe him closely. When we had filled the ranks of my squadron with recruits then we would have to start a new troop and that would need sergeants.

I made sure we all wore our best uniforms and that the horses were well turned out. Badger had enjoyed the rest and Trooper Sharp had trimmed both his mane and his tail. His coat shone and I knew that we would attract a crowd. We headed into the centre of Canterbury. The outbreak of war had meant that many workers had lost their jobs. The army might be a more attractive proposition, especially in peacetime. In addition, the smart uniform was said to attract the ladies.

The infantry had a drummer to attract a crowd but I would use my bugler. We rode close to the Cathedral and the nearby alehouses. After tying up our horses I nodded to Jones who began to go through all the calls that he knew. He was a good musician and he stitched them together so that they almost made a tune. We soon had a crowd who gathered around to see what we were about.

Quartermaster Sergeant Grant had done this before and he began his routine, a little like a fairground barker. "You see here men of the finest cavalry regiment in Great Britain. Look at this fine uniform and admire the magnificent horses. Now we have a few places left for any suitable men who can ride." Like a conjurer a coin suddenly appeared in his hand. "Now for those lucky few who join up today I will offer a King's Shilling." The coins disappeared again and he rubbed his hands together. "Now then, my lads, who'll be the first?"

I knew it would not be as easy as that and no-one came forward. Corporal Seymour shook his head, "You see the trouble is, Quartermaster Grant, that these lads think they will be marching up and down hills with the Grand Old Duke of York." Many of the crowd laughed thinking of the satirical rhyme. "They probably don't know that he isn't leading our troops anymore. They probably don't know that the rest of the regiment is, even now, sunning themselves at the Cape of Good Hope where it is warmer weather than here." He winked at a couple of young lads and, lowering his voice, said, "Probably being waited on by a couple of dusky maidens I wouldn't doubt. They'll be enjoying the pleasure of a rich man and a summer cruise."

It was as though the flood gates had been opened and the two young men started it. By the end of the day we had ten recruits all of whom had either signed up or made their mark. As we led them back to the barracks I said, to Grant, "But suppose they can't ride? The colonel won't be very happy."

He grinned, "Don't you worry about that sir. We can make anyone into a horseman given time and if the Sergeant Major is correct and the rest of the regiment won't be back for a couple of months then the colonel will have another troop of trained men."

He was right. I went on the next three recruitment drives and then realised that I was superfluous; Grant and Seymour were like a double act and they worked well together. I sent Lieutenant Jackson, who had realised that commanding an empty barracks was no fun, with them and it did his confidence no end of good. I joined Percy training both men and horses. Those three months were glorious. I had never had three months of peace and never had such power. It had to end and it did when two things happened. War was declared in May and the regiment arrived back two weeks later.

Chapter 7

The talk in the mess the night the regiment returned was depressing. Many horses had suffered after months at sea; a sea voyage is always stressful and these poor animals had barely landed before being returned to the torture of a transport. The troopers were no longer fit, but even worse was the memory of so much time being wasted.

"Politicians, Robbie, they haven't the first clue. They must have known before we left that they were going to give the Cape away." Even David was no longer his ebullient self.

I tried to cheer them up with positive thoughts. "Well at least we can now build up the strength of the troopers and the horses."

"If that Bonaparte fellow gives us time. When we were sailing north we passed Nelson and his fleet. Our captain told us that there was a French fleet in the area. Good old Nelson, trust him to sniff out the Frog's plans."

I smiled. I could hardly divulge that we had intercepted the plans. I gestured with my head, "And how did the DeVeres take it?"

"If you thought they were bad here you should have heard them whinge and complain on the transport. I am sure that was why the major and the colonel sailed on another ship. They did not have to endure their incessant moaning." He shook his head and then his face became serious. "That wasn't the worst. They had men flogged for the most trivial of misdemeanours. The morale of the troopers is at rock bottom. Between the floggings and the disease we couldn't field a whole troop let alone a squadron. The only squadron which would do justice to the regiment now is yours. Well done."

I shook my head, "It was these two lieutenants. They managed to get the best remounts and more recruits than we needed. We can start E Squadron as soon as the colonel gives the order."

"I think he will have to leave that until the men have recovered."

That was a luxury we did not have. The next morning I was summoned to the colonel's office. We had all seen the courier arrive and then leave. I had wondered what he had brought and I was intrigued when I was summoned. Part of me wondered if Colonel Selkirk had another plan for me. I had heard that Napoleon had occupied mainland Italy and only Sicily remained free. Was I to be sent there? Speculation was of no use. I would find out soon enough.

The colonel was red with anger. "Politicians Matthews! I'd sooner shoot them than the French!"

The major was calmer, "There is little use upsetting yourself sir. We can do nought about it. You know as well as I do that we have to obey orders."

The colonel subsided and nodded. He waved at me to enter; obviously he was too upset to speak. The major gestured for me to sit. "We have been ordered to Swedish Pomerania." I had never even heard of the place. The major smiled at my dumbstruck expression and strode to the map of Europe on the wall. In terms of who ruled what it was highly inaccurate but at least the coastlines were the same.

He picked up a letter opener and used it as an improvised pointer. "It is here on the southern side of the Baltic. It is close to Prussia but, more importantly, it is close to Hanover and Brunswick. They are amongst our only allies, save Portugal, on the continent. Bonaparte is already eyeing them up and we are being sent, along with a battalion of infantry and a horse battery, to be on hand should the French invade."

It was ludicrous. My mouth must have dropped open for I saw the major smile again. "Sir, if Bonaparte decides to invade Hanover, it will be with whole Corps. What could a mere brigade do?"

"It is a gesture Robbie. It is the politicians at work. It shows that Britain will not allow the French a free hand in Europe and it encourages those who might be wavering. The good news is that we only have to send a squadron." His face became serious. "The bad news is that as you have the only squadron ready then it will have to be yours."

I began to work out the logistics of taking my squadron abroad. I was at least one officer short and I was about to mention that when the major said, "As you are a captain short and in view of your relative inexperience then I shall be accompanying you. We will take the Sergeant Major too. His experience and organisation will be worth another twenty men. We will have to take the doctor as well."

I was pleased that we were taking Sergeant Major Jones; his experience and reassuring presence would make up for any deficiencies in either the two lieutenants or myself. Having just prepared three squadrons for foreign service it was no problem for us to organise merely one. It was made easier by the fact that we had spent the last couple of months drilling and preparing for just such an event. The colonel paraded the whole regiment the day we left. The contrast in the mounts and the men was remarkable. The horses and men which had been to the Cape drooped and sagged. Our squadron paraded with a spring in their step and a smile on their faces. I rode behind the major as we took the road to Dover where the transports would be waiting. The other elements, the infantry battalion and the horse artillery would be proceeding from Harwich, close to their base.

I had loaded Badger on to a ship before and he took to it calmly and easily. Some of the newer horses became agitated. I wondered if the vet might have been more appropriate than the doctor. The transport was hired from the East India Company and was therefore both comfortable and adequate for the task. The stalls for the horses were well ventilated and roomy. There was a good system to secure them in bad weather and a small area for them to be exercised.

As officers, the five of us had a cabin each, while the men had hammocks just as the sailors did. I was looking forward to the voyage. I enjoyed seeing new places and we would pass Denmark as well as Sweden and Hanover. These were new lands to me.

I did not get much time to see the coastline as we passed north. We were far too busy preparing for the forthcoming campaign. The officers and the Sergeant Major spent every day examining maps of both Pomerania and Hanover.

"I am not sure what Horse Guards intend us to actually do but I suspect we will be scouting for the infantry."

"How many infantry will there be sir?"

"If it is a full battalion then it could be nine hundred. On the other hand it might be as few as five hundred men and the guns will just be four or six pounders and only six of them. We are a token gesture and we are expendable." I saw the looks on the lieutenants' faces. I think they thought there was planning in all of this. "Be under no illusions gentlemen we will be on our own over there."

"And who will command?"

"The commanding officer of the 5th is Colonel Mackenzie so I assume it will be him." The major spread his arms. "I know nothing about him. The 5th are from Northumberland and have a good reputation. That is something any way. As for the battery, I think it is Johnston's Battery."

"How do we address him sir?"

"Brigadier or Colonel. Sometimes they can be a little prickly so we will use Brigadier until we see the lie of the land."

I do not know what I expected but Stralsund, the capital of Swedish Pomerania, was not it. It was a walled city which looked as though it had been preserved in time. We could have been entering a town in the Middle Ages. Everything looked old as we entered the port. The harbour only had small ships within it and the guns which protruded from its bastions were ancient pieces. A couple of frigates could have captured it.

We disembarked the men while the horses were hoisted over the side and it gave me the opportunity to observe the soldiers who were guarding the guns. They wore strange little shakos with a turned up brim and a large feather. They looked to be as antique as the town. Their muskets were also longer and looked older than any I had seen, even amongst the Austrians. It did not bode well but, as the major had told me, Sweden was not at war with France yet but their king, Gustave, liked Britain. He had given permission to cross his land and enter Hanover.

A small carriage halted next to us and a fussy little man with a fur hat emerged. The hat seemed strange as it was almost June. He had a pair of glasses perched precariously on the end of his nose and a harassed looking assistant behind him hovered with a mass of documents.

"I am the Consul here. James Whittingham is the name. This is my assistant, Postelthwaite." He shook his head, "I know preposterous name what? But at least he speaks the local languages." I felt sorry for the young man but he must have been used to it for he smiled.

"I am Major Hyde-Smith and…"

The Consul waved an impatient hand away, "Yes, yes, I know who you are and these are your men. Now I have secured an area outside the city walls for you to camp. The other forces aren't here yet. I have arranged for some supplies to be sent to you but the city elders made it quite clear that they do not want you in their town. "He saw the major's raised eyebrows. "I know what you are going to say major, that your men will behave themselves and I do not doubt that you are correct. However this part of Sweden is surrounded by armies who would like to take it from them and they are suspicious. Added to the fact that Admiral Nelson was a little high handed when he sank the Danish Fleet a couple of years ago, you can understand it. Besides as soon as the other units arrive you can toddle off to Hanover." He smiled as though that explained all.

"Do you know how long we are likely to be in Hanover?"

"Good gracious, no. It all depends upon the French eh what?" He suddenly became serious and gestured for the major and me to close with him. "To be honest I have heard rumours of French armies massing on the borders of Hanover so I suspect that you will be busy sooner rather than later." He smiled as though we would be pleased to be facing huge French armies.

Once the horses were unloaded we saddled them and waited for the wagons with the other equipment to follow. We would be sleeping under canvas and I was grateful that this was summer. I would not enjoy having to spend time here in winter. The Texel had been cold enough and this country was rumoured to be even colder.

Since our visit to France, Trooper Sharp had seemed to grow in confidence. He was no longer the diffident young man who was put upon by all and sundry. He now gave instructions and orders to the same troopers who had mocked him before. He was also able to banter and joke with the NCOs too. The change made my life much easier. I no longer had to watch him and make sure that he was not suffering at the hands of another Jem Green. I knew that my equipment would arrive at our new camp and my tent would be erected before any other tent. He was efficient.

The major followed the little carriage with Mr Whittingham on board and we lumbered through the town. The streets were narrow and people peered at us as we rode through them. The men had been ordered to adopt a serious demeanour and we rode in silence. It was almost a funeral procession. The field we had been allocated was, mercifully, dry. I hated wading through mud in the morning.

Sergeant Major Jones nodded approvingly, "If you gentlemen would like to take yourselves off and explore the area I will get this lot organised."

It was a polite way of telling us that he did not require officers around to interfere with his systems. Major Hyde-Smith smiled and said, "Thank you Sergeant Major, we will be back for dinner."

"Very well sirs, enjoy yourselves."

We needed to know how far it was to the border and we rode west. No-one spoke to us, which was just as well as none of us could speak Swedish. They all stared at these officers in the strange helmets and blue uniforms. I glanced over my shoulder at Austen and Jackson; they were both staring back at the civilians.

"I realise that you two have never been abroad before but try to avoid staring with your mouths open. You are officers after all."

"Sorry Captain Matthews."

Major Hyde-Smith inclined his head, "I suppose we all had to experience this once although you are still an enigma, Captain

Matthews. One of these days you must tell me your background and how you gained the experience you obviously have."

"When this war is over sir there will be time for such tales."

"At the present rate we will both be old men."

"Then it will make a pleasant diversion after dinner."

We had left the town and were well into the countryside. It began to remind me more and more of parts of Austria. The churches were different but many of the buildings had a similar appearance and design.

We rode for a couple of hours and then the major stopped. "We could have crossed the border already. How the devil do you know?"

Just then a cart with an older and a younger man came from a tiny side road and they stopped to stare at us. "If we smile, sir, we won't frighten them as much."

The major smiled and then said, "Hanover?" They gave us blank looks. "Brunswick." He repeated them a little louder as though they were deaf.

The old man turned to the young man and said something. I found I could understand a little of it. They sounded as though they were speaking a language similar to Austrian. I tried some Austrian and asked them where Hanover was.

It did the trick and they both grinned and began to jabber at me as though I was fluent. I held up my hands and asked them to speak slowly. They did so and then the older one asked me if we were Austrians or Prussians. When I told him that we were English his face broke into a grin. I guessed we were welcome.

"I didn't get all of it, sir but I think he said that we crossed over the border at the last farm we passed."

The three of them stared at me. "You speak Swedish?"

"No Major, I understand and speak a little Austrian and they speak German."

Major Hyde-Smith shook his head, "Remarkable!" I merely shrugged and he added, "We might as well go back then. Now we know how close we are."

As we trotted back along the road I ventured. "I would have thought that someone from the Hanoverian army would have been here. It would have made matters much easier."

"And just when I was thinking how clever you were Captain Matthews you let yourself down. The role of the War Office is to make life difficult for the ordinary soldier. When did they ever consult on anything which would help us to do our job better? It is just luck that we have a good sword and it is down to keen cavalrymen that we have such a fine carbine. No, we shall muddle along, improvising as we go. It is the British way. Thank God for Sergeant Major Jones." He lowered his voice so that the lieutenants would not overhear us. "I am more worried about our Brigadier. In my experience colonels of infantry think that cavalry can travel as fast as a bullet and surround ten times their number. I hope our chap is more of a realist."

The camp was all set up with cook fires burning and a general look of order when we returned. The tents were in immaculately straight lines and the horse lines were far enough from the tents so that we would not be too discomfited by the smell.

Trooper Sharp was there to take my horse as soon as we reached the flag and guidon which indicated the headquarters. "I'll take your stuff sir and see to Badger." He pointed to a tent three down from the headquarters one. "That's yours sir and mine is just behind it." He took my helmet, sword and pistols and handed me the forage cap. It had been the first time I had worn my new helmet for such a long period and it was a relief to take it off.

Sergeant Major Jones flourished towards a laid table with his arm. "We have no regimental silver but I managed to get a couple of bottles of some white wine for you gentlemen. I chilled them in the river sir. Your food will be along shortly."

"Thank you Sergeant Major; you are a godsend." As he left the tent Major Hyde-Smith said, "You know I was thinking of having a wash but the thought of a chilled German white has put all that from my mind. What's say we taste this unexpected treat?"

The wine was delicious and chilled enough to refresh and get the taste of salt from our mouths. The food was filling albeit dull but Sergeant Major Jones outdid himself when he arrived with a bottle containing a clear liquid. "The locals drink this sir. It's called Schnapps."

I nodded, "Like whisky but even more fiery."

The major said, "James, do join us." The Sergeant Major looked as though he would refuse but the major said, "I insist."

When we had filled our glasses he nodded at Lieutenant Jackson. The youngest officer stood and said, "Gentlemen the King!"

I sipped mine but Percy took half of it in one go and I saw his eyes widen at the shock.

"By God sir, that'll wake you up in the morning." The major then nodded to Jackson again who said, "The regiment." I noticed that we all sipped it this time; even Sergeant Major Jones.

The other transports arrived during the night so that we were awoken before dawn by the arrival of six hundred infantry and a battery of six guns. Sergeant Major Jones had chosen the best part of the site for our camp. I did not think that the infantry would appreciate being that close to our horses. However, as it turned out, they did not have to suffer long.

By the time dawn had fully broken our men were breakfasted and on parade. Major Hyde-Smith came over to me. "We had better discover what is expected of us. I am not sure that we will be moving today."

When we reached the infantry camp we saw that Mr Whittingham and his assistant were there along with a very young captain of the Royal Horse Artillery. Brigadier Mackenzie was also younger than Colonel Fenton. He looked very upright with a monocle and a fine moustache. He would not have looked out of place in Bonaparte's Guides. He strode over to meet us.

"Ah glad you are settled in already. Rum place what?"

"It is interesting sir."

Mr Whittingham obviously felt we had spent enough time chatting. "Well gentlemen we need to get on. I have heard that a French Corps is already on the borders with Hanover. You need to get across the border and offer your assistance as soon as you can."

The major and Brigadier Mackenzie exchanged a look of exasperation. "Sir, my men have been up half the night unloading the transport and erecting tents. They are in no condition to march…" he obviously did not know how far we would have to march and he waved a vague hand, "however far it is."

I thought the little official would explode. Major Hyde-Smith said, "We have rested for a day. I could take my squadron south and reconnoitre. If you followed tomorrow then we should have a suitable camp set up and be able to have a clearer picture of what is going on."

The relief on the brigadier's face was obvious. "Thank you very much sir. That will help."

The young captain piped up. "Sir! My chaps are raring to go. We can go with the 11th."

"Very well. I expect you to keep me informed though. None of this death and glory sort of thing."

Major Hyde-Smith saluted, "Of course sir."

The little official fixed the major with a keen stare. "Thank you gentlemen, and if you would keep me informed also."

"Of course Mr Whittingham and where will you be?"

"Why behind these fortress walls of course."

The captain trotted along behind us, "That's a stroke of luck. I didn't fancy moving at the pace of the infantry." He held out his hand, "Captain Johnston's the name."

We introduced ourselves. "We will lead off," the major pointed down the road. "Hanover is just a few miles in that direction. If we have to move quickly then I don't want to have to plough through your artillery pieces so keep your chaps at the rear with the baggage."

I could see the disappointment on his face but what the major had said was no different from his comments about the infantry. Ignoring the artilleryman the major turned to me, "As you can speak a little of the language then take a sergeant and half a dozen men and act as scouts."

"Sir. How far should we go?"

"Until we find some Hanoverian troops," he laughed, "or a French Corps."

I disobeyed my order; I took Corporal Seymour rather than a sergeant. He was reliable and the men liked him. I allowed him to choose the four other men who would accompany Trooper Sharp as the sixth man. As we left the camp I spoke to them. "I am not certain that our allies know we are coming so keep your weapons holstered. It is their country and we are strangers here." I tapped the helmet. "Luckily only the British wear these but we will have to tread warily."

We had ridden half a mile when one of the troopers said, "Sir, what if we meet the French?"

Corporal Seymour answered for me, "Then we will be in the deep shit, my son. It will mean the French have beaten the Hanoverians before we got here." He turned to me, "That right sir?"

"Succinctly put, Corporal Seymour."

I noticed that Sharp was riding as confidently as the corporal and they were, in fact riding side by side. That was a good sign. I missed the camaraderie of the 17th Chasseurs. The sooner I could create that in D Troop the better. We passed the farmhouse and I said, "Right boys; we are now in Hanover. Keep your eyes peeled. We need our allies and a good camp."

We rode through one small town and I halted the men. I found an old man smoking a pipe outside his home. I told him we were British and asked him where the nearest troops were. His accent was thicker than the others had been and it took a couple of attempts to both ask the questions and receive the answer but I deduced that we were fifteen miles from a garrison of Hanoverian troops. It was a town called Gustrow. I headed towards it, hoping that we would find some troops there.

The countryside was filled with growth and life. It had been a good summer and they would have good crops. I was busy wondering about the people and how they lived when Badger suddenly pricked up his ears. As I bent down to stroke his mane I heard the crack of a pistol and felt a ball whizz above my head. The other horses began to prance as their agitated riders went for the weapons.

"Keep your hands away from your weapons." Then I shouted, in German, "We are English. We are English."

Twenty riders suddenly appeared from the hedgerows. Their weapons were levelled at us. I put my hands up and waited for the officer to approach me. I recognised him by the fact that he held no carbine but had a sword the equal of mine. "Do you speak English?"

He shook his head and I sighed, I would have to give him a mixture of Austrian and the odd German o I knew. The languages were similar but, as I had discovered with the old man there were enough differences to be dangerous. I explained that we were part of a brigade sent to help the Hanoverians. It was obvious that they were not expecting us but when the weapons were lowered I knew that they believed us. But for Badger it could have had a tragic outcome. Had I been shot I think my men would have all fired and died.

The officer agreed to escort us to Gustrow. I turned to Trooper Sharp. "Find the major and tell him we have gone with this officer to his regiment."

I didn't need to explain to Sharp that he was my insurance in case this did not go the way I had planned. As we rode towards the distant town I noticed that his men rode on either side of my handful. Were we allies or prisoners?

Chapter 8

It was a garrison of infantry. There were no artillery pieces and the cavalry which escorted us was merely brigaded with the four companies. I realised that I did not have enough of the language to be able to converse with our allies but I was desperate to know if the French had crossed the border.

The major in command of the garrison listened to the lieutenant who had met us. He nodded. He spoke slowly to me, "I understand you speak a little of our language."

I caught most of it and said, "A little." I used a hand gesture as well which made him smile.

"I have sent a message to the commander of…" he said a word which I did not understand and he waved his hand around. I took this to mean the district and I nodded. "Until then, rest."

"Corporal, we are amongst friends. Water the horses."

As they strode off the major gestured to a table set outside the headquarters building. We sat and he smiled. I noticed that he was definitely rotund. I suspected that he sat more than he marched and he had the florid face of a drinker. He smiled a lot and seemed pleasant enough. "Hot day. Yes?"

"Hot day, yes."

He suddenly seemed to get an idea and barked an order. His orderly left the office and raced across the main square. I wondered what was afoot. When he returned with two brimming tankards of foaming beer I knew what it was.

He beamed, "Good beer. From Hamburg!"

"Cheers!" I drank and it was delicious. I felt sorry for my men who stood by the horses at the trough jealously watching as the foaming liquid slipped down. I was taking it steady but my host shouted for his orderly again and soon we had another in our hands. Hospitality meant that I could not refuse but much more and I would be roaring drunk. I was relieved when I heard the hooves of the rest of the squadron arriving.

Major Hyde-Smith turned to Jones and said, "I can see I have much to learn about campaigning from Captain Matthews."

I jumped to my feet and introduced the two majors. "I have not had time to find a camp site yet sir. The major here has sent to the Commanding General of the district for guidance."

Sergeant Major Jones said, "There is a good little spot just north of the town. There are trees for shade and a stream for water."

"Ask him, Matthews. You are the expert."

"I am sorry sir but my knowledge of this language is limited." By a series of hand gestures accompanied by the few words I knew which would be useful I conveyed the major's request. It was granted and we rode to the new camp. I think the Hanoverian major was disappointed that we would not carry on drinking.

We had just erected the tents when my erstwhile drinking companion brought the news. He was beaming from ear to ear. He shook me and the major by the hand. "The general says we are friends. He comes tomorrow to speak with you and your general."

It took a couple of attempts to glean all that information but at least we had performed our first task successfully. After he had gone Major Hyde-Smith took me to one side. "So far Mr Matthews I am somewhat superfluous. You have done a good job here. I can see why that Colonel Selkirk uses you. You are very resourceful."

I couldn't tell him that growing up bilingual seemed to make it easier for me to learn other languages. I was also keenly aware that the English did not take to other languages well. They seemed to believe that the rest of the world ought to speak their language.

Their general arrived with an honour guard of heavy cavalry. He had with him some staff officers. As they rode up Major Hyde-Smith said, "Well this is a bit of a problem. The brigadier isn't here yet and I am not sure of the protocol."

"You will have to speak with him sir. It would be rude otherwise. If these are anything like the Austrians they believe in doing everything properly."

"Ah another chink into Captain Matthews' background. You have had dealings with the Austrian army."

The general stepped down and looked towards the staff lieutenant next to him. Thankfully he began to speak in English. "This is General Amperstadt and he is delighted to have his British allies come to join him."

The major nodded. "I am Major Hyde Smith and the Brigadier in charge of this expedition is Colonel Mackenzie. He will be along shortly."

As if on cue we heard the drum beat of approaching soldiers. Colonel Mackenzie rode at the head of the red coated infantrymen and they looked a fine sight. I could see that the general was impressed. Major Hyde-Smith was worried about the brigadier's reaction but the infantryman was just happy to have found some Hanoverian troops and someone who could speak English.

The four of them retired to the major's headquarters while the infantry were assigned a camp. The general and his entourage left after an hour and our two senior officers came out. Colonel Mackenzie said to his aide, "Officer's call if you please."

When we were all assembled an aide unrolled a map. "It seems we have arrived none too soon. The French are massing across the border and the Hanoverians do not have enough men to watch all the crossing points. Nor are they organised enough yet to meet them in the field. Our job is to help plug the gaps and buy that time." He jabbed his pointer at a red spot on the map. "This is Dannenberg. The 11th Light Dragoons and the Horse Artillery will make a forced march and build a defensive position there. The Hanoverians are pulling their troops from there to fortify another part of the line. The 5th will also force-march and join you again tomorrow."

Lieutenant Jackson said, "Just like a game of leap frog."

Major Hyde-Smith silenced him with a glare but the brigadier laughed, "Yes it seems that way doesn't it? We are replacing two batteries of artillery, four regiments of infantry and a full regiment of cavalry."

Major Hyde-Smith asked, "Questions?"

I stood. "Sir, what is our purpose at Dannenberg?" He seemed to see me for the first time and his look was one of puzzlement. "What I mean sir is are we to stop the enemy there or is there a more strategic function to our role?"

He seemed relieved by the question. "We are keeping the road open as long as we can. If the French break through then the Hanoverians intend to get as many of her soldiers out as possible. They will head to Rostock and Stralsund. We have to go to Stralsund but they have the option."

I nodded, "We are covering a retreat."

"Quite. Now the general is leaving that lieutenant with us and a dozen of his horsemen. They will wait for us in Dannenberg and facilitate the changeover. I will be leaving my headquarters staff here at Gustrow to keep an eye on the equipment and to begin to pack it up. Your men will have to billet in Dannenberg. Good luck."

And that was it. We went to our horses and left. We carried everything that we might need: blankets, greatcoats and ammunition. It reminded me of Italy when we had moved so fast that we had left our supplies far behind. Here it was more desperate. I knew how fast the French could move and I feared for the lumbering 5th.

We did not ride at our normal pace but trotted at a healthy nine miles an hour. We stopped every hour for ten minutes but we still managed to reach the town in eleven hours. Many of the men had never ridden so far before and I knew that many would be weary and saddle sore.

Lieutenant Von Doren was waiting with a happy grin on his face as we rode into the small town. The ten dragoons with him looked as though they knew their business and it added to our ability to find the enemy.

"Welcome gentlemen. There is a small barracks here. It will accommodate you but not your infantry colleagues."

"We will sleep there tonight and allow the 5th to use it tomorrow."

The lieutenant looked surprised. "What is it you English say? The early bird catches the beetle."

"It's worm and we need every soldier to be as comfortable as possible. We will switch and switch about so that every man has at least one night in two in comfort. Now Lieutenant Von Doren, any more news of the French?"

"Not yet sir."

"Good. Captain Matthews and Sergeant Major Jones go with Captain Johnson and position the artillery at the end of town. While there is still light begin to build some defences. "

All three of us snapped a, "Sir!"

"7th Troop fall in and follow me."

When we reached the end of the town we found an old wooden bridge which crossed a stream. "This looks good to me Captain Johnson."

He rubbed his hands together. "It certainly does. I'll have one gun on the bridge loaded with grapeshot and the other two on either side."

I pointed to the hedgerow which tumbled down to the river. "If we cut some of that we can bring it closer to the bridge and make life harder for them."

Quartermaster Sergeant Grant said, "Leave that with me."

"Corporal Seymour, see if you can find a couple of axes. Cut down the trees opposite the bridge. It will give us a better field of fire and we can use them as a barricade in front of the bridge."

Sergeant Major Jones said, "I'll see if I can get some empty hessian sacks and filled them with river sand. It will give some protection to the gunners."

Suddenly I was alone with Trooper Sharp. "Come on Sharp. Let's cut across the bridge and scout out the other side."

The ground was flat and filled with farms. The edges of the farms were marked with trees and hedgerows. I reckoned that we would have plenty of warning of an enemy approaching the bridge. We explored for three miles and found just a couple of sleepy hamlets. We returned to the bridge and I was pleased to see half a barrier in place. More importantly, the artillery was in place, ready to sweep away anyone who attempted to cross the bridge.

"Tomorrow, Sergeant Major, we will make those banks a little more difficult too eh?"

"Yes sir."

The watches arranged and the sentries set, we ate. The officers and the NCOs had to eat together, which was not a problem. Jackson was on duty which made Lieutenant Austen the junior officer. He watched all those around the table, even the NCOs with a little awe on his face. All of them were older than he was and many had already seen action. He was as silent as I had ever seen him.

A thought struck me. "Sir, I know that there was a garrison here but, to my mind the crossing of the Elbe some five miles back is a much better place to hold up a pursuing army. Here they can cross the river further up and flank us."

"I know. The same thought struck me. We will see what the brigadier says when he comes tomorrow, or tonight. In the meantime we will deploy a troop on each flank to stop just such a flanking move."

Captain Johnson, who seemed the most affable fellow ever kept smiling and nodding. "I agree with you chaps and if you want me to I'll send a gun down there now in preparation."

"No thank you, Captain Johnson. That is unnecessary. Your men seem quite skilled at limbering and unlimbering. It won't take them long to do that."

"Oh no, sir. A piece of cake! Back at the barracks we have competitions to limber and unlimber. Losers get to shovel out the stables!"

Lieutenant Von Doren was, like Lieutenant Austen, taking it all in. I was curious about his mastery of our language. "Your English is excellent Lieutenant. How so?"

"My mother was English and I grew up speaking German and English." How strange, I thought, that we had such similar experiences and yet our lives could not have been more different. He had grown up, he had told us, as a pampered son of a Hanoverian aristocrat. He had wanted for nothing and could have chosen both his regiment and his branch of the army. I had been illegitimate, ignored and lucky to be taken on as a trooper. Yet I felt an affinity with him. "It has proved fortunate for I get to enjoy the company of the soldiers of my mother's people."

I turned to Percy, "There you are Percy, have a go at speaking another language. You might get your promotion that way." He nodded, "The alternative is to wait until a Frenchmen takes off my head and you get a battlefield promotion."

He looked visibly shocked, "Oh sir. Don't say that! I want promotion but not that way."

We all laughed and the sergeants shook their head. They all had to earn their promotions. They could not buy a commission.

The infantry arrived at noon the next day and Colonel Mackenzie wasted no time in deploying his men. We apprised him of the situation. "I agree with you two. This is nowhere near as good as the Elbe. Captain Johnson, leave one gun here with your best sergeant and then make a defensive position at the Elbe." He gestured to a lieutenant. "Lieutenant Dunston, take a platoon and help the artillery defend the bridge back there."

Although he looked disappointed he shouted a, "Yes sir," and led his men away.

"Right Captain Matthews, you take the right flank and I'll take the left. Ride until you find somewhere else they can cross. Sergeant Major Jones you remain here with the headquarters staff and be ready to leave as soon as the Brigadier gives you the order."

"You can rely on me sir."

As I led my troop west I realised that we had depleted our own numbers already with the men left at Gustrow and those at Stralsund. We were like thinly spread butter; in places the toast was a little too visible.

We found a crossing less than a mile north of us. The sign was hard to read but it looked to be the Luneburger Road. "Seymour, take a couple of men and ride east for a mile or so; let me know what you see. The rest of you dismount. Take out your carbines and make sure that they are loaded and primed." Thanks to the three months training they did so efficiently and well.

When I heard the thunder of hooves I ordered them to stand to. We had a double line. The first rank were dismounted and using their mounts as a shooting platform, whilst the ones behind were mounted.

Corporal Seymour reined his horse in. "Cavalry sir, hundreds of them."

"Whose?"

"Couldn't see any flags sir. They weren't redcoats."

I smiled, "Which doesn't help us as the only redcoats for hundreds of miles are the 5th."

"Sorry sir."

"Never mind. Rejoin the others." I turned to Percy. "If this is the French Corps then you take half the men back to the Brigadier and tell him."

"And what about you sir?"

"I will follow when we have knocked them about a bit."

As soon as I saw them I recognised the uniforms. "Don't worry. They are Hanoverians."

I could see, as they crossed the bridge that they had been in action. Once again I had to resort to a limited vocabulary and hand gestures, but they seemed to understand and they trotted safely down the road towards the 5th. Although they had been beaten they still retained their order and I saw their sergeants making them straighten up as they marched past us. These soldiers would fight again. The question was, would the French give them time?

As the numbers dwindled I began to worry. In my experience the French cavalry were always keen to chase down stragglers. "Lieutenant Austen, take charge of the dismounted men. Sergeant Grant bring the mounted men with me. Have your carbines ready.

Bugler Jones, stay by me. You may to have to play a few tunes yet."

"Excellent sir. I do like playing my bugle."

Jones was irrepressible.

When I saw men beginning to run towards us then I knew the French were close. "Sergeant, take half the men on the other side of the road and leave the road clear for the stragglers."

As soon as they were in position I shouted, "Now there will be French cavalry coming down this road soon. When I give the order fire your carbine and then drop it and take out a pistol. You will fire that and then listen for the bugle."

I saw two grenadiers half carrying a wounded comrade. The look on their faces told me that they would die rather than leave their comrade to the French. I saw that a handful of men were trying to organise some sort of defence to help these wounded to escape. They clustered around their flag. "At the trot forward. Keep your lines."

My original plan might still work but I could not leave these brave soldiers to be massacred and their flag to be captured. Now that I was close I saw that the cavalry were French Dragoons. The men around the flag had a square of sorts but with less than a hundred men within it they were shrinking and dying. It would collapse long before they reached the bridge.

"Jones, when I give the command, sound recall."

He never questioned, he just said, "Yes sir."

We were eighty yards away and remained unseen, mainly because of the smoke from the grenadiers' muskets. "Halt!" I looked down the line. "Fire!"

The fifty carbines all barked as one and a wall of smoke filled the space. "Sound recall!" As the notes rang out I hoped that the

Hanoverian call was similar to ours. They would, at least, know that they had friends behind. "Ready pistols!"

The Dragoons had seen the new danger and they charged towards us, eager to get at horsemen they believed now had no guns. They came at us in a ragged mass with little speed. "Fire!" As the smoke enveloped us I shouted, "Draw sabres!"

The pistol we used was the 1802 land pattern Pistol and the ball it fired was a hefty .65 of an inch. The Dragoons and their mounts were scythed down. We now had a chance. "Sound the charge!"

As he put the bugle to his lips Jones said, "Now I do know that one!"

We launched forward as a line. We had no speed but we were hitting dishevelled, demoralised and disorganised Dragoons. They had gone from the verge of victory to disaster in a heartbeat. I slashed down with my sword and struck a major in the neck. He fell to the ground. Badger was bigger than the Dragoon's mounts and she barged past two of them. I stabbed one Dragoon as I went by and hit the other with my fist. I glanced ahead and saw another regiment of horsemen. This time they were Chasseurs and they were in line. I looked for Jones. "Sound retreat!"

Jones must have been waiting for the command and the notes were almost instantaneous. As I turned Badger around I saw only one empty saddle. We had been lucky but one man had still died. The Hanoverians were now racing towards the bridge. When we caught up with their rear I shouted. "Halt and reload." I could see the Chasseurs were half a mile away and the bridge about the same distance. We had enough time to load again. With my carbine ready I looked down the line. None of the men looked to have panicked and their confidence was apparent in the calm way they loaded.

"These chaps will make a lot of noise. Just fire on command and then retreat towards the bridge. Lieutenant Austen will look after us. Fire! Sound recall." As the rest turned I drew two of my pistols. Three of the Chasseurs had managed to evade the wall of lead and were hurtling at me. I fired both pistols and drew my sword. As one of the men fell dead and a second clutched his arm I wheeled Badger out of the path of the last man and sliced across his back as he passed me. He fell to the ground and I followed my men. As I neared the bridge I heard the cheers of both my men and the Hanoverians.

As soon as I had crossed the small bridge I heard Percy shout, "Fire!" The French were discouraged from following. I saw them dragging their wounded out of range.

The Hanoverian captain who had led the rearguard was wounded and had to be helped by his sergeant. He made his way over to me.

His English was poor, but it was better than my German. "Thank you sir. I am in your debt."

I shook his hand and it came away bloody. I said, in German, "You and your men are too brave to leave."

He nodded and they began to trudge down to the bridge where the 5th resolutely stood.

"Reload. We will give them one more volley if they try to cross. Sharp, go and inform the Brigadier that we have another Division coming this way and ask him what are his orders?"

The men dressed their ranks under Quartermaster Grant's keen eye and we waited to see what the enemy cavalry would do. Percy nudged his mount next to mine. "That took nerve, sir."

"What did?"

"Facing down three of them."

"I had every advantage. I had two pistols primed, and a third if I needed it. They were riding fast and, therefore, easier to evade and they all rode much smaller horses. Had I missed with my pistols I would have charged them and they would have sailed by me and missed."

He shook his head, "I thought you were a dead man for sure, sir. I was remembering what you said before and thought that I did not want promotion in that fashion."

"Sir! Look!"

Grant's voice drew me to the sight across the bridge. They were deploying artillery.

"Thank you Quartermaster Sergeant. I think we will trot back down to the Brigadier eh."

We rode in good order the mile or so. Sharp was still there trying to get the Brigadier's attention. I shook my head in irritation. "Percy take command. Face the enemy horse."

"Colonel Mackenzie there are at least two regiments of horse and a battery of guns heading from the other bridge. They will be here within the next fifteen minutes."

"You don't say. This puts us in a pickle." He pointed across the bridge and I could see the column of men marching forwards.

"Sir, if we wheel this gun around it will buy some time and help us to withdraw in good order to the Elbe."

"I suppose you are right. You fellows cover our retreat but don't get yourselves caught eh? You had better send a messenger to your major then. Wouldn't want him with his backside in the wind eh?" he then turned to shout his orders to his redcoats who began to shoulder arms and march at double time down the road.

"Corporal Seymour. Ride to the major and tell him we are withdrawing."

The cannon had been turned to face the road we had just withdrawn down. I could see the cavalry already coming down. "Well Captain Johnson, whenever you are ready."

The happy gunner shook his head. "This little popgun has been loaded with ball and grape. If we wait until they are fifty yards away it should be quite spectacular."

The other gun was already firing ball at the approaching column. I glanced down the road and saw the small ball carve a line through ten files of men. They just closed ranks and kept on coming. We would thin them out but that was all.

"Captain, I will place my men in front of the cannon and disguise it. When they are a hundred yards from us we will fire and then move. They should get a shock!"

"Capital idea. But do be sharp or you may get a whiff of grapeshot up your arse!"

"Ready men. As soon as this gun fires the captain will limber up and then it will be up to us to hold up the enemy."

The day was fading fast and I hoped that we could withdraw before dark. I suddenly noticed that Lieutenant Von Doren was next to me with his men. "I thought you went with the Brigadier?"

"He doesn't need me. If I don't fight now I may never get another chance."

"What do you mean?"

"That was our main army you saw retreating. The French have my country. There is just this little strip from here to Pomerania that we hold. Our war has not lasted very long has it?"

I felt sorry for the lad. "You can always bring your men back to England with us. I am sure the rest of your army will try to get there. I mean where else is there for them to go?"

"You are right." He brightened. "I shall go to England." He drew his gun which was an old musket. "But first I shall kill a Frenchman or two."

The French cavalry had filled the land. They were in a line ten men wide and eagerly leaning forward. I dare say they were anticipating us fleeing. They must have been bemused to see just eighty men facing them and not moving.

"Ready lads! Fire! Fall back!"We did not wait until we saw the results of our shots. The smoke hid them from us in any case. We had just cleared the gun's barrel when it went off. The double shotting made it even louder and many of the trooper's horses reared.

I reined in Badger and looked down the road. It was carnage. There were horses and men lying as far as the eye could see. Dying horse's legs jerked in the air and I saw troopers dragging themselves away from them. Already our guns were being limbered. I hoped that Seymour had reached the major.

"Reload and fall back once the gun has moved. Keep your eyes on the French." I was not particularly worried. The French cavalry would be warier now. They had been bitten twice.

Captain Johnson's cheery voice came to me, "See you at the bridge!"

I heard hooves from behind me and turned to see the major and the other troop. He took the scene in quickly. "I see you have been busier than we have."

"Yes sir. We are the rearguard. The 5th should almost be at the Elbe by now and the guns have just gone."

"Right, you chaps get along. We will keep the Frenchies occupied."

"I don't think that they will be rushing sir. They have lost a lot of men and horses. It is the infantry I would worry about." I pointed down the main road where the column had reformed and was marching resolutely across the bridge.

"Off you go." He turned to his sergeant, "Form the men into two lines. Lieutenant Jackson, go on the right hand side." The men quickly formed up and prepared their carbines. "Number 8 Troop, on my command, fire." He waited until they were just fifty yards away and shouted, "Fire!" The smoke rippled along their front and, before it had hidden them I saw half a dozen men and as many horses fall. Take out your pistols! Fire!"

"Come on Quartermaster Sergeant Grant let's go."

"Yes sir."

Chapter 9

We had a clear road all the way to the Elbe. The 5th were already lined up on either side of the bridge and the two guns were unlimbering. The Northumbrians gave us a cheer as we trotted across. The Brigadier gave me a questioning look, "The major will be along shortly sir. Where would you like us?"

"If you would be so kind as to place your men on the right then I will be happier. Lieutenant Von Doren, your countrymen have headed north towards Rostock would you make sure that the road is clear for the next fifteen miles. When we leave I don't want to have any unpleasant surprises."

"Sir." The cheery Hanoverian trotted off with his escort.

I made sure that the men dismounted when we reached the end of the line. Our horses had been ridden hard and the day was not yet over."Percy, make sure they have all loaded their guns and feed them if you can."

Just then I heard a deep voice behind me, "Glad you made it sir. Is Major Hyde-Smith safe too?"

"Good to see you too Sergeant Major Jones. Yes he is just delaying the French and will be along shortly. All the equipment in one piece? "

"Yes sir I sent it back to the port with the men. The farrier sergeant can handle that. I thought I would be more use here." He glanced down the line. "You didn't lose too many troopers then sir?"

"Just one man missing, Trooper Bradley." I waved a hand at the others. "A few of them have cuts from our run in with the Chasseurs and Dragoons but they acquitted themselves well."

He nodded, "You can't beat a bit of real combat to make them into better troopers. You can have all the drills in the world but until you have faced another man who is trying to kill you then you won't be a real soldier. This squadron will be the best in the regiment now sir."

"Don't tell Captain DeVere that, he will have a fit."

We both looked up as the other troop trotted across the bridge. "I'll go and report to the major sir. Glad you are all in one piece."

The French cavalry were hard on their heels as the troop cleared the bridge. I heard Colonel Mackenzie shout, "Fire!"

The three cannon belched their deadly missiles and then the 5th began volley fire which cleared the enemy from the end of the bridge. They would not try that again.

"Better get some food organised for the men Sergeant Grant. We don't know when we will get a chance to eat later.

"Sir."

"Take charge, Lieutenant Austen. I'll go and find out what is happening."

I walked back. There was no point in riding Badger; it was less than four hundred yards to the bridge. I saw that the infantry had already reloaded and were busy talking about the effects of their volley. It was the first time they had been in action since we had arrived and I knew that they were eager to prove themselves.

The major was with Colonel Mackenzie. "Ah glad you came. We have a slight problem now. How long do we wait? The Hanoverians were not going as fast as I would have hoped we need to buy them some time."

"Yes sir, but at the same time we need to leave ourselves enough time to get to Stralsund." The major pointed to the redcoats. "Even with a forced march it will take a day at least possibly a day and a half and with no bridges to stop them their cavalry can outflank us."

"Quite. Bit of a problem all around."

"Could we not blow up the bridge?"

"A good idea Captain Matthews but it is made of stone and we don't have enough explosives."

"Yes sir, but if they thought that it was mined they would be cautious. It might buy us some time."

"What do you mean? I don't understand."

"Well sir, if we pointedly had men putting barrels under the piers of the bridge and running fuses back here they would think we had mined it. They wouldn't know that the barrels were empty. We leave a handful of men to light the fuses when the enemy begin to cross. They will pull back and by the time they have seen the trick then the rearguard could be well away."

Major Hyde-Smith nodded, "It could work but it would have to be the 11th that were the rearguard."

"Quite. Well if you think you can do it Captain Matthews…"

"All we need is some fuse and some empty barrels."

Captain Johnson had both and he was delighted with the idea. "Let my chaps do it. They would look more realistic and we can put a little powder in the barrels to make them pop. They will think twice before coming over. Capital idea."

I was pleased as it saved me a job. We now watched as the French brought up infantry and their own artillery. Captain Johnson's men had erected a barrier of logs and they were afforded some protection. As the French guns were being brought up there was an infantry duel augmented by the Royal Horse Artillery's guns. The range was almost point blank for the cannons and we were delighted to see at least two cannon destroyed as they laboured to build defences. It was towards dusk when Lieutenant Von Doren rode in.

I watched as he spoke with the Brigadier. The bugle sounded for officer's call and we raced to the temporary headquarters at the bridgehead. He looked at Captain Johnson who said, "The bridge is mined sir and all ready to be lit. They now have cannon on the other side and they have protected them. Come the morning they will be able to fire and I fancy they will have something bigger than horse artillery tomorrow."

"We won't be here tomorrow. At least not all of us. Lieutenant Von Doren has found somewhere to ambush them about twenty miles away. There is a blind summit on the road. If we can lure their cavalry there then my boys can make mincemeat of them. We will begin pulling out now. We will do it section by section. Captain Johnson can you limber up quietly?"

"Yes sir but if we leave one gun with the rearguard it would aid the 11th."

"Quite. Now who is staying to light the fuse Major Hyde-Smith?"

We hadn't decided but I knew who it would be. "That would be me sir with half a dozen men."

"Good! Thank you Captain Matthews. Then let's be about this. Major Hyde-Smith if you would send a rider to that Mr Whittingham and ask him to make sure that there are enough transports to take us off eh?"

"Yes sir."

I could have asked for volunteers and I would have been inundated. Instead I chose my men. "Corporal Seymour, Bugler Jones, Troopers Sharp, Green and Wilson you are the rearguard."

None of them looked unhappy and the rest, including Lieutenant Austen did. He came over, "Sir, let me have the honour."

"It is my hare brained scheme and I need you with the troop."

Sergeant Major Jones came over, "I'll keep an eye on the young chap sir. Now you be careful here. These Frenchies can be sneaky."

As soon as it was dark the soldiers began to slip away quietly. I wondered if the enemy might try to creep across under cover of night but Captain Johnson had that problem solved, every ten minutes or so he would blast a shot from his one remaining gun across the bridge. He was a clever officer and his timing was not regular. One of his shots caught a party of light infantry who were scurrying across the bridge. Half of them were blown to smithereens and the rest were despatched by the carbines of the 11th. As the false dawn appeared Major Hyde-White led the two troops away.

"Now be careful and don't wait too long."

"I won't and I will sound retreat when we do leave. Just in case they come early and the column is still close to here."

"I would imagine that the first elements of the 5th will have reached the ambush area by now. Good luck chaps."

It suddenly felt very lonely with just one gun crew and my few men. As dawn broke they would see, quite clearly that the red coats had gone. What would they do then?

We had our answer just before dawn. We heard a huge crack as a French twelve pounder shattered the barricade. Captain Johnson looked at me. "Well Robbie, the game is up."

"Get your gun limbered and out of here. We'll be behind you." I turned to Jones. "Sound retreat. Sharp, hold Badger for me."

I dismounted and made my way to the fuses. I had my flint ready. "Corporal Seymour, tell me as soon as you see them begin to move"

I was protected by a small barricade. They could see me but not hit me. I heard the cannon gradually demolishing the barricade and I was glad when I heard the sound of the Royal Horse Artillery leaving. There were just my men left now and, as the cannon ceased firing, it seemed eerily quiet. The smoke from the demolished barricades spiralled up in smoke rings towards the emerging sun. I could hear the French officers giving commands. I even heard some of the words, for there was total silence on our side of the river.

I heard an officer saying that we had left and ordering the light infantry to rush the barricades.

I lit the fuse just as Corporal Seymour shouted, "They're coming sir."

As soon as I was sure that the fuses had caught I leapt from the barricades like a startled rabbit. The light infantry on the other side and on the bridge popped a few ineffectual shots at me. I reached and mounted Badger quickly. "Sound retreat again and let's go!"

As we galloped away I turned in my saddle. I could see the light infantry caught in two minds. Could they reach the barrels before they exploded? Half decided that discretion was the better part of valour while some of the others hurried forwards. I reined in Badger when I was a hundred yards from the bridge. I was intrigued. What would the explosion look like?

The infantry were just ten yards from the barrels when the first of them popped, crackled and then lit up the sky with an explosion. It looked mightier than it was but the light infantry frantically hurled themselves into the water. The other barrels all went off together and the bridge was covered in a pall of smoke. It was like a giant firework display. They would have to wait until the smoke had cleared and its structure checked before they crossed. I kicked Badger on. I had bought us a precious half an hour. We knew that we could rest when we reached the others but the French did not. Badger's powerful stride soon overtook the others and we galloped up the road. We caught up with Captain Johnson and slowed down to ride with him.

He looked at me expectantly, "Well?"

"An excellent ruse. Even I thought the whole thing would blow up. We have half an hour."

"That will be more than enough time. We are almost upon them."

He was wrong. We had another five miles to go before I saw a summit which looked to fit the description given by Lieutenant Von Doren. It was not the steepest incline but I could see nothing beyond the ridge and the top of the road. As we crested it I saw the 5th lined up in two lines on either side of the road whilst the middle of the road was filled with the two guns of the artillery troop.

Captain Johnson was impressed. "They won't have a clue. A damned fine spot."

Captain Fraser of the 5th waved to the captain. "Brigadier's compliments and could you ride up the road and set up another ambush. There is a company of our chaps waiting for you with the major."

The captain nodded, "Sergeant, do as the captain asked. I think I shall stay here. I have a mind to see the expressions on their faces when we blast them."

Captain Fraser looked bemused, "But Captain Johnson the Brigadier asked for you."

He dismissed it with a wave, "Nonsense, my sergeant is a good chap and besides I have two of my guns here."

He dismounted and led his horse to his two guns. The infantryman shook his head, "Artillery men! Mad as fish the lot of them! Sir if you would join your troop behind our men, I believe your young lieutenant and Lieutenant Von Doren are going to be the bait."

I hoped that Percy and Von Doren would not try to outdo each other. We could not afford any glorious deaths. The major and Sergeant Major Jones awaited me. The major saw my expression. "You should not wonder that the boy volunteered. He has been watching you perform such actions since we first landed."

"Don't worry sir. He'll be alright. He has plenty of sense."

I hoped they were both right. I watched as he and half of my troop rode down the road towards the unseen enemy. He had a difficult task ahead of him. He had to appear as though the enemy had surprised them. They would not ride into a trap easily. I assumed that they would have the Chasseurs chasing us with the Dragoons and Light Infantry in close attendance. I knew from experience that the French Light Infantry could almost keep up with cavalry for short distances.

In the end their general must have decided to keep the infantry with the cavalry for we heard the crack of muskets some two hours after we had arrived. The Sergeant Major of the 5th shouted, "Stand to and await my command!"

The crest of the ridge was less than forty yards away. That was lethal range for the Brown Bess musket. I knew that the cannon would be loaded with grapeshot and they too would make a mess of an attacker. Percy's bugler sounded the retreat and I watched as they thundered over the rise. The two lieutenants were, as I had expected, at the rear of their men. Sabres in hand they whooped over the crest. I saw Major Hyde-Smith grimace. Percy would pay for that frivolity later on.

The men rode around our left flank and then the horsemen appeared. They had spread into a semi circle to out flank our horsemen and the Brigadier waited until they were almost upon us before shouting, "Fire!"

The 5th kept firing and reloading and their volleys almost became a continuous wall of fire. After five volleys I heard the command, "Cease fire!"

Then the major turned to his bugler. "Sound the charge if you please."

I drew my sword and we trotted forward through the smoke. As soon as we were clear it was as though we had entered an abattoir. We had not time to take in the grisly sights. We had to hit their survivors whilst they were disorganised. We galloped through horsemen whose ears were still ringing from the firing and were disorientated and confused. Which way was the enemy?

I stabbed a sergeant as he was turning to organise his men. I saw Sharp's sabre slice through the arm of a Dragoon like a knife through butter. Suddenly we were through the cavalry and into the light infantry in skirmish order. It was a cavalryman's dream and we drove them before us. Barely three of them fired before being struck and skewered. Some lay on the ground in the belief that a horse will not step on a prone man. It was a good theory but the horses were not looking down and their hooves crushed many a skull.

Badger was well ahead of the rest of the squadron and I saw, ahead of me their horse artillery unlimbering and the infantry column deploying into line. "Jones, sound the recall!"

As the strident notes rang out my men all slowed. Those French men unfortunate to be within sword's length died where they stood and in some cases cowered but, to my horror, Lieutenant Von Doren and his Hanoverians charged recklessly at the line. The

French battalion must have been inexperienced too for they fired far too early. Even so all but two of the Hanoverians fell. I saw Lieutenant Von Doren shout something to his comrade before turning to flee. His companion was shot in the back and fell from his horse. I saw Von Doren's horse stagger.

"Sharp, grab a spare horse and follow me. Jones, keep sounding recall."

The artillery had unlimbered now and began to hurl cannon balls at us. I knew they were not aiming specifically at me, but it felt like it. I saw Von Doren's horse stumble and begin to fall. I was close enough to be able to shout, "Jump clear!"

Just in time, he leapt from the horse. I could see another regiment of Dragoons leaving the flanks and riding towards us. I wheeled Badger around. I leaned down, took my foot from the stirrup and grabbed his arm. "Put your foot in the stirrup and jump up!"

The Dragoons were now less than a hundred yards away. I turned Badger and she gamely tried to gallop towards the retreating 11th. Sharp appeared next to me, with a French mount. I could not stop to make it easy for Von Doren to mount it. I shouted, "Jump"

He was young and he was reckless. Fortunately he was also lucky and he managed to jump without catching his foot in my stirrup. As Badger leapt forwards I drew my horse pistol and fired behind me, blindly. I didn't think for one moment I would hit anything but I wanted the nearest riders to give us a wide berth. We reached the crest and we rode to the right. The Dragoons suffered the same fate as their comrades and the 5th fired five volleys to empty saddles and discourage a chase.

Major Hyde-Smith said, "Well done Robbie." Then he glowered at Von Doren. "If you were in my regiment you would be on a charge! You lost your men there for no good reason!"

"I am sorry sir, I didn't recognise the call."

"Stuff and nonsense. You saw the rest of us stop!"

He hung his head and I could see tears forming. "Sir, he has lost all of his men. There will be a time for recriminations later on but...."

"Quite." I thought he had finished but he had a parting shot to deliver. "And you nearly got one of the finest officers in the regiment killed too!"

The Brigadier ordered a retreat to the next ambush point; once again we were the rearguard. This time it appears that the French had decided not to pursue us as recklessly and we saw them making camp at the top of the hill. They had many casualties to attend to and many fleeing survivors to gather.

I was exhausted when we reached our next camp and ambush point. After a frugal meal of iron rations we were again summoned to an officer's meeting.

"You all did well today gentlemen I am hopeful that we will reach Stralsund tomorrow. However that depends on two things: the desire of the French to catch us and the ability of the 11th to continue to do so such sterling work as our rearguard."

Major Hyde-Smith stood. "We can continue to be the rearguard sir but our horses will not be able to charge again. We will have to discourage them by other means."

The adjutant of the 5th stood, "But you will be able to stop 'em?"

"If we do not sir, then the transports will not have to load horses for we shall all be dead."

"Then let us hope that we have to take a long time to load the horses of the valiant 11th Light Dragoons."

Later that night as we sat beneath a wonderfully old tree which must have been planted when they still fought with lance and shield, Lieutenant Jackson asked, "What did you mean, sir, other means?"

"Take a leaf out of Captain Matthew's book and use our superior firepower. I can see why you have so many pistols."

"They do come in handy. A little tip sir, if we find any dead cavalry then it pays to take their pistols."

"I shall bear it in mind. Any more questions."

Von Doren sheepishly asked, "Can I ride with the 11th tomorrow sir?"

"If you obey orders then the answer is yes but woe betide you if you fall foul of me again."

Riding rearguard is one of the most thankless jobs any cavalryman can do. To avoid getting a stiff neck constantly turning around we found that the best method was to stop every half a mile and face towards the pursuers and then move on. We also rotated the troops every five miles just to give the troopers some relief.

I was in command when the Dragoons caught up with us. We had just crossed a ford and we heard the thunder of their hooves. "Turn at the water's edge."

We formed a double line at the ford and waited for them. They did not charge but came at the walk with their own musketoons at the ready. I had used the weapon and knew its limitations. It was not as short as the carbine and took longer to reload. I took a leaf out of the 5th's book. "Front rank, fire."

Percy shouted, "Second rank fire!"

In that way we kept a constant rate of fire up. They did hit my troopers but we hit more of them. After twenty minutes we saw infantry appear and I ordered the retreat. This scene was repeated many times until we finally reached the farm which marked the border. There the 11th halted. I did not think that the French would risk the wrath of Sweden by invading but I did not know for sure.

Out horses were exhausted and we were almost out of ammunition. We knew that the 5th had reached Stralsund already, one of the RHA gunners had ridden back to tell us.

We dismounted and we walked the last few miles into the port. Colonel Mackenzie must have had a lookout for as we entered through the city gates the 5th lined both sides and stood to attention as we trudged in. They did not cheer but they smiled and we heard their comments as we walked by.

"Well done bonnie lads."

"Ye'll do for me."

"Proper soldiers y'are."

"I'll stand ye a pint next time we are in England!"

We all walked a little straighter. We had done a good job and we were appreciated. What more could a soldier ask?

Chapter 10

We had to wait for two days for the transports to be completely loaded. It was decided not to allow leave for the men. Everyone agreed that there was just too much temptation in the little port of Stralsund. The officers were allowed to wander the town and I thoroughly enjoyed the experience. Lieutenant Von Doren was my shadow. To be fair he and Percy got on so well that it didn't matter. The Hanoverian was desperate to please both of us and proved an able guide. I knew what he wanted. He wished to return to England with us? He was keen to fight the French again and get some revenge for his dead troopers. It was not the right frame of mind to make such a decision. He asked me to intercede with the major who was still annoyed with the reckless young man. He was like Percy; he would make a good officer some day but he needed to have someone to guide him and give him advice.

I broached the subject after dinner on the East Indiaman. "Sir about Von Doren, he is keen to return to England with us."

" I am not having that fellow in the regiment. Too foolish and a foreigner to boot!"

I wondered what he would say if he knew of my origins. "But could he not come to England with us. We know that the Hanoverians who fled the battle went to Rostock to take ship. Some may have gone to England. Perhaps they may be able to form a regiment."

"And what good would that do?

"Well sir we have a regiment of Chasseurs Britanniques made up of émigrés from France."

"And damned useless they are too."

I sighed, "Sir, have we so many men in England to fight Bonaparte that we can afford to shun volunteers?"

He calmed down and smiled, "Probably not. "Yes the boy can come with us but keep him away from me."

"Yes sir. I dare say he will bunk in with Percy."

"Now he has settled down. You have done well with him. He leads the men well and is composed and competent."

I bit back my retort that Von Doren would be just as useful when trained. And I knew that we needed more officers. We were at least one captain short and, with the new recruits, a couple of lieutenants light as well.

When we set sail I stood at the side watching the old city slip by. We could spend the voyage home looking at the sights we had missed on the way out. It struck me that the whole of Denmark was flat. The cliffs appeared huge when you saw them because the land around was so low. Once we went through the Skagerrak the sea became both colder and rougher. We spent the next few days below decks trying to get warm.

The captain told us, one night, that the French Fleet had been chased by Nelson but there was a danger of invasion from France. There were rumours that huge camps were appearing all across the northern part of France and that invasion barges were being constructed. For that reason we would be putting into London and not Dover. When I told Trooper Sharp the news he grinned. "That was us sir! We found that out! Will you be getting a medal or something? You should, you know."

I laughed and shook my head, "Sharp, when will you get it into your head, we don't exist. If we had been caught then we would have been shot as spies and Colonel Selkirk would have denied all knowledge of us."

"Then why did you do it sir?" The young man looked genuinely puzzled.

"Alan, why did you join up?"

"To fight for me country and because my dad would have wanted me to do just that."

"And that is why I do it. To fight Bonaparte. It is what my dad would have wanted me to." It was strange, there was no-one left to ask but I wondered if the Count would have been proud of his illegitimate son. I don't think he would have appreciated my fighting for Bonaparte but I think he would have approved of my actions as a soldier both in the French army and the British. Perhaps, if he had still been alive, he might have smiled at me and told me, '*Well done*.'

It was still wet when we reached the Thames. It might have been July but the weather was still dismal. It took us forever to find a berth. There was a good signals system along the coast and I knew that our arrival had been noted for, as we tied up, I saw a familiar figure on a black horse. It was Colonel Selkirk. My heart sank a little. I had hoped for some time back at the barracks. Obviously that was not to be.

He waited patiently at the bottom of the gangplank. Major Hyde-Smith eyed him, suspiciously. "Who is that? It looks remarkably like a staff officer."

I sighed, "That sir, is Colonel Selkirk."

"Then I suppose he has another task for you. Come let us see what the desk bound warrior wants this time."

The two lieutenants and Lieutenant Von Doren followed us down the gangplank. He spoke to all of us but his eyes were on me. "I hear you acquitted yourselves well in what could have been a disastrous misadventure. You are all to be commended." He spied the Hanoverian. "And you sir have arrived at a most propitious time. Sir John Halkett is now forming regiments which will be called the King's German Legion. He is recruiting from the many Hanoverians who have fled your poor country."

I now felt I knew the man. He gave you a smile and a sweetener and then hit you with the sucker punch. He smiled the cold smile of a crocodile about to make you his dinner and said to the major. "I am afraid I must take young Robbie and his capable servant from you for a while. Just three months at the most."

"I protest sir. Captain Matthews is the most capable captain we have ever had in the 11th. If you take him away we will be short handed."

"Quite so, quite so. Well," he dived into his coat and pulled out a document, "perhaps this might assuage your conscience. It is a captaincy for Lieutenant Percy Austen." He smiled at Percy. "That would be you I believe?"

"But sir…"

"Tush, tush, your bravery in Hanover is reason enough."

"But sir all of that was Captain Matthews…"

His cold smile turned upon me, "And I am sure that the good captain will not mind sharing his good fortune with you. Would you captain?"

"Congratulations Percy, you deserve it. Well done."

I could see that he was torn between his heart's desire and a feeling that he had somehow been duped. I turned to the major. "I am sorry for this sir but with Percy a captain and no war, as yet, perhaps I might be excused for three months or so?"

This time the smile was genuine, "Of course." He shot a cold stare at Selkirk who seemed oblivious to the animosity. "You come back to us, you hear, you are too valuable to be wasted on some mad Machiavellian scheme."

The colonel calmly said, "You would think so wouldn't you. But that is not the way the world works now is it?" He looked at me again, "Robbie get your servant and your things. You can stay with me tonight. You won't need your horses. I shall wait at the Coal Hole Inn. One of your drinking haunts I believe."

As I went back on board I wondered just how the colonel got his information. "Trooper Sharp, get our things. Colonel Selkirk needs us again." I hesitated, "You can refuse you know."

His face broke into a grin, "You are joking sir. Miss all the fun? Besides I want to try my French out this time."

Lieutenant Von Doren and Captain Austen were waiting for me at the bottom of the gangplank. Percy held out his hand and his voice was thick with emotion. "I want to thank you sir. I don't know how you make things happen but you do. I dreamed of being a captain and I despaired of making it a reality. You come along and here I am."

"You just needed a little push Percy and I am pleased for you. Watch over Badger for me and the men of my troop. Jackson is a good man but he is still learning. Look to Sergeant Grant."

"I will sir. You can rely on me."

"I know and don't let the DeVeres bully you, stand up for yourself." The emotion was too much for him and he just tightened his smile and nodded.

Lieutenant Von Doren shook my hand, "I have learned much since serving with you and I hope that, in this new regiment, I can be as good an officer as you."

"You will. You have learned your lesson and those dead men will always ride at your shoulder reminding you."

"I know sir."

We left them and headed through the maelstrom that was the disembarking troops. I was back in England, but for how long?

There was a carriage outside the Coal Hole Inn with a liveried footman waiting. He gave a half bow. "Captain Matthews, sir?" I nodded. "Allow me to take your bags. The colonel is waiting inside."

"Shall I wait with the bags sir?"

"No Sharp. You will be part of this too so come along with me." I saw the eyebrows of the footman rise but he kept his counsel. I suspected that he felt that servants did not need to understand the reasons merely to carry out the plans. I cared not; Trooper Sharp would be vital to my mission on the Continent- wherever the colonel sent us.

He was in a quiet alcove with his back to the wall and he gestured us over. I saw three mugs of ale on the table and a plate of sausages. He smiled as we sat down. "I may have a fine house and a good cook but you canna beat hot sausages in a tavern washed down with some ale. Dig in." He saw the hesitation on Trooper Sharp's face. "Go on son, there's plenty and I can see you're hungry."

It was true. Sharp now had his sea legs but we had not eaten for twelve hours and he began to eat the greasy hot little parcels of pork. I too was grateful for the hot steaming sausages. Colonel Selkirk was not a delicate eater and he briefed us through a mouthful of food.

"The information you brought last time was really valuable. Our lords and masters were very impressed. Our friend, little Nel, managed to chase Villeneuve away to the West Indies. However our blockading ships tell us that he has camps close to the coast in northern France. He is planning an invasion." Sharp stopped eating as the import of the colonel's words. "We need you two to find out the troops he has there and, if you can, when they are likely to come."

I put down my ale and sat back. "Let me be blunt with you Colonel Selkirk. I can find out where the troops are but I think it is unlikely that I will find out when."

"The when is not as important as the numbers besides Bonaparte needs to have control of the Channel for a number of hours to achieve his ends. The problem is he is a cunning chap and he could land anywhere. The powers that be assume that it will be along the Kent coast but I am not so sure. You should be able to discover that information."

I sighed. "There are still two problems that I can foresee: how do I get there and get back. We are at war and I cannot just go on a packet can I? In addition to which I assume that the coast will be heavily patrolled. Even if you could land me I cannot see how we would escape."

"If they are your concerns then rest easy. A Royal Navy sloop will land you and they will ensure that you are unobserved. We have some expertise in this area. We have been landing émigrés for years. As for the picking up, that is slightly more problematic. The sloop will return to the French coast every four days. It will not be to the same place. That would risk capture. You and the captain of the sloop will have the landing sites. You have a maximum of sixteen days. If you have not been picked up by then we will assume that you are lost."

I nodded. I had to smile when I saw the look on Sharp's face. "When do we leave?"

"As soon as you have finished your ale and Mr Sharp has demolished the last of the sausages we shall go to my town house where I have suitable clothes. You will be able to leave your uniforms there and my carriage will then take you to Gravesend where the 'Black Prince' awaits."

As Trooper Sharp swallowed the last of the sausages he mumbled, "Don't give a body time to turn around."

Both the colonel and I laughed, "Welcome to the world of espionage Sharp."

The carriage's curtains were closed and we sped anonymously through the streets. There was a courtyard at the back of Colonel Selkirk's house and we left the carriage as swiftly as we had entered it. "If you follow Barrington he will show you to a room where you can change."

It was less of a room and more of a suite we were taken to. Our clothes were all laid out on the bed. Both were French made and the only difference was the quality of mine. I strapped my sword on. It was Austrian and would not be remarked upon. Sharp had a French sword I recognised. Barrington hovered close by while we dressed, adjusting when necessary.

"We will clean your uniforms and hang them in the robes until you return." He gave an apologetic smile, "If you return." He handed Trooper Sharp two bags; the larger one was obviously mine. "There are a couple of changes of clothes in the bags along with two French pistols and a small bag of gold Louis. The colonel has some papers which might be useful. Now if you will follow me. I believe the tide waits for no man, not even the colonel."

The colonel was, indeed waiting for us. He held a leather document wallet in his hand. "These are papers which identify you as Henri Ricard and his American servant Alan Sharp. There is an American passport for Mr Sharp." He shrugged, "It may expedite an escape."

"It is a real passport then?"

"It is. It accurately describes Mr. Sharp although, truth be told, it would match many men." He handed them to me. I would examine them later on and give Sharp his own passport. I felt happier knowing that he would have a way out of France if disaster overtook us.

"Now time is pressing. Are there any more questions? If so ask me in the carriage. We have to be quick to make the tide."

The ride through London was frenetic. I heard the curses both of the driver and the pedestrians who were driven from the road. Once we reached the outskirts the journey became quieter. It was something of a relief when we halted and he door opened. I could smell the river and the sea. The driver and guard unloaded our bags and deposited them on the quayside. There the 'Black Prince' awaited us.

Colonel Selkirk was quite spritely despite his age and he hurried us to the gangplank where a young lieutenant, who looked to be about twelve, awaited us.

"You have cut it fine sir."

"Listen you young whippersnapper I have been told that you are the best sloop officer in the Channel Fleet so I will overlook your impudence. Just get these two men to France and back safely and there may be a promotion in it for you."

He did not seem at all put out by the rebuke and he smiled, "That doesn't matter sir, I like the Prince. Now gentlemen if you would like to come aboard. I will try to live up to the reputation I appear to have."

I liked Jonathan Teer; he was an affable, spirited and cheerful young man. He reminded me of François the French captain who had rescued me from Egypt. Perhaps it was something about the captaincy of such small and vulnerable ships that made them that way.

We had no sooner stepped on board than the gangplank was run in and the tethers tying us to the shore released. Colonel Selkirk gave an absent minded wave and entered his carriage."I am

Lieutenant Jonathan Teer. Your bags are below. If you would join them I will get us to sea." He obviously felt he had to explain. "We wouldn't want any prying eyes eh?"

I could see that despite his apparent youth this was an experienced captain for this sort of venture. I felt more confident already. Once below I took out the documents and gave Sharp his passport. "This may well save you if we are unfortunate enough to be captured. Just keep to your story that you did not know I was anything other than a Frenchman who hired you in America."

"Will it come to that sir?"

"It may well. We do not need you to be dumb this time. You can just speak French badly. The more you speak it the better it will become. It will also explain why I have to occasionally speak English to you but I shall do so badly."

We both checked through our bags to familiarise ourselves with the equipment. The pistols, powder and ball were all French and there were even some French toiletries in my bag. I did not think I would use them but it was not something I could guarantee.

The ship's bosun knocked on the door and, knuckling his forehead, said, "Mr Teer's compliments and as we have cleared land would you care to come on deck. "

We followed him up the narrow stairs to the stern of the ship. The lieutenant was lounging on the taff rail. "We are making good time and it is blowing up nicely. This should keep prying eyes indoors although the place I am going to land you is deserted... hopefully." He handed me a map. "Now here is the map with the landing site and the places I will wait to pick you up. They are number one to four. I will wait from ten o'clock at night until two in the morning. If I miss you then go to the next one." He paused, "You have a time piece I take it?"

"Yes."

"Good. Now you must memorise the places for I do not want the map going ashore with you. We will do all that we can to aid you gentlemen but there are just four pick up points and a narrow time limit. We have spread them out as you will have a large area to cover. You choose your own route, of course."

"I understand. And are there security measures?" I remembered how François had used signals to make sure we were alone.

"Yes, good man. I am impressed. Some of the chaps I take seem to think they are on some damned ferry. I will show the same number of lights as the number on the map. You will flash a light the same number as the number on the map. If you are under duress then flash five times."

"And..."

He grinned, "And I shall be prepared. My men are quite competent." He leaned in and said, "Between you and me if they hadn't been pressed they would have either been smugglers or pirates... or both! Now take that below deck, the light is better, and memorise them. The steward will give you something hot eh?"

I opened the map and looked at the points. They were not sequential. Number one was in the far north, north of Calais. Number two, the first pick up point was in the south, close to Etaples. The last one was between Calais and Boulogne. We would need horses. I handed it to Sharp. "Memorise it too."

The motion of the sloop became more extreme as it was buffeted by the Channel waves. I knew it would help us to slip ashore unnoticed but I wished it was a little flatter. The cook appeared with two huge sandwiches filled with hot fried salt pork and two mugs with steam rising. "Here y'are sirs. Something to stick to your ribs while you are in Johnny Frenchman land."

I took a sip of the drink. It was cocoa laced with rum. It was delicious. My face must have displayed my thoughts for he chuckled, "That'll keep you warm even if you fall in the old Tiddly Oggy."

Sharp also enjoyed the drink and, as he munched his hot sandwich he ventured, "Sir, what is the Tiddly Oggy?"

"I think it must be sailor's slang for the sea. They seem to have their own language. Look at the plate. What do you notice?"

"It's square and has a raised edge around the side."

That is to stop the food falling out during a storm but it is called the fiddle so in the Navy if you are 'on the fiddle' then it means you have got more than your fair share and must have bribed the cook."

"How do you know all this sir?"

"I have sailed with men who had been in the navy once and they told me. There's many more, 'let the cat out of the bag', 'pay through the nose', they have their own language."

We had just finished when we were summoned to the deck. Two seamen humped our bags across their shoulders and followed us up the narrow stairs.

"Gentlemen, there is France. My men will row you ashore. The clock is now ticking. Four nights from now we will be at rendezvous two." I nodded. "Have you any idea how long this might take?"

"Last time it was just a few days but you never know. Sorry."

"Oh don't apologise. We shall just swan up and down. It is quite lucrative. We look for smugglers and the like. Brings in a healthy income and the navy has given us sixteen days to enjoy ourselves. You are doing us a favour sir."

I shook hands, "It has been a pleasure to meet you and I hope to see you one of these nights."

The small skiff seemed precariously close to swamping as we were rowed ashore, but the bosun, who steered seemed unconcerned. Two men hauled the boat on to the shingle and helped us off with our bags. The bosun cheekily pointed down the beach, "That way to Calais sir!" I nodded and then he added, whilst pointing north, "and just up there is a bloody big French fort so pick the right direction eh sir?"

Within a few strokes they were lost in the spray and we were alone in France.

Chapter 10

We headed inland from the sea. The land was made up of dunes and marshes. Luckily there was a path of sorts. I wondered if smugglers used this particular beach. Eventually we reached a tree lined road heading along the coast. It looked well used and, if there was a '*bloody big French fort*' just north of us then that made sense. It was hard to judge time but I was concerned about arriving in Calais at the wrong time. Too early and we would be viewed suspiciously. Too late and we stood more chance of questions about our lack of transport.

"We'll walk down this road until we reach the outskirts of Calais and then we will wait until dawn and begin moving when the streets start to fill up."

The captain had dropped us as close to Calais as he could and we soon found ourselves in the outskirts of the port. We walked to the edge of the harbour where a few hardy fishermen were heading for their boats. We stood and watched them for a while. I have noticed that people who do that sort of thing are generally ignored. I even passed a few pleasantries with a couple of them, wishing them a good harvest. They smiled and thanked me. The fact that we were talking also made it less suspicious. As the last boat was leaving I asked, "Is there anywhere close to get a decent meal?"

"Try Jacques, just along from the Customs House. Tell him Pierre sent you." He laughed, "I might get a free drink out of it; if you eat enough."

"Thank you."

We reached the small establishment. I did not know quite what to call it. It was hardly a restaurant and yet it wasn't a bar. It looked the kind of place that hard working fishermen would use.

Up ahead I saw the Customs House and the National Guardsmen at the barrier. They did not even give us a second glance. Already our choices were reaping rewards. The place was almost empty. I suppose the fishermen must have just left. The owner was wiping down the tables although the cloth was so dirty I was not certain how effective it would be.

"Sirs?"

"Pierre told us we could get some decent food and drink here at a reasonable price."

His demeanour changed instantly. We had gone from casual enquirers to customers. "Certainly sir, the best in Calais, if I do say so myself. Just arrived have you?"

I gestured towards the Custom's House. "Just." If asked later on he would say that we had arrived legally.

"Just take a seat and I will bring you a menu."

"Don't bother with that. Just bring us what you think is your best meal and your best wine." It was a little early for wine but it would help us to fit in.

He rubbed his hands together, "I do like serving gentlemen of quality. I shall bring your food in a moment."

He disappeared into his kitchen whistling happily and I winked at Sharp who grinned back at me. I realised how relaxed he looked compared with our first foray. He was learning.

The food was adequate and I knew that he was rooking us but it was worth it to become established. When the men from the Custom's House arrived for their breakfast it was confirmed. They smiled at us and said, "Good morning." There was no suspicion and we even chatted about the weather and the effect of the British Blockade on the trade in Calais.

As we left I gave the owner a healthy tip and the officers both smiled and wished us a pleasant stay. We were safely in France and I prayed that it would be as easy to get out.

I had discovered, through chatting in the bar, that the best hotel was the 'Mercure'. I headed there. It would be where any officers involved in the planning of an invasion would stay or at least they would frequent it at night. I also deduced that there would need to be civilian contractors supplying the army and they would also stay there. Our story was that I was trying to import cotton from America. Now that the relations between America and Britain were strained it would be logical to try to steal that lucrative trade. I doubted that any one in Calais would know more than I did about cotton- that was precisely zero- but it was a peaceful occupation.

The hotel was delighted to take a customer who paid in gold Louis and not the requisitions from Bonaparte. We were given a fine suite with a separate room for Sharp. I said we would be there for at least a week and paid in advance. It was not my money I was being so lavish with. The manager was delighted to have money in the bank.

After we had changed and Trooper Sharp had put our clothes away I went to the front desk. "Is there somewhere I could rent a couple of horses? I am thinking of buying some property n the area."

"Of course sir. We have some in the hotel." He gave me an ingratiating smile. "I will add it to your bill." We were a lucrative goldmine to the 'Mercure' and its staff.

"Of course."

The horses were much better than the ones I had hired the last time I had been in Calais. I made sure that we steered clear of that area of the harbour from where we had fled previously. Our appearance was different as I had grown a moustache and Sharp had allowed his hair to grow longer. I doubted that Sergeant Major Jones would have approved but needs must.

As soon we as left the old town I noticed soldiers marching towards the port. That meant that there were camps nearby.

To make it less obvious that we were spying, Trooper Sharp had a stick and he made notches on it with his pocket knife. To an observer it would look like idle whittling but we had a system worked out so that, at night, we could convert our notches into regiments. The camps were really obvious and were just outside the town. There were just four regiments of foot there. When we had not seen any more for two miles I turned around and we headed back into Calais. As luck would have it we fell in with a couple of infantry officers heading into the port to pick up new uniforms.

After the normal peasantries I said, "That is a large camp."

The officer laughed, "You are joking. We are the smallest. Now Boulogne, Bruges and Montreil, they are the big camps. They are like small cities."

His companion seemed less ebullient, "It makes no difference. Until we drive their Navy away how will we cross."

I played Devil's Advocate. "But it is such a small stretch of water. Surely it would not take long to cross it."

He shook his head. "Have you looked out to sea? The British blockade the port."

His friend laughed, "Do not worry our admiral will defeat them and then there is always the tunnel."

"The tunnel?"

"Yes, General Bonaparte has engineers digging under the sea."

It was his companions turn to laugh. "And I have seen how much they have dug. Our children can travel that way or possibly our grandchildren! They have barely scraped a hole."

They walked ahead of us. I slowed down and followed. I wished to hear their conversation. "I suppose the colonel will give us another test tonight on the map."

"The names are unpronounceable! I do not know why we are landing in Essex. It seems like mudflats to me."

"I think out little general believes they will not expect us there. Besides, Kent has too many hills and places where the British could hold us up. Essex is, at least, flat."

We could return to England right now. We knew where they were landing. I had discovered the most vital piece of information on the first day.

Back in the hotel Sharp said, "I don't like the idea of that tunnel sir."

"I am not worried about that. It would take a long time to build a tunnel but we need to investigate these other camps."

There was a map of northern France in the lobby and we went down to look at it. "It looks to me like Boulogne is the closest." Sharp didn't say anything but he drew a line from Etaples to Montreuil. I nodded. It was close to our last rendezvous point. Bruges was the furthest. We would look at Boulogne and then finish our reconnaissance at Montreuil.

Back in the room we dressed for dinner. "After dinner I will go to the bar and see what I can pick up."

"I will transfer the information from the notches to paper."

"Good." I was keen to have a written record to take back to the colonel this time. I had sensed a little disappointment at the oral nature of my report the last time we had returned.

The restaurant in the hotel was a fine one. The menu was extensive and expensive. The clientele matched the menu. There was no-one below the rank of colonel and the women all wore fabulous clothes. I suspected that Calais would not normally have such attraction for the well heeled but the prospect of an invasion by the mercurial Bonaparte made it the place to be.

I ordered for Sharp; by now I was accustomed to his taste and knew that he would enjoy the food. We were largely unobserved in the rear of the restaurant and that suited me. I was mentally identifying the ranks and, where possible, the regiments.

As I was eating I noticed a colonel of engineers with a small, pretty woman. She looked nothing like the other flashily dressed women who adorned the arms of the other soldiers. She seemed like a little bird and nibbled at her food. She had me intrigued. What interested me was the fact that the engineer appeared to be serious in nature. He was listening to all that the woman said. Whilst the other women were giggling and laughing she was actually drawing on a paper napkin and talking in an animated fashion. I resolved to discover more, if they stayed.

After we had had coffee Sharp nodded and went to our rooms. I signed for the meal and adjourned to the bar area. Many of the officers and their ladies had had too much to drink and were being quite lively. I headed for the small table occupied by the engineer and the bird like lady. I took the table next to them. I ordered a brandy and lit a cigar. I did not often smoke but found it a useful disguise to mask my spying.

I could barely hear what they were saying because of the cacophony of noise from the women and their escorts. Suddenly one of the officers dropped a bottle of champagne and it crashed to the floor. The woman jumped and gave a small squeal. I took the opportunity to lean over and say, "Are you all right Madame? The noise is intolerable."

She smiled at me and lowered her eyes. "Thank you sir but I am a little nervous."

The engineer ventured, "Some of my brother officers need lessons in being gentlemen."

"They do indeed sir. May I buy you both a drink?"

I think that the colonel of engineers was going to decline but the lady fluttered her eyelids and said, "Why thank you sir. Would you care to join us?"

I saw the flash of irritation on the man's face before he stood and said, "Of course, sir, do join us."

I waved to the waiter and circled my hand around the table. I introduced myself, "I am Henri Ricard." I shrugged apologetically, "A business man."

The colonel smiled, "Do not be ashamed of that. France needs all the trade it can get so that we can strangle England. I am Colonel Robert Mandeville, an engineer." I nodded and shook his hand. "And this is a celebrity; this is Madame Sophie Blanchard who is an aeronaut and balloonist. She is the first woman to ascend alone in a balloon and she is a very clever engineer."

I had heard of balloonists who ascended into the skies on either hot air or hydrogen balloons. I was impressed. I took her hand and kissed the back of it. "I am honoured." I waved a hand at the other ladies in the room. "They are noisy and without thought but you, Madame are a true vision of the future; a woman who can think and is beautiful at the same time."

She giggled and the colonel rolled his eyes. "You are too kind sir."

"And tell me what are you doing here? Do you plan an ascent? Please tell me that you do. I would dearly love to watch you."

The colonel answered for her. "Nothing so frivolous. She is working with me so that we might defeat the English at long last. Their fleet will be useless."

It is strange how you can get a sudden moment of clarity. A thought comes to you from seemingly nowhere. This time I gave voice to it. "You are going to fly an army across the waves!"

Her face told me the answer and it was confirmed by the colonel's denial. "No sir! What a ridiculous thing to say. Come Madame, we have tarried too long and we must away."

I could see from her face that she wished to stay but the colonel almost dragged her from the room. As I sat and finished my drink I thought of the idea. It was fantastical but if even women had ascended in balloons then the logistics would allow for a large enough balloons to transport large numbers? The tunnel and then balloons; Bonaparte was deadly serious this time. He intended to invade Britain and it looked like he was almost ready to do so. He was using every means possible. I knew that he liked using science whenever he could. Whatever one might say about him, he was forward looking and an innovative thinker.

As I ascended the stairs to my room I could not get the pretty little woman from my thoughts. She seemed too tiny to be such a daredevil. I could see why she had come to the attention of Bonaparte. He always liked to use new inventive ideas and this was one such.

The next day we took the horses again, and headed down to Boulogne. I had decided that, as it was so close to Calais, we would see what ships there were in the harbour. The blockading fleet had reported no large ships with masts in the northern harbours of France but I wondered if they would use barges, perhaps, to cross the narrow strip of water.

As we headed south and closed with Boulogne we saw the camps. They were well organised and Trooper Sharp found it easy to mark them down on his stick. When we neared a uniform he hid the stick but we still received suspicious glances. The closer we came to the port the more aggressive was the attitude. Eventually two of the Gendarmerie held up their hands and stopped us.

"Papers!"

It was a peremptory command and the second soldier held his musket as though he was ready to fire. I handed mine over. "What is the problem? I am a simple businessman travelling with my servant. Why are you stopping me?"

My papers seemed to satisfy him but he still viewed me with suspicion. "This is a military area. What are you doing here?"

"You may have camps here officer but this is the main road to the port so how else am I to see if it is suitable for my ships eh?"

"Your ships?" His tone was now almost placatory.

"Yes, I intend to import cotton from America and I need to know which port would be the best to use and to build my warehouses." I wagged a finger at him, "The First Consul would not be happy at your attitude."

His face paled, "You know Consul Bonaparte?"

I smiled, "I have supped with him." That was not a lie but it felt like one.

"I am sorry sir." He hurriedly wrote something on a piece of paper. "Here you are sir; a pass which will prevent you having similar problems closer to the port."

"Thank you. The next time I see Napoleon I will tell him of your kindness." I used his first name to suggest intimacy.

Boulogne turned out to be one huge military camp. If the other two were of the same size then there could be almost two hundred thousand men ready to invade England. Of course only a few would use the balloons, if they ever materialised, but they had the barges to do so. I know that the British Army had a good reputation but they could not field half that number. If they landed in Essex than half of the men who would be opposing them would be stuck south of the Thames.

The pass proved a godsend and we were able to get quite close to the harbour and see the many barges which filled the inner harbour. They would have been impossible to see from the sea. Bonaparte was ready to invade; all that he needed was the Channel free from the Royal Navy for six hours and he would be in London within the week.

The coast road was, mercifully devoid of any soldiers. I could see watch towers, in the distance, but there were no camps. Calais harbour proved to be a copy of Boulogne and there were nearly as many barges there as there had been further south. Once back in the room we compiled the information into one document. It made frightening reading. The cannon we had seen would have made our generals pale let alone the infantry and cavalry. The French must have used the peace to build as many twelve pounders as possible. I knew that we had nothing with the range and power of that gun.

Dinner that evening was a repeat of the first night, save that the lovely Madame Blanchard was not there. I felt disappointed. There was nothing to keep us there and we retired early.

I had decided to risk riding to Bruges. It was much further away than Boulogne had been but I intended to visit Montreuil just before we were picked up by Lieutenant Teer. As a result we rose early and breakfasted just after first light. I was happily surprised to see Madame Blanchard eating alone and she looked just as pleased to see me.

"Good to see you. Would you two gentlemen join me? I do so hate eating alone."

"Of course. This is my servant, Sharp. I am afraid he is American and so he does not speak our language."

Sharp bowed and she beamed. "Oh I would love to visit America. They say that anything is possible there. This awful war prevents such travel does it not?"

The waiter took our order. "It seems a shame that you cannot visit America and yet here you are in the middle of all these preparations for war."

"I know but I need to be here."

"Amongst all these soldiers? I confess it is difficult to find warehouses which I could use. They are all filled with the paraphernalia of war."

"When they leave then you will not have a problem will you? There will be many of them and they will be available at a low price."

"So far I have seen precious little evidence of them moving."

She gave me a smug smile. "I think they will move sooner rather than later."

Our food arrived and we ate in silence for a while. "Your balloon, is it here in Calais?"

"No, it is further south, close to Boulogne."

Enigmatically, that was all that she said. I felt at a loss how to proceed. There was something going on with the lady and it was to do with the invasion. "Perhaps I could see your balloon one day. I confess I have never seen one. The idea of flying above the earth intrigues me."

She hesitated and then smiled, "Of course. Why not? I need to get out of this hotel soon and the colonel will not be back from Paris for another day at least. Could you arrange for a carriage?" She saw my look and giggled, "I can fly a balloon but I have never mastered a horse."

While she went to change I said to Trooper Sharp, "A change of plans. We are going to see the lady's balloon. I have a feeling it has something to do with the invasion. Keep your eyes open."

I went to the reception and arranged for a carriage. From the smile on the assistant manager's face I suspected I would be paying a fortune for it. "You will, of course require a driver. That will be extra."

I did not mind that for it meant that I would be able to get more information from this intriguing and intrepid lady. She was a lively conversationalist and happily chatted about how she had taken to ballooning. I gathered that she had stolen her husband from his first wife. The attraction of ballooning had made her determined to achieve her heart's desire. She might be tiny but she was determined. It soon became obvious that Bonaparte himself had been involved in her plans. She was discreet but I was able to deduce certain facts from what she didn't say. She had designed a balloon which could carry up to thirty men. As I stared out of the window I worked out that thirty such balloons could carry a battalion. They could land anywhere. They could even land in London, at Hyde Park and then the Royal Family could be captured. It was a brilliant idea.

The workshop was close to Gris Nez, just south of Wissant and it was situated on the cliff top. There was a company of engineers guarding it and it was an enclosed encampment. Had we not been with Madame Blanchard then it is unlikely that we would have been allowed within a hundred yards of the perimeter.

The captain in command looked to be under the spell of this lady and he caved in to her smile when she said she wished to show her new friends the balloons. This was the first time she had used the plural and that intrigued me. We were taken to a large oblong building. Once inside I was disappointed. There were just three enormous sacks lying on the ground. She saw my face and she laughed. "They do not look much lying there do they? Yet when we light a fire and fill them with hot air they can rise into the sky. Come let me show you one which is a little more alive than these three sleeping beauties."

We exited the building and found ourselves on the cliff top. There was a basket and above it an envelope which was filling with air. It was tethered to the ground and a soldier was feeding the fire.

"Now do you see? The air is heated and it expands the balloon. Eventually the skin becomes tight and we would rise into the sky if we were in the basket."

I was genuinely amazed and surprised, "How do you steer it?"

"Ah, that is the problem. You do not. You go where the wind takes you. But you are fortunate. We can ascend…" she gave me a cheeky smile, "if you have the courage."

I was a little fearful but I could not, in all conscience, back out now. "Of course!"

The captain seemed worried, "Madame Blanchard, are you sure?"

"The wind is from the west and I do not intend to free us from the ground, merely to rise and show my friend here the joys of a balloon." Despite her sex and her size she had real authority when she spoke.

We headed over to the balloon. I could see Sharp's worried expression. He had only caught a little of the conversation. "Madame, I will just explain to my servant what we are about. He will worry."

I then spoke to Sharp. I used a dreadful accent and pronounced the words badly; much as I had heard Englishmen massacring French before now. "Sharp, I am going up in the balloon. Do not fear. Keep an eye on how they operate this contraption." I saw the captain's surprised look. "He is American and cannot speak French." He nodded his understanding.

"You will need to take off your hat. It can be quite windy up there." I handed my hat to Sharp. "Now climb into the basket and I will join you."

As I stepped in I wondered how she would fit in the basket with me. The fire took up half of the interior and I am not a little man. The captain brought a small stool and she used it climb over the side of the wicker basket. I had been correct and we were almost touching once she was inside.

She giggled again, "It is a little cosy. We shall know each other a little better by the time we have descended. Now put some more wood in the fire and we will begin to rise." As I did so I heard her order the soldiers who were around the basket. "Let go of the anchors."

I stood upright as the ropes holding us to the ground were loosened. Nothing happened for a while and I wondered if I was the victim of an elaborate hoax. She patted my hand. "It is not sudden but it is inevitable." I wondered if she was speaking of the ascent or the thrill I had just felt from the touch of her tiny hand.

I felt a little wobble and then I saw Sharp and the others begin to move farther away. I realised that they were not moving; it was us and we were rising. One rope only held us."Do not worry, Henri, there is little wind today we shall just rise, gently, into the sky."

The sensation was so unbelievably subtle that it was hard to believe that we were actually moving. A furtive look over the side showed me that we were and the faces below us were much smaller. I gripped the side of the basket.

"Well what do you think?"

"I think it is quite remarkable. How many people could you fit into one of these?"

"Oh this is a small one, just the two of us." She touched my hand, "Why would you wish someone else was here with us?" She had moved quite close to me and lowered her voice so that I had to bend down to hear her words. I had almost forgotten that we were in a balloon. I was intoxicated by her. I suddenly had a whiff of her perfume as her face neared mine. I have no idea what made me do it but I suddenly moved towards her and kissed her. I thought that she would back away but she kissed me back. I put my arms around her and she did the same.

When we came apart I saw that her face was flushed with excitement. "You see what the air does to us Henri? It frees us not only from the ground but the conventions of the earth. Here we are free, just like the birds and the bees." Her voice became husky as she said, "Kiss me again!"

Suddenly the balloon stopped rising and seemed to hang in the air. She looked disappointed. "Ah we have reached the end of the rope and soon we shall descend and, once again, become mere mortals. As much as I would love to kiss you again I think you must appreciate the view. It is spectacular."

I too wanted to carry on kissing but as I looked out I saw that we had ascended quite a long way and I could see all the way to both Calais and Boulogne. She pointed west and, to my amazement, I could see the English coast. It looked close enough to touch. I realized that it would be impossible to damage these balloons. They would be able to travel with impunity. How could anyone stop them?

I continued looking as I said, "So you can only carry two people then?"

"In this one, yes but the ones you saw in the workshop can each carry up to thirty people. Perhaps not such huge people as you are, but ones like me. As soon as the wind is from the west we will try them out. I am quite excited by the prospect." We were descending now and I knew that the kisses would not start again.

"Why do you need wind from the west?"

"We only need an east wind when we wish to cross the sea. I am not just a balloonist; I also have to know about wind and weather. It is complicated and you need skill."

I can see that Madame and I can see that you have skill"

She touched my hand again as the ground moved towards us even faster. "I have many skills." As we bumped to the ground she squeezed my fingers and then she laughed as she disengaged herself. "There, how did you enjoy your first flight?"

"It was magnificent!" She seemed genuinely pleased that I had enjoyed the trip.

The ride back to Calais seemed mundane after the excitement of the flight. We both had to behave on the journey back as Sharp was with us and the driver could also see us. I confess that I was thinking of what might ensue later that evening for I was under no illusions; Madame Sophie Blanchard had wanted to do more than kiss.

As we entered the hotel I was planning a way to get to her room later that night. My hopes were shattered when the manager handed her a letter. "Madame Blanchard, this came to you from Paris."

She looked disappointed as she read the letter. "It seems I have to go to Paris to meet with First Consul Bonaparte."

"When?"

Her hand briefly touched mine as she said, "Now." She turned to the manager. "I will go to my room to pack a few things. Could you change the horses? The First Consul will reimburse you."

"Of course Madame."

As he left she looked into my eyes and said, "I shall see you when I return. It will only be a day or two. Then we can continue to get to know each other a little better."

"Of course." Life has a way of tempting you and then tearing away the temptation before you can enjoy it. I was not to know it but that would be the last time I would ever see Sophie again.

Chapter 11

While we ate dinner early in a deserted dining room I explained to Sharp what I had learned. "Well sir, what I did notice was what looked like wagons without wheels. I think that they must serve the same purpose as the baskets. They looked as though they could hold quite a few men."

"The question is what do we do about them?"

"Sir?"

"Those are the only three balloons they have. They are prototypes. They have yet to try them out. If they were destroyed then it would put them back considerably in their plans to invade England."

He nodded as he took it in. "But I thought that we were just here to observe."

"We were but Colonel Selkirk can't have known about this, can he?" I think I was trying to persuade myself that we needed to do something about them.

Sharp said, "Tonight is the first boat sir. We could go back with this information and let the colonel decide what to do. We have plenty of information for him."

I nodded. "I know but I think we should do something about them."

Sharp's face fell. "What do you mean sir?"

"I mean let's try to destroy them."

"But there are a company of engineers there."

I could see that I was being unreasonable. I was asking Sharp to risk his life and it was not necessary. "You are right." He looked relieved, "I will go with you to the rendezvous point and you can take the information back to Colonel Selkirk."

His face became angry, "That's not what I meant sir. I am not afraid! I am not deserting you but why should you put your life at risk?"

"Because I wear the uniform and there is no one else. It's just us."

"Then we will both do it."

Later that night we finalised our plans. We would borrow the horses the following day but we would take with us spare clothes. Our luggage we would leave. Once we had destroyed the skins- I still had to work out how- we would head for the second rendezvous point. It would mean risking Calais again, for our second point was close to Dunkerque. The hotel would raise the alarm but not until the evening of the following day.

As we rode down the road I was busy trying to work out how to get past the guards and then destroy the skins. It was Sharp who had the idea. "It strikes me sir, that the building is made of wood and it should burn."

"I can see that and there would be plenty of inflammable material close to hand but how do we get the soldiers far enough away so that we could start the fire?"

"Sir, when you were in the balloon what made it rise?"

"We put wood into the stove and it inflated."

"So if we could make the balloon rise, without anyone in it they would try to get it back."

"We still have the guards on the balloon to worry about and we have to hope that the fire is sill lit."

He laughed, "Well we can think of something else then, can't we sir?"

He was right. We had to improvise and think on our feet. We hid the horses north of the site for we would be travelling back through the night to reach our rendezvous. I realised that I could have guaranteed success by waiting until the small hours of the night when everyone would be asleep but that would have meant us missing our boat. I had no doubt that once we fired the workshop the French would not rest until we were captured.

We found a place, close to the cliff, where we could observe them. I had left my sword on the horse as it might trip me up and we would not need such weapons. We both had our two pistols and that, along with my stiletto, would have to suffice.

"Let's count the guards and watch their routine."

"You know they will have a relief at some point. If it is like our army it will be every four hours."

He was right of course. We had a good point from which to view. The cliff we used overlooked the camp, not by much, but enough. We counted the men and there appeared to be sixty of them. Assuming that they had some who worked inside that would give us, perhaps, seventy men. We were both dressed in dark clothes and, if we fled at night they would have to spread out to find us. It was not much but it was all that we had. We discovered that they changed guards at four hourly intervals. If they relieved them at eight then we had our pattern. There were two guards at the balloon which was still inflated although it was deflating. There were four at the main gate and, annoyingly, another two who seemed to patrol the perimeter. They would be the wild cards.

We had brought bread, cheese and wine. We ate at six. It was mainly to fill the time before darkness fell. It would be dark at about nine thirty; by ten thirty the guards would be relaxed enough for us to strike.

"Sharp have you ever killed a man with a knife?" He shook his head. "It is not as easy as it sounds. You have to be ruthless. Here I will show you." I demonstrated with him. "You put your hand over their mouth to stop them screaming and pull the head back with your knee in the small of their back. It exposes the throat and stops them elbowing you in the stomach. You have to watch for them pushing you backwards or head butting you. You have to strike quickly. You slice hard across the throat. The warm blood can be off putting but it is your life or theirs. Just make sure you follow through with it."

"Yes, sir. I won't let you down." He was like a puppy trying to please his master. I began to feel guilty about putting him in this position.

When the guards changed at eight I felt much better. I felt even happier when, at ten past eight, ten of them, mainly officers, mounted their horses and left the camp and headed north. The whole camp took on a deserted feel and I could see lights in two of the mess tents. The third was obviously the officers and they had left the camp. We gradually edged our way down the gentle slope. We knew the route the two patrolling guards took; our problem was that we could not predict when they would arrive. Our first job was to take them out of commission.

They obliged us by talking as they wandered along. I did not enjoy the prospect of killing the two of them but we risked capture and death if we merely knocked them out. With Sharp on one side of their path and me on the other we waited until they were close. We rose like two wraiths. Mine died silently as the knife ripped though his jugular vein. Sharp's victim gave the slightest of moans before he too fell dead.

We took their powder with us as it would help to start the fire. We now knew that there were just two guards on the balloon and four on the gate. We had not been able to see the workshop and we didn't know how many guards were there. That would be our next problem.

To my amazement there were none. It struck me as bizarre that they guarded the small balloon but not their secret weapons. Later I decided that they feared theft and not sabotage. The door was, miraculously, unlocked and we slipped inside. We found a great deal of material which would burn and we made a mound of it in the middle of the workshop. Then we dragged the three skins over. That was a harder task than we imagined; they were not light. Eventually we managed it. We poured the black powder all around the skins and Sharp emptied the oil from two oil lamps he found to soak the envelopes.

"Go and open the rear doors a little. That way we can escape across the cliff tops to our horses." As he went to do that I began to use my flint to make a spark. Perhaps I had used too much powder or maybe the oil aided the flames but whatever the reason, when the spark came the whole pile erupted into flame which almost singed my hair. We didn't need to worry about being able to start a fire. We had done that successfully, too successfully.

I ran for the door. Unfortunately the fire showed us up quite clearly in its light and the two sentries from the small balloon both opened fire. They would have been better to have waited for a better shot but, thankfully, they missed us. The alarm was now raised and we ran up the slope towards our hidden horses. So much for escaping in the dark!

I did not bother glancing over my shoulder. It would only slow us up and I was certain that they would not be able to hit us in the dark while running. As long as we could reach our horses we had a chance. The two animals were chewing grass as we raced up. We untied them and threw ourselves on their backs. I felt confident that we could out run engineers on foot and we gradually pulled away from our pursuers as we headed north towards the road. We only had to reach the rendezvous and we would be safe and we would have succeeded.

I have found that sometimes fate plays tricks with you. We had just reached the road when we ran into the ten men who had ridden out of the camp some time earlier. Perhaps they had heard the noise, or seen the flames and returned. I will never know. We crashed into them. I drew my pistol and fired at one officer. He disappeared from his horse. I drew my sword and stabbed another. I heard a pistol, I think it was Sharp's and a third trooper fell. I began to think we might escape when I heard a scream as Sharp was slashed by a sabre.

"Ride south!" I turned to face the remaining engineers and galloped at them, slashing wildly with my sword. They did not expect that and fell back. I managed to cut one of the men and caught a horse with the edge of my sword, causing it to buck its rider. I remembered my second pistol and I drew and fired at the four men who faced me. The flash and the crash made a couple of their horses rear up while my ball hit one of the engineers squarely in the face. I did not wish to push my luck and I wheeled my horse around and galloped off into the dark.

I dreaded finding Sharp's empty saddle and I was happy when I caught up with him still mounted. I heard the sound of pursuit. We were not out of the woods yet. We had to pass the front of the camp and there were four guards there. I just prayed that their attention was elsewhere. "Sharp! Can you ride?"

His voice was weak but full of determination, "I'll hang on, sir. It's my left arm."

I could see the blood dripping from his arm. We would have to stop as soon as we could. My plans were now in tatters. We could no longer head north. The pursuit meant we had to head south and that in turn limited our escape to the boat from Etaples but that would be in eight day's time! We would have to hide out for eight days! I put that thought to the back of my mind. First we had to escape our pursuers and then see to Sharp. The guards at the gate were too busy looking at the workshop which was now an inferno to be able to react to us. By the time they heard our hooves and turned we were beyond them and they wasted powder and ball firing at us. I think what saved us was that the horses of the engineers had ridden more than ours had and they began to fall back. After half an hour I halted and could hear nothing.

I rode next to a white faced Sharp and grabbed a belt from my saddlebags. I tightened it around his upper arm and was thankful when the bleeding stopped. I saw then that the sword had raked his face as well. It was a superficial wound but one which would leave him scarred for life. My arrogance had left him disfigured. We could have been on the sloop now, heading for England with all of the information if I hadn't wanted to go back covered in glory.

I took the bottle from Sharp's saddlebag. "Here Alan, have a drink of brandy."

"Sorry about this sir."

"Don't be a fool it was my fault. We'll get out of this."

"How sir? They'll be scouring the country for us and we have nowhere to hide."

"You concentrate on staying in your saddle and I will get us out of this." I sounded far more confident than I actually was. How would we get out of this predicament? Then it came to me. Pierre. I knew I was only about eighty miles from Breteuil. If we stopped somewhere in between we might be able to reach it before we were caught. Would they expect us to take the Amiens road? I didn't think so. We would have to take that chance.

We rode until dawn. I stopped every hour to loosen the belt and allow blood to flow. Trooper Sharp needed food and rest, as well as the wound cleaning. He never complained but I worried as he swayed in his saddle. I found an abandoned barn just outside Amiens. I counted on the fact that we had outrun our pursuit. For the next few hours we were safe. I laid him down on the ground and tied his horse up. "I will go and get us some food. Rest while you can."

As soon as I laid him on the ground he fell asleep. He had been exhausted. I took out the brandy and cleaned up the wound. It was deep and would need stitching. I rode into Amiens just as the city was coming to life. I found one of those shops which appear to be open all the time and which sell almost everything. I managed to buy some needles and some cat gut. They also pointed me in the direction of a small tavern which was open.

I was the only customer. "Have you any hot food?"

"Yes sir. We have some soup from yesterday. We can heat it up."

"Good. Have you bread?"

"No , but the bakers is three doors down. "

"Heat up the soup I will buy it all and the pot."

"And the pot?"

I flashed a handful of coins. "And the pot." They nodded and smiled.

By the time I returned the soup was hot and I handed over far too many coins and took the hot soup and the bread. I did not go directly back to the barn. I was not certain that I hadn't aroused interest. I went by a circuitous route and made sure that I was not being followed. Eventually I reached the barn. I checked that no-one was around and then entered. Before I saw to the sleeping Sharp I led the horses to a patch of grass and let them graze. They would need water but that would have to wait. As Trooper Sharp was still asleep I decided to have a go at stitching his wound. It was vital I stopped him losing blood. I might not be very good with a needle but it would be better than nothing.

I poured some brandy into a mug and dropped the needle and the cat gut into it. I then ripped a piece of shirt and used the brandy to clean the wound on Sharp's face. He murmured a little but did not wake. I remembered the old housekeeper at Breteuil telling me that sleep was always the best medicine. I hoped so. I could not put it off any longer and I threaded the cat gut into the eye of the needle. It was only then I realised what a big needle it was. It was too late to change now and I began to stitch the savage wound. I tried to make the stitches as small as possible. Halfway through he woke up and I thought he was going to shout. I clamped my hand over his mouth. His eyes were wide with terror.

"Don't worry Alan. It's almost over. Be brave. I have nearly done." When I had finished I gave him another mouthful of brandy. "Let's see if it has done the trick." I loosened the belt. A few droplets of blood dripped from the wound but they soon stopped. "Thank God for that. Now sit up." I brought the small pot of soup over and gave him the bread. "Eat. I am going to water the horses. When I come back I want that pot emptied and the loaf eaten."

"But what about you sir?"

"I had my soup already and there is a loaf for me." I hated lying to him but I knew he would want to share the food with me and I needed him to be stronger quickly. We would have to travel in daylight and travel soon. He had to be as alert as possible. He did, thankfully, obey me and the pot was empty by the time I returned from seeing to the horses' welfare. He had colour in his cheeks too.

"Thank God for that." I began to wolf down the second baguette I had bought.

"What now sir?"

"Now we ride to a place called Breteuil. It is close to where I was brought up and an old friend of mine has an inn there. Well, at least, I hope he does. We will rest up and then head back to Etaples in seven days."

"Sir, if you left now you could make the third rendezvous point."

I shook my head, "No, we couldn't. It is too far to the north for us to reach it in time. We would have to pass close by Boulogne and they would be looking for us. I have made my mind up, we shall head for Etaples and by then the hue and cry should have died down and the roads empty." I had almost convinced myself that that would be true but I did not think they would. Bonaparte was a vengeful man. He would have his men hunt us down. We had thwarted him and that made us his enemies. The roads would be filled with men searching for us for months.

We rode along the back roads for safety. Had Sharp not been wounded I would have sought out the Amiens lawyer, Francois, who had helped me to buy the inn for Julian. As it was I owed it to the trooper to help him first. We rode through Ailly-sur-Noye; it was a tiny town and we passed through it without a problem.

The inn was called 'The Chasseur'. Julian had named it in honour of my old regiment. I saw the sign, newly painted, swinging jauntily in the sun. It felt welcoming. I hoped that I would receive a welcome from Pierre and Julian but both had fought for France and might now view me as an enemy. If they turned me away I would understand but it would probably result in my capture and, ultimately, death. There was a yard and a stable. We ducked under the roof and dismounted in the cobbled courtyard. I heard someone in the stables.

"I'll be with you gentlemen in a moment. Some of these horses seem to be having a shitting contest at the moment."

I recognised the voice, it was Pierre. "Well Lieutenant Boucher as a Chasseur you should be used to being in the shit!"

He suddenly erupted from the stables and picked me bodily up. "Robbie! We heard you were dead!" He cupped his hands and shouted towards the inn, "Julian, it's Robbie!"

Julian had lost a leg in Italy so I was surprised when he walked out grinning from ear to ear. He had a peg leg! "Good to see you again, Captain!"

They crowded around me and I was aware that Sharp was still standing close by and looking like death warmed up. "Listen my friends, I am in trouble and my friend here is wounded."

Both had been good soldiers and like all good soldiers knew when to be decisive. "Julian, take them inside and I will get these horses out of sight." He grinned at me. "They are stolen aren't they?"

I nodded, "Technically just since midnight, but yes, stolen."

He laughed, "I have missed you Robbie. Life is never dull around you is it?"

The inn was, thankfully, empty apart from Monique, Jacques' wife who was nursing a baby. Her face beamed as she saw me. "Captain Macgregor, we heard you were dead."

"No, I am afraid that I am alive and bringing you trouble once again."

She put the baby into its cot and pulled her dress up. "You can never be trouble sir. Without you, who knows where the three of us would be." She noticed that Sharp was in danger of swooning. "He is hurt. Please, sit."

I helped Sharp down into a chair and took off his jacket. Monique shook her head when she saw the wound. "That is not good, captain." She poured a large glass of brandy for Sharp and made him drink it.

He said, in English, "Thank you." Then he passed out.

They both looked at me. I nodded. "As I said I bring you trouble. He is English and a soldier."

Julian smiled, "It matters not. If you could carry him upstairs to one of the rooms. He needs rest and the good offices of my wife."

I hefted the injured man and, trying not to aggravate the wound, I carried him, somewhat awkwardly up the stairs. Monique was at the top of the stairs and she gestured to the bedroom. "Put him there and I will clean his wound and see to him."

I laid him on the bed and then stood looking down at Sharp who was now white as a sheet. Monique patted my arm. "Go, you look tired too. You know that I will care for him." She hesitated, "What is his name?"

"Sharp, Alan Sharp."

She mouthed the word, "Alan… yes that is a good name."

By the time I had descended, Pierre was there. He had a bottle of wine open and there was cheese and bread on the table. "Come old friend and eat. Then you can tell us the tale."

"Thank you, I am famished," I began to eat.

Pierre and Julian toasted me, "Cheers!"

Pierre lit his pipe. "We heard that the 17th were finished in Egypt. The rumour was that you were all either dead or prisoners. A few soldiers eventually made it back and they said that the whole regiment disappeared in the desert. Is that true?"

"That is fairly accurate but they did not disappear; they were betrayed and slaughtered. Jean and I were the only ones to escape the carnage."

"Jean too is alive then?"

I shook my head, "No he died of his wounds I buried him and Killer together."

"Killer died as well? He was a magnificent horse. And those who betrayed them, what of them?"

"I killed the man responsible in a duel but I became a fugitive. I had to flee for my life and I ended up in Sicily where I met the Knight of St.John that we met. Eventually I returned to Scotland."

Pierre looked intrigued, "You found your family then?"

"I did but it was not a good meeting. I was not made welcome. I had to change my name for I killed some men in England. I am now Robbie Matthews."

Pierre and Julian both laughed. "So you are wanted in Egypt, wanted in England and now, unless I miss my guess, you are wanted in France."

I found myself laughing with them. "That about sums it up."

"So what brings you to this backwater?" I hesitated. Pierre continued, "We are your friends first and last. We fought together. You and I are the last of the 17th. Those bonds are stronger than any other. Besides this Bonaparte is not a republican. He will proclaim himself king one of these days. Albert will be turning in his grave at some of his antics."

I sighed. "Bonaparte is planning to invade England. I have seen the camps and I have seen the boats. I have been sent to find out how far along his plans are."

Julian sipped his wine. "So you are a spy."

There was no point in denying this; I would not lie to friends. "Yes I am a spy."

He nodded, "Continue."

"I discovered that he had a plan to use balloons to ferry men across the Channel. I destroyed the balloons and Sharp was wounded in the encounter."

"And how did you intend to leave France?"

"A sloop will come and pick me up. There is a boat in a couple of nights and then, four nights later, the last boat."

Pierre tapped his pipe out on the fire. "Well you can stay here until your next boat or the last one."

"But I am an English spy."

Pierre gave a grim laugh, "Many Frenchmen will die in the invasion and for what? So that Bonaparte can gain the glory. At least in Malta we were invading an antiquated medieval army. The British are a different kettle of fish. They will fight tooth and nail for their island. No, my friend, I am happy for you to get to England with news which might stop the maniac." He pointed to Julian, "We both fought to defend France and I would do so again. What I will not do is try to take another man's land. I like this place. It is my home. We travelled in Italy and Germany but I would not want those lands. Let the Germans and the Italians keep them. And I do not want England."

"It is a fine country."

"But how do you eat the slop they serve as food?"

"It is not that bad besides have you ever eaten their food?"

"No, I have heard too many stories about how bad it is."

"You would like their beer and their inns."

He stood and stretched, "They cannot compare with 'The Chasseur'. We are the best inn for miles and we even have visitors from Amiens. Why, even Francois, the lawyer brings his clients here when he wishes to impress them. Julian and Monique are good cooks and I keep fine beer and wine."

Julian nodded, "He is right and we owe it all to you. Now the inn will be filling up and it might be best if you were scarce. If, as you say, they are hunting you then today and tomorrow will be the most dangerous times."

"You are right and I do need to sleep." I clasped them both around the shoulders; they appeared to have shrunk while I had grown. "I want to thank you comrades. I did not think you would let me down and it is good to know that we are all still the same."

Pierre grinned, "Perhaps there must be something in English food and beer for you are almost a giant now so perhaps we are not all the same."

I went into Sharp's room. I saw that he was naked beneath the bed sheets. Monique gave a smile. "It is better to let the air circulate. I will wash these clothes."

"Thank you Monique. You are kind. How is he?"

"I will not lie it does not look good. There is bruising which makes it hard to see but I think there is redness there and it feels hot to the touch. He too is beginning a fever. It may be the shock and the lack of sleep but we will watch him. I will bring Guiscard's bed in here and a mattress. I can look after them both."

I cocked my head, "Guiscard?"

"Yes our son is named after his grandfather."

"The old man would have liked that and he would have adored you."

I could not help a yawn. "And now, Robbie, you must sleep. Your room is across the way."

I had barely undressed and put my head on the pillow before I was asleep. I think I felt safe for the first time since we had arrived in France.

When I awoke it was dark. I suddenly panicked, wondering where I was. Then it all came back to me. I put on my breeches and shirt and went to Sharp's room. Monique was in a rocking chair feeding Guiscard and she put her finger to her lips and mouthed, "He is sleeping."

I realised that it must be the middle of the night and I went back to bed. As I lay, this time trying to sleep I worked out that I had not had a night in a bed since before we left for Pomerania. My body demanded sleep and I dutifully obliged.

Chapter 12

The next time I awoke it was morning. The nearby cockerel informed of that as did the sound of movement in the street below. I washed and dressed. Monique was just leaving Sharp's bedroom when I emerged. Her face told me the story.

"He is no better then?"

"No, I am afraid he is worse. His arm is hot and red. It is infected." She paused, "He could lose an arm."

One again I was filled with guilt. We had to do something. Pierre and Julian had a table laden with food and the four of us ate together. Monique told the others what she had told me and their faces showed the same concern. Then Pierre began to smile. "Sir, do you remember when we were in the 17th. What did we do with a bad wound?"

For a moment I could not remember and then it struck me. "Maggots!"

Monique shook her head, "Do you mind? I am eating."

"No Monique, we put live maggots on the wound and they eat all the diseased parts when there are none left alive then the wound is healed."

She looked dubious but Pierre said, "It does work."

"I will let you gentlemen deal with the wriggling little creepy crawlies."

Pierre leapt up and sought some maggots. There was always something dead along the road and the maggots would soon be feasting. As he left he shouted, "Robbie, we will need a clean bandage."

Despite Monique's words she was interested enough to watch as we cut away the bloodied bandages. I could smell the wound and feel the heat. There had been dirt in the wound and I had not cleaned it well enough. When he returned, Pierre packed the maggots around the injured arm and I began to wrap the bandage tightly until the scarf was completely covered.

"Now we wait and we watch."

We watched for two days before there was any change. They were two days of a solitary existence for me as I kept out of the way of the customers. Pierre had done a good job of changing the appearance of the horses. He even went so far as to let them graze with a friendly farmer who liked to use the tavern. Although my friend did all that they could to keep me amused and occupied, I hated the boredom and the inactivity. In addition to the ennui I was also worried sick about poor Trooper Sharp who seemed to show no signs of improvement.

Monique kept feeding him soup in his rare moments of consciousness. Even when he was inert she still managed to open his mouth and pour the healthy broth down. I watched her as she did it. She shrugged, "It's just like Guiscard, only Alan is a little bigger."

Julian was lucky to have found such a woman. I am sure they must be rare; women who are kind yet can cope with any hardship. It made me think of Sophie. I knew it was highly unlikely that I would ever see her again and, after what I had done to her balloons, I could not expect a good reception. I still wondered what would have happened had she not had that message to go to Paris. Would we have ended the night in each other's arms and what would have happened after? It was all speculation but I had plenty of time to speculate.

After two days the fever broke and the arm appeared cooler. I was relieved. We all crowded into his room when Monique gave us the news. He tried to sit up but Monique snapped at him like a naughty child. "Do not undo all my good work! Lie down."

I do not think he understood a single word but the tone was obvious and he lay back down. "How long have I been here sir?"

"About three days."

He nodded and closed his eyes. Then he must have worked out the times of the sloop and he tried to struggle up. "Sir the rendezvous. We have to get to the…"

I held up my hand. "You are going nowhere until Monique is happy with your improvement. We are not far from the last rendezvous point and we have a few days yet. Get better. We will get home, trooper."

That evening I joined Julian and Pierre in the bar. There were just a couple of locals present and they were trusted by my friends. Pierre had news. "I have been into Amiens to get some provisions and there are still groups of the Gendarmerie looking for two saboteurs."

"Do they have a description?"

"They have your name and they know that Sharp is an American. Otherwise the description could apply to most Frenchmen."

Monique joined us, "My two babies are sleeping."

We laughed and Julian told her of our plight. She moved away from me and said, "If you shave off your moustache then you will not look like the man who came here and if we do not shave Alan then he will look totally different too. You came in clothes that were burgundy and brown in colour. We dress you in blue and green. Do not wear a hat, instead use a bandana around you head."

Julian put his arm around her and kissed her. "Gorgeous and clever. I think myself lucky every day and thank God she took pity on a one legged man."

She ruffled his hair. "There was no pity; I grabbed the best man I had seen in a long time."

They were wonderful people and I found myself envying them a little. They had few luxuries but a comfortable life. The two men had been invalided out of the army and would never have to suffer for another's ambition.

The change in Trooper Sharp over the next three days was quite remarkable. When we removed the dead maggots the arm looked much cleaner. On Monique's advice we removed the stitches and we saw that the flesh had joined itself. Monique had applied creams and ointments to the scar on his face and it, too looked less angry. The beard also helped to disguise it.

Disaster almost struck the day before we were due to leave. Perhaps we were complacent, I don't know. I had shaved off my moustache and was seated in the bar drinking with Pierre when the soldiers came in. There was a young lieutenant, a sergeant and a private.

The lieutenant looked angry when he walked through the door. He glared at us all. "We are looking for two British spies!"

I was not sure if he expected someone to say where they were but we just looked at each other. Pierre laughed and said, "We haven't got any."

The sergeant grinned and then, as the lieutenant shifted his ire to him became stoic. "I have checked with the local officials. It seems that some notables were murdered not far from here some years ago and this inn was implicated."

It was Julian's turn to laugh, "I think the inn might also be innocent."

This time the private stifled a laugh and turned it into a cough. The lieutenant reddened. "I mean that those in this inn were implicated."

Julian tapped his leg. "I lost this leg serving France. Even if I was a spy I wouldn't be a very good one would I?"

Pierre tapped his chest, "And I was invalided out after Egypt and I couldn't even lift a sword now."

Frustrated the lieutenant glanced at Monique and then his gaze settled upon me. "And you! The one who keeps quiet. Who are you?"

I shrugged and pointed to Pierre. "I served with Pierre here and I too left the Chasseurs after Egypt. I came here to relive old times." I decided to go on the offensive. "As you can see we are three old soldiers. Where did you serve lieutenant? In which campaign did you serve your country?"

This time the private and the sergeant looked at the lieutenant to see his reaction. He blushed, "Then, as old soldiers you should respect what we are doing for we are searching for enemies of France."

I nodded, "Then perhaps it is the manner in which you search. If you were more polite and respectful to old soldiers them you might find out the information you seek. We have seen no strangers here. Does that satisfy you?"

He nodded. He then glared at all of us and then stormed out.

The sergeant gave an apologetic shrug. "I am sorry gentlemen. I served in Italy as did the private. Now they promote boys who have yet to shave. We will not return."

After they had gone we all breathed a collective sigh of relief. Pierre said, "Remind me never to play cards with you Robbie. I thought we would have to kill all three of them."

"No, Pierre, I only kill those now who try to kill me."

We would have to travel by day to ensure that we reached Etaples by nine o'clock. That would be dangerous. Pierre solved it. "They are looking for two men. I will come with you and they will not see anything to raise their suspicions. It will also mean that we can talk in French while Trooper Sharp plays the half wit."

Alan had been taking French lessons from Monique and although his accent marked him as English he could, at least, understand some of what Pierre had said. He joined in the laughter.

We left before dawn. I hugged Monique. "I can never thank you enough." I took out two of my gold Louis. "Here is one for you two and one for Guiscard when he is older. A present from his Uncle Robbie."

She nodded. "Will he ever see his Uncle Robbie when he becomes older and can understand more?"

"This war cannot last forever. I will return. I promise."

The three of us rode towards Amiens and reached the busy town just after eight. The streets were filling up. Many of those on the streets knew Pierre and shouted greetings to him. It meant that the Gendarmerie almost totally ignored us. A cursory glance was all that they gave us and then we were on the road to Abbeville. We managed to get through that town too and we were on the last leg to the coast.

Pierre and I spoke at length of our dead comrades. We were not certain if we would ever meet again and there were things which needed to be said. He wanted to know how each of them had died. It might sound both morbid and macabre to anyone else but I knew why he needed that knowledge. He felt guilty as he had not been there. He had been saved by a pirate's sword thrust into his back. He would grow old. Tiny, Charles, Albert, Michael and all the others would never grow old and it was important that Pierre knew how they met their end.

We smelled the sea and felt the ozone laden breeze long before we saw it. We had ridden steadily and reached the sand dunes by six o'clock. We had made good time.

"You might as well return to the inn."

"No, old friend. I will see you safely aboard this ship and then I will be happy. You have come a long way from the young boy who was barely shaving; the young lad who put us to shame with his sword and pistol skills, not to mention how you tamed the aptly named Killer. You see, my friend, you were something of a mascot, a lucky charm to the 17th and you are the only survivor. I owe it to our dead comrades to make sure that you get back to England. So long as you live then so do they. They stand like guardian angels at your shoulder."

And so he waited with us. We ate the picnic Julian had made for us and we watched the sun set in the west. We had brought a lantern for the signal and I kept checking the time on my watch. Ten o'clock came and went. I would like to say that I was not worried but I was terrified. If the sloop went then how would we get back to England? The blockade of ships from both sides meant that it would be impossible. We would have to travel far to the south and that did not bear thinking about.

It was at eleven fifteen when we saw the four flashes. I flashed the lamp four times and then we saw the sails of the sloop as they were lowered. We had tethered the horses and Pierre walked with us to the sea. "I have never seen one of these roast beefs up close, not alive anyway. I think I will talk with one."

We had just seen the boat begin to be lowered when there was a flash from the south and then the crack of cannon. It was a French Man of war! I saw the dingy being pulled up and the sails lowered as the lieutenant tried to get away from the trap. Five flashes came from the sloop- they were leaving. The pop of his own cannon sounded minuscule in comparison to the thunder from the French ship. The French ship was much bigger- probably a frigate. As much as I wanted him to come back for us I wanted him to escape more and he did. I heard the rip as the cannonballs ripped through his sails but he escaped. We were trapped in France once more.

"Well sir, that's torn it then."

"Aye it has." I turned to Pierre. "Well we had better come back with you then Pierre."

He tapped the side of his nose. "We are not defeated yet. Do not be so pessimistic. Let us go."

As we rode he explained. "There is a small port some five miles away. St Valery. I know a couple of smugglers and they occasionally go to England to sell brandy."

"And how do you know them?"

"Who do you think supplies the brandy?"

If I thought that the whole village would be asleep I was wrong. The tavern was busy. When we entered the room everyone stopped their conversation and stared at us. They all looked to be working men who could handle themselves. The gnarled knuckles and weather beaten faces told the whole story in an instant. Had we been alone then I think that Sharp and I might have come to harm. As it was Pierre's presence must have reassured them for they visibly relaxed when they recognised him.

The owner, a tiny, shifty looking ferret of a man, cocked his head to one side. "Pierre what brings you out here at this ungodly hour?"

Pierre laughed and clasped the man's hand. "Why to be amongst the ungodly of course." The whole room laughed and went back to their conversations. "This is Robbie and Alan. They are friends of mine." He lowered his voice. "Is Jean around?"

With an equally quiet voice the owner said, "No, he left a couple of hours ago."

"Damn. Listen, Serge, my friends here need to lie low until Jean returns. Can you help?"

The ferret showed his teeth as he smiled, "Of course…for a price." He held out his hand and I gave him a couple of silver coins. He smiled, "A brighter colour would help." I dropped a gold Louis into his palm and his smile widened. "There is a room upstairs and I will even throw in food and ale."

Pierre snorted, "For that kind of price you should have thrown in your wife."

He laughed, "She would have been included in the silver if she hadn't run off last year with a wine salesman from Bordeaux. Come I will take you upstairs."

"We have horses."

"Put them in the stable. They will be safe enough."

The room we were given was little more than an attic. There were four beds with horsehair mattresses and three grey blankets. I suspect the blankets had once been white but time and the lack of washing had turned them into a grey. I decided that, once the ferret had gone I would be discarding his blanket.

"I will bring some food and ale to you. Make yourself comfortable."From his tone one would have thought he was offering us a room in the Louvre Palace.

Sharp had picked up a few of the words and I explained to him what our host had said. "How are you holding up?"

"Better than I thought I would. The arm aches but I haven't had to use it much yet."

I threw the blankets to the floor and watched as insects leapt, briefly from them, and then disappeared once more. I shook my head. "It looks like we have company tonight." Sharp laughed. I picked up one of the mattresses and shook it violently. This time the insects and bugs leapt for the safety of the pile of blankets. I repeated the action with the other two mattresses. It would not deal completely with the wildlife but it would serve to thin them out.

Pierre and Serge returned with three plates of some offal based stew and a large tankard of ale. Once again Serge's expression and gestures suggested we had been give food cooked by Bonaparte's chef.

"I will see you gentlemen in the morning. You are quite safe here. Sleep well."

After he had gone I asked, "Are we safe, Pierre?"

"No, the robbing bastard will assume you have more gold Louis. We will take it in turns to stay awake."

I pointed at the pile of blankets which were almost moving of their own accord. "That won't be a problem."

We ate the food, which filled a small hole, and we drank the ale which was drinkable. "Sharp, you get some sleep. Pierre and I will watch."

"Sir, I want to take my turn too."

I shook my head, "You only have one arm at the moment. Do not worry, Alan, I had plenty of sleep at the 'Chasseur'. This will not be a problem."

He was soon asleep and Pierre and I turned down the lantern and talked as we peered through the attic windows at the dark Channel beyond. "If this Jean went out tonight then he might not want to go out again tomorrow."

"You still have gold Louis?"

"A few, yes."

"Offer him one he will ask for four and you settle on two. He will take you. Besides, the English can't get enough of French brandy and wine. I am sure he will be able to make a second trip."

"I want to thank you for what you are doing for us."

"Don't be daft, Robbie. I have enjoyed it. I like my life in the inn, don't get me wrong. But I do miss the excitement we had doing those little jobs for Boney. I know that in a couple of years I won't be able to do this sort of thing, so thank you. I feel rejuvenated. For a while I am a young horseman again." He smoked his pipe in silence for a while. "To be honest I had been getting a little low lately. Julian and Monique are good people but I have no one. I was never a lady's man, you know that. I enjoyed the camaraderie of the regiment. Seeing you again has brought the memories back. Seeing you and young Alan there working together is reassuring. The life I knew still goes on. When you are back in England and I am in the corner of the bar I will be imagining what you are doing. When I read the reports of the battles I shall look out for Light Dragoons and know that it may be you who is performing so heroically. To me you will still be little Robbie Macgregor and not the English spy."

"You could come with us to England, Pierre. I am a successful businessman too and I have money. I even have a ship."

"No, it is far too cold for me. But it is good to know that you have done well. Not so bad for a French bastard eh?"

"And I have contacts in Sicily. I know that you liked it there."

"Ah yes, Naples and Sorrento." I could hear in his voice that he was tempted by that idea as he remembered our visit there. "When you go there, write and let me know. I might take you up on that but I wouldn't just turn up with your relatives. That is not my way."

"They wouldn't mind but I promise that I will let you know when I go there." I began to think of a way to keep in touch. "You say you still keep in touch with Francois?"

"The lawyer from Amiens? Yes. He reads all our legal documents."

"Good, then tomorrow we will get pen and paper and I will write a letter to him. He is still my lawyer and I will use him to pass information to you. He was always a bright young man and, unusually for a lawyer, honest."

We sat in silence, each planning the future. I was pleased we had had this conversation for I could see that I had brought a little hope into his life. Our meeting had helped us both and that pleased me.

Suddenly I heard a creak on the stairs. Neither of us needed to speak. We both stood and went silently to the door. We stood on either side and waited for whoever came through. I took out my stiletto and my pistol. I reversed the pistol so that I held it like a club. The handle of the door began to move slightly and then it groaned open. In the dim light from outside I saw a hand. Pierre grabbed the outstretched hand and pulled. As the bald head came next to me I struck it with my pistol. Pierre punched the second man who lumbered into the room and I wrapped my arm around the ferret who hovered just outside and held my stiletto to his throat.

"So Serge, my gold Louis was not enough. You decided to rob me too." I pricked his neck so that a tendril of blood dripped down his throat.

"No sir, this is a misunderstanding. We merely came to collect the dishes."

Pierre had lit the lantern again and revealed the two men who were struggling to their feet. Their cudgels lay on the floor. "And they came with cudgels in case there were mice?"

Defeated he hung his head. Pierre snorted. "Slit their throats Robbie. It's all that they deserve."

I could see the terror in the ferret's eyes. "Shall I Serge? Shall I do the world a favour and rid it of three rats?"

He dropped to his knees, "No sir, please. I beg of you, spare us."

Pierre kicked one of the men in the ribs. "You two, piss off. I am going to watch out of the window and if you are not at the end of the village by the time I count to two hundred then your boss dies. Clear?"

They nodded and Serge almost screamed, "Do it! For the love of God, do it!"

They scurried away, leaving their weapons on the floor. Pierre went to the window. "Well they can run that's for sure." He turned to Serge. "Anyone else around?"

He shook his head. "Just those two."

Pierre chuckled, "I don't think I believe you. I'll take him downstairs Robbie and lock this place up. You can sleep now. I'll watch our slippery friend here."

I didn't sleep. I watched the sea and listened. I thought of the journey I had had to reach this point. There was a time when I had thought I was a traitor. Now I did not. I was not fighting the French people; after all they were half of me. I was fighting a tyrant. I know that those people in America who had been of English stock had not thought they were traitors when they fought against King George for they, like me, were fighting a tyrant too.

I watched dawn's light sparkle on the water and Sharp awoke. He saw the cudgels on the ground. "What did I sleep through?"

"The landlord decided to put up the rent in the night and these were his collector's tools. Let us just say that we discouraged him." He rose. "Let us go down stairs. Pierre has been watching the ferret all night."

Serge was asleep on one of the benches. Of Pierre there was no sign but I could hear the spit of fat. I went into the kitchen and found him frying up hunks of ham. "The bread is a bit stale but there are plenty of eggs. I am sure our host will not mind us helping ourselves eh?"

We ate well that morning and wolfed down huge amounts of Serge's food. I did not doubt that we would have had much smaller rations had he brought us breakfast. There was a sudden rapping on the door and a rough voice shouted, "What the hell is the door doing being locked? Open it Serge or I will gut you like a fish!"

Pierre did not seem at all put out by the threat and he left the kitchen. I heard the bolts slide back and the Pierre's voice, "Well Jean, I see you are still a bad tempered old pig. Come in there's some food on the go."

Jean reminded me of every caricature I had ever seen of a pirate. He had a long flowing beard and hair. He stood on two tree trunks and his belt was festooned with weapons. "Jean, these are two of my friends and they would like you to take them to England."

Jean did not seem discomfited by the request. He picked up a huge piece of ham and slapped it on a piece of bread and then he shovelled an egg on to the top and finally another piece of bread. He bit into it and gobs of yolk and fat spurted out, dripping down his already heavily stained coat. He smiled. He swallowed some of it and then turned to me to speak. It was disconcerting to have pieces of ham and bread fly at you.

"It will cost you. I did my business last night so it will be a special trip."

I flashed a gold Louis."One of these."

"You didn't pay Serge with one of those did you?" I nodded. "I bet the bastard tried to rob you." Again I nodded. He emptied his mouth and wiped his hands on his jacket. "Four."

"Two, and that is all."

He nodded and he held out his left hand for the coins. I dropped them in and he shook hands with me. "I will be back at six. We sail at seven so do not be late. I have your money and I will not wait for you."

Pierre asked, "Where are you off to then? Going to get more brandy and wine?"

Jean laughed and I saw that he had a gold tooth too. "Of course. No point in wasting a trip over is there?"

Serge spent most of the day sulking. Pierre rarely took his eyes from him. "Won't this cause a problem to you?"

"Nah! Serge is a pain in the arse to most people. The only reason we tolerate him is because of where this place is. Jean is the one I wouldn't upset. If anything this has helped me. Serge now knows not to cross me."

"And his men?"

"They are alright at sneaking up on sleeping men but that is about it. They haven't got the balls to try anything else. If I tell you none of them have ever served France you will have a better idea of what kind of men they are."

Alan nodded. I smiled at him, "I see your French is improving?"

"Yes sir, I got most of that and I even worked out the French for 'balls'!"

"Always a handy word to know, Sharp."

The day dragged because I was worried that someone might arrive at this small port who might be an official or a soldier. The Grand Army was less than twenty miles from where we were. Who knew when they might decide to include this small port in the list of places from which to embark.

Pierre was certain that they would not come. "If I know my soldiers then they want to go as short a distance from their camp to get legless as possible. The officers would only go to the best hotels in the bigger towns and wouldn't come here. The only danger you will have will be the French navy and the Royal Navy.

They both try to stop smugglers. Old Jean is a past master at escaping them and they have not even come close yet. But there is always a first time and, as we know well, everyone's luck runs out sometimes."

Jean's ship was bigger than I had expected. It had a mainmast and a lateen sail aft of the main one. It looked to be too big to be a fishing boat and too small for a trader. Pierre saw my puzzlement. "Are you wondering how much she can hold?" I nodded. "A lot! She has plenty of hold space. You will have to stay on deck; below is infested with rats and God alone knows what else. Luckily for you it is only a short voyage but keep everything to hand."

I held up my leather satchel. "We both have one of these. Everything we need is in them." Sharp had spent the morning copying out all the information in case we were separated. I had also written my letter to Francois and sealed it with my mother's ring. Although Francois knew and trusted Pierre it was a guarantee that the missive came from me.

Pierre walked us to the ship. It had the unlikely name of 'Mathilde'. It seemed somehow, incongruous, given Jean's appearance and the nature of his business.

"Come on lads step lively. Pierre, give your mate a kiss and then we'll shove off."

Pierre made an obscene gesture at Jean but his eyes were smiling. "You take care Robbie and I hope we meet again."

"You take care too."

Pierre grasped Alan's hand, "You are the first Englishman that I have met that I didn't try to kill. You're all right you are."

Sharp laughed, "Enjoy your tavern my friend."

And then we were aboard and the boat was edging west towards the setting sun. Jean grinned amiably at us, the sun glinting off his tooth. "Now I am not going anywhere special for you two. I have a little place I am heading to close to a place call Hastings. You go ashore when the barrels do. Is that clear?"

"Yes captain and that suits us."

"Good, now try not to get in the way. My lads are a bit handy with their fists if you catch my drift."

We headed north and the setting sun illuminated the coast of France. I had achieved the first part. We had left France. Now could we avoid two navies and a rough set of seas and make it back home? I suspected we were already being written off as dead by Colonel Selkirk. Would he have told the regiment? There was little point in worrying about that. We had this little bridge called the Channel to cross first.

We passed close to Montreuil. We could see little save the massive fires from the huge army which was camped there. We had not managed to get close to it but we had enough information from the other camp to be able to estimate the numbers. We had just begun to leave the French coast and head west when we hit trouble. As the sun disappeared over the horizon one of the lookouts spied what he thought was a sail to the north. It was barely a glimpse but Jean took no chances. We were standing close to him and he explained, "It might be nothing but we are not the fastest smuggler around. We are just the best and the luckiest. We will sail west for a few miles and then resume our course north."

It was a more uncomfortable journey as we struck breakers head on. Trooper Sharp became a little green again. It was understandable. He had not sailed on such a small ship before. Even the 'Black Prince' had been twice the size of this little tub.

"I reckon we can head north again now." The captain grinned at Sharp, "It might make life easier for the young man."

Suddenly, out of nowhere, a small cannon ball ripped a hole in our lateen sail. The captain threw his helm over to try to out run this mystery ship. Surprisingly there was no second shot. Had we not the evidence of our eyes and the hole in the sail I would have said that we imagined it. We peered astern but the sea and the sky were melded into a large black hole.

A shape materialised out of the dark and a ship appeared; it was twice our size and moving much faster than we were. A voice told us, in French, to haul down our sails or risk being sunk. I saw the resignation as Jean gave the order and his shoulders drooped. "Well, my friends, it appears that my famous luck has finally run out. I am sorry. It looks like you will not be seeing England after all."

We drifted to a bobbing halt. The ship came next to us and its deck was a good eight feet above ours. I struggled to see a flag but the masthead was obscured by the spars. When Lieutenant Teer leaned over and saw us, he burst out laughing.

"Well 'pon my word. What a stroke of fortune this is. We thought we had lost you last night and here you are, large as life and twice as welcome. We'll have you aboard in a jiffy."

A couple of seamen jumped down to the deck and two ropes snaked down. They grinned at us. "Right sirs, if you would like to climb up these ropes."

I shook my head, "I can do so but this soldier was wounded last week and he can't use his left arm."

"Not a problem me old cocker." He was a barrel of a man. He turned to Sharp. "Jump on me back and hold on with your good arm. I promise I won't drop you."

Sharp did as he was bid and the seaman clambered up the rope as easily as I might walk down the street. I felt a fool as I struggled up with no body on my back to slow me down.

Lieutenant Teer greeted me as I struggled over the side. "Good to see you."

"And you." I gestured at the 'Mathilde'. "Any chance you could let him go. We would not have escaped otherwise."

"It's a nice little prize but we can always catch him again." He leaned over the side. He spoke in French. "Captain, I will let you go this time but the next time I catch you then I will have your little boat."

I saw the relief on Jean's face and he grinned up, "If you catch me sir, you deserve to have my boat. Farewell Englishmen!"

"And now let's get below deck and you can tell me your tale."

Chapter 13

Once we were under way I finally relaxed. Sharp and I grinned at each other. When I had heard the French voice I thought we had been captured by the enemy. Lieutenant Teer had an excellent accent.

He entered the cabin, "I am sorry about last night. A damned frigate was snooping around. I didn't want you caught as well so I slipped away and hoped I could return later. The damned ship kept chasing every which way.... Sorry."

"Do not worry yourself Jonathan. We were delayed because Trooper Sharp was wounded within a day or so of our arrival. We have spent much of the time hiding out."

He looked disappointed. "Then you did not discover much about the invasion."

"Oh yes, we know all that. There are huge camps at three places close to the coast and the harbours are filled with barges which the blockading ships cannot see as they have no masts."

"Then I shall have to get you back as soon as possible. I just went to Dover and sent a message from there. Colonel Selkirk thinks you are lost."

The winds were in our favour and we fairly flew across the waves. By dawn we were sailing up the Thames. "I will land you close to Horse Guards and give you an escort. Would never forgive myself if you were to fall foul of some felon in London."

When we landed at the wharf on the Thames the bosun and four of the toughest seamen I have ever seen took us directly to Horse Guards. I wondered if the people who started at us thought that we had been pressed. It must have looked a strange sight. When we saw the red coated sentry the bosun knuckled his head and said, "Here you are sir. I must say, for a soldier, you are a rum 'un."

I suspect it was a compliment but I had no time to find out for the bosun about turned his men and strode back towards the river. I had a feeling that Lieutenant Teer was going back to try to capture Captain Jean.

The guards gave us curious looks at the main door and I had to explain that we were both soldiers. Even then the duty officer appeared unwilling to admit us until I mentioned Colonel Selkirk's name.

"Ah, you are a couple of them. Let them through, private."

I never discovered exactly what the officer meant by a couple of them although I suspect it was nothing complimentary. We knocked on the door and a tired voice grumbled, "Enter!"

The colonel's head was buried in some papers and he did not look up as he snapped, "Well, damn it, what is it?"

I said, quietly, "We thought we had better report sir."

His face was a picture as he stared at us and then he laughed and banged the desk. "I thought you were dead or captured. But you are here!" He opened a cupboard and pulled out a bottle of whisky and three glasses. He poured a healthy measure and said, "Here's to you! You are a sight for sore eyes."

We swallowed the fiery liquid and he waved us into the two seats which were there. He leaned forwards, "Well then, did you find out what I needed to know?"

I nodded and handed him the report. "Save my old eyes and give me the gist of it. Is Boney coming?"

"The bad news is that he is and he has three huge camps at Boulogne, Bruges and Montreuil. We didn't manage to see them all but I estimate that there could be over two hundred thousand men in Northern France at the moment. He has barges in the harbours all ready to bring them."

The colonel's shoulders sagged, "Is there any good news?"

I nodded cheerfully, "He cannot invade so long as you blockade the coast and keep ships outside the harbours."

"Well that is a relief. Admiral Nelson is more than a match for any two of their admirals." He poured us another whisky. "How did you manage to miss all the rendezvous and why did it take you so long?"

"That would be my fault sir. We discovered that Bonaparte also has a tunnel he is building. That will take years but he also had plans to use balloons to transport men and they would have been able to avoid the navy."

He laughed, "Well that is more fanciful than the tunnel idea."

"No sir. He had three balloons ready to try out and I believe they would have worked."

He sat up, suddenly serious, "You say 'had' as though he no longer does."

"We destroyed them and the workshop where they are being built but Trooper Sharp was wounded during our escape and we had to lie low in France until he healed."

Colonel Selkirk looked at each of us in turn. "It was a damned stupid thing to do Robbie but I am damned glad that you did." He scribbled on a piece of paper, signed it and sealed it. "I cannot acknowledge what you did for England, Trooper Sharp, but I can promote you to sergeant. You might as well get paid more for risking your life following this lunatic around Europe."

He came around the desk and handed the letter to Sharp who said, "Thank you sir I…"

"It's nothing. It isn't like I will be paying you the money now is it?" He sat and sipped his whisky again, "Just as a matter of interest were there any guards at this workshop?"

"Yes sir. A company of engineers."

"And you two sabotaged their efforts and escaped from them?"

"It would appear so."

He shook his head, "Too modest by far. You two better get back to your barracks then. Take the mail coach." He took a document from a small pile and signed it. "Here is a travel warrant."

"But sir, our uniforms."

"Of course. I'll tell you what, let us go to my town house and you can stay the night. I daresay you need the sleep and I would like to hear in detail just what went on. Let us go to my house now. I will need to change if I am to report to the Prime Minister and the powers that be."

As we walked through the streets to Colonel Selkirk's house he smiled wryly. "Perhaps a bath might be in order as well gentlemen. You smell of horses and… well let us say that a farmyard springs to mind."

"Believe me, colonel, we both desire to be clean again, more than anything. It has been a hard few weeks days."

The old colonel's eyes looked sad and careworn as he looked at me, "You have done well, Robbie, and I do appreciate your efforts. I have sent many young men like you but you are the only one who consistently delivers. Hopefully you will now have time to recover."

"I think you said that before sir."

He laughed, "I did, didn't I? Well this time I will try to keep my word."

The colonel had two baths run. I soaked in mine for a good hour until a servant came along and asked me if I was all right. When I dressed and shaved I felt much better. I had decided to keep my moustache. Although Monique had shaved it off it was growing again. I had missed having one and I could see no reason not to. Sharp had shaved too. The effect was to highlight the scar which was still red and angry. When the colonel saw it he commented, "It will soon fade and become just a thin white line." He pointed to the side of his face. "There is a faint one there. It has moved and become thinner over the years so that you can barely see it unless you know where to look."

We relaxed for the afternoon and napped. When the colonel returned he clapped me on the back. "Well done young Robbie. The news was a good kick up the backside for the politicians. Your news had the same effect as putting a stick into a wasp's nest. They thought that Bonaparte meant what he said about peace. They have learned the truth at last. And now let me change and then we will eat. You can regale me with your stories."

The next day we left his house together. As we stepped outside an ensign gave him an officially sealed document. The colonel read it and he frowned. "I have to change my plans today. Damned armchair generals. Why can't they let soldiers just do their job without interference." He folded the letter and put it in his pocket. "Take care. I know I need not remind you that you cannot speak of what you have discovered. When the French do not invade no one will know that it was your courage and your effort which enabled it to happen. That is the way of our world."

We were lucky in that there was no-one else in the mail coach which hurtled us back to Kent. It enabled us to talk and discuss what had happened.

"You now know the dangers of what we do and if you do not wish to accompany me again I will understand."

"No sir, I do not mind but I must ask one thing. Now that I am a sergeant, I can still be your servant can't I?"

"Of course but I thought that you would want to be in command of men."

"I would rather be your servant sir. If I can't be then I will refuse the promotion."

"That will not be necessary. If you wish to be my servant still then that is fine by me."

The journey flew by but we both nodded off and the driver had to wake us when we arrived in Canterbury. We still had money left from the trip and we went to the tailors. I had learned that a handmade uniform lasted longer than the ones issued by the Quartermaster "You might as well have your sergeant's uniform made up as soon as possible."

Carruthers and Co was an old established tailoring firm. They prided themselves on quality and speed. They were not cheap. That was not a problem. It was Mr Carruthers the elder who took our order. He was a tiny precise man who constantly smiled as he measured and scribbled on the tiniest piece of paper I have ever seen. I could barely make out that they were figures. How he would translate them later I had no idea.

"If you gentlemen would give me an hour then your new uniform will be ready, sergeant."

We wandered the busy streets of Canterbury. There were many fine inns and taverns. We found one, 'The George' and took a small dining room to the side where we could eat in private. I did not relish the thought of bumping into some of our comrades before we had had a chance to report to the colonel and the major. The waiter took our order and we sat in silence. We had been together for such a long time that a conversation was unnecessary. I knew that Sharp would be reflecting, as I was, on the fragile nature of our existence. There were many times we could have ended up dead but we had survived and that was reassuring.

"Have you ever noticed sir, how many inns and taverns are called George? I wonder why that is sir?"

"I suspect it is because our kings for the past few years have all been George. As soon as we get a new king then the names will change." We drank the ale the waiter had brought.

Suddenly I heard voices from the next room. The walls were little more than plaster and our silence afforded us the opportunity to listen to another conversation. Normally we would not have done so but I recognised Lieutenant DeVere's voice.

"I have told you before, Ramsden, there is no risk to you. All you need to do is put the items in the captain's room and we will do the rest. My brother has promised you that he will see that you are promoted."

"But sir, Mr Austen is a good officer and the lads all like him. If they find out what I have done then I will not be able to stay in the regiment."

"Nonsense! I have it on good authority that my brother will soon be promoted to become Major DeVere and then he will get rid of any troublemakers who do not toe the line. Besides now that Matthews is dead it is us who control the regiment." There was silence. I looked at Sharp who was also listening. DeVere's voice became more threatening. "Let me put it another way, Ramsden, if you do not comply then it will be you who is leaving the regiment. I am sure that my brother and I can find some dirt to ruin your career. You have a simple choice to make; join the winning side or lose everything that you have."

The conversation ended and I heard the sound of disappearing footsteps clattering on the stone floor. I peered out of the door and saw the two soldiers disappearing. Sharp spoke first, "That was Trooper Ramsden sir. He is Captain Austen's servant."

"Then we must get back before the deed can be done." Our food arrived. We did not do the fine fare justice for we wolfed it down as though it was iron rations. We paid our bill quickly and left. The tailor had just finished the uniform. We paid for the clothes and we hurried the mile or so to the barracks.

As we passed through the guard house I asked, "Has Trooper Ramsden returned yet?"

The trooper looked surprised, "I thought you were dead sir. Both of you."

"Well we are not! Now answer the question!"

I raised my voice more than I normally do and the trooper shrank a little. "Sorry sir, yes sir. Just five minutes ago. Him and Lieutenant DeVere."

I smiled, "Thank you." As a sort of apology I said, "Long journey."

He smiled back, "No problem sir. It is a long way back from the dead isn't it?"

As we hurried along I said to Sharp, "Get to Captain Austen's rooms and do not let Ramsden enter." I nodded at his new uniform. "Use your new stripes if you have to!"

"Yes sir!"

I went directly to the Headquarters Building. Neither the colonel nor the major were there but Sergeant Major Jones was. He just nodded, "I knew you weren't dead sir. Welcome back."

"We will have the pleasantries later." I closed the door. "I just overheard Lieutenant DeVere threatening Trooper Ramsden. He wanted him to plant some things in Captain Austen's room."

I saw his face darken. "That explains a lot sir. Many of the officers have had things stolen over the last week or so. It seemed that the only person who could have done it was either an officer or an officer's servant. The DeVere brothers were making a little too much of it."

"Where are the colonel and the major?"

"In London; they were ordered to present themselves at Horse Guards." I saw a thought dawn upon him. "Captain Austen is with him."

"Then come with me and we will deal with this matter ourselves."

When we reached the officer's quarters I saw Sharp standing in front of Percy's door. He gave a slight shake of the head. "Ramsden has not done the deed yet." I nodded to Sergeant Sharp, "You stay here. Come with me Sergeant Major."

We reached Ramsden's room. The door was slightly ajar and there were voices within. I nodded to the Sergeant Major who threw open the door. I stood just behind him. There we saw Lieutenant DeVere taking objects from a bag and handing them to Ramsden. As soon as he saw us his eyes widened in panic.

"Thank goodness you have come, Sergeant Major. I have just discovered the thief. It is Captain Austen's servant. I think the two of them must have been in collusion."

I stepped out from behind the huge Sergeant Major. "I think not Lieutenant. You are the one handing the objects to the trooper."

"No, you misunderstand... "

"Trooper Ramsden did you hand the objects to the Lieutenant?" He looked relieved, "No sir."

"Did you or Captain Austen take those objects from their rightful owners?"

"No sir."

"Well lieutenant? We are waiting for an explanation."

His face darkened and he spat out, "You cannot believe an enlisted man over an officer." We remained icily silent. "It makes no difference. My brother will soon be in command of this regiment…"

"However until that dark day dawns he is not. Sergeant Major Jones place Lieutenant DeVere under close arrest and those stolen items in the regimental strongbox."

"With pleasure. Guard!"

"You can't do this." DeVere tried to barge his way out of the room. Sergeant Major Jones grabbed his arm.

"Take your hand off me you big ape!"

Sergeant Major Jones leaned forward and said very quietly, "Sir, if you don't stop wriggling I will break your arm. Now hand me your sword and try to behave like a gentleman."

His shoulders slumped and he gave his sword to me. The two guards appeared at the door. I pointed down the corridor, "Take the lieutenant to his room. He is not to leave it and not to have visitors."

The two guards looked at each other. "Not even Captain DeVere?"

Sergeant Major Jones roar almost made them recoil in fear, "You heard the officer. No-one!"

After they had left I turned to Ramsden. "I want you to go with the Sergeant Major and write out what the lieutenant asked you to do." I paused, "I was in 'The George' and heard it all. Leave nothing out and you will be safe."

"Thank you sir."

"Wait for me in office, boy." After he had gone he said. "Captain DeVere will not like this you know sir."

"I know. When will the colonel be back?"

"This evening."

"Then we weather the storm until then. If you get Sergeant Sharp to write his own statement out it will help."

He looked surprised, "Sergeant Sharp?"

"Yes, Colonel Selkirk promoted him but he still wishes to be my servant."

He nodded, "It is good to have you back sir."

I went to my rooms and deposited my bag. I headed for the mess. There was no point in hiding away. If Captain DeVere wanted to cause trouble then I was ready.

It was something of an anti-climax when I discovered only Captain Stafford in the mess. "I see the news of your demise was greatly exaggerated."

"It was."

My serious tone and expression must have warned him that something was amiss. "Is there a problem?"

I told him all that had transpired. He smacked his hand against the table. "It all makes sense now. Everything that was taken was from officers. It had to have been either a servant or an officer. Only Percy and James escaped the thief and they were under suspicion. The DeVeres and their cronies were making snide remarks. Captain DeVere will not take the arrest of his brother lying down you know."

"I know. It is up to us to hold the fort until the colonel arrives. Tell me, why does DeVere think he is getting the regiment?"

"There is a rumour that his uncle at Horse Guards was bringing charges of incompetency against the colonel and the major. Something to do with equipment going missing when you were in Pomerania."

"But the major was there with us how he could he be involved?"

"Ah that is the clever part. It is said that the major needn't have gone to Pomerania and that was part of the plan to defraud the government out of a fortune."

"And why has Percy been summoned?"

"With you presumed dead he was the next senior officer and he was called to give evidence."

It all made sense to me now. DeVere had waited until he thought that I was out of the picture and then used his family to pressurise the two officers. The colonel was close to retirement anyway and Major Hyde-Smith's family had no influence. The DeVeres were powerful and ambitious.

"Right then, come along with me to the regimental office. This needs careful thinking and planning. When we reached it Sergeant Major Jones was just reading the two statements. He glanced up at me and nodded, "Both signed sir. They present a clear cut picture if you ask me."

"Right Sergeant Sharp, you take Ramsden and take him back into town. I want you two off the base for at least three hours."

Sharp looked worried, "Will you be all right sir?"

"I hope so sergeant, I hope so." As the two men left I ran through my thinking again and hoped that I had planned it well enough. "Well Sergeant Major, will those two guards be able to keep Lieutenant DeVere in his room and, more importantly, Captain DeVere out?"

He grinned, "I reckon they are more scared of me than of him."

"Good. I want them to confront us in here."

"In here sir? But why?"

"Have you got a copy of the standing orders handy?"

"Yes sir but..." realisation dawned. "Very clever sir. That will work. I am sure he has not read them."

David looked confused, "Standing orders? How does that help us?"

Jones dropped the document on the desk. "It is too much to read at the moment sir but it is what Captain Matthews asked for when he arrived. I can see why. This is the regimental Bible. Every eventuality not written in King's Regulations is in here."

I sat down as did David. "Who is this relative of the DeVeres then that gets them so much freedom to do as they like?"

"Their Uncle is a Major General and a close friend of the Duke of York. As far as I know he never commanded a unit in action and he was one of the Johnnies who made such a mess of the war in America."

I was baffled, "Then how does he have so much power?"

"They kept promoting him to get him away from real soldiers. So long as the Duke of York is there then he is fireproof. I just hope that Colonel Fenton uses his influence too."

"Does he have much?"

"He knows a lot of the generals and they respect him. Captain DeVere might have underestimated how much respect Major Hyde-Smith gained in Pomerania. I hear the Elector of Hanover is singing his and your praises as the men who saved the Hanoverian Army from the French."

"So more men managed to escape?"

"They certainly did and Sir John Halkett is forming the first regiment. They are to be called the King's German Legion."

That was a good thing anyway. Von Doren would get to fight the French and I think he had learned his lesson when he lost his men. It was a costly loss but in the long run might have made Von Doren a hope for the future.

We heard a commotion down the corridor and suddenly a very angry and irate Captain DeVere burst into the room. As soon as he saw me he became even more animated. "I might have known that you would be involved in all of this." He pointed an accusing finger at Sergeant Major Jones. "Jones, I will have you reduced to the ranks for this! I want my brother released immediately!"

Sergeant Major Jones stood up. He towered over DeVere. "First of all, Captain DeVere, it is Sergeant Major Jones. I have earned the rank and the respect and secondly you brother has been found guilty of theft and that means he is under close arrest."

Captain DeVere got a sly look on his face and turned to Captain de Lasalle and Lieutenant Wolfe who had followed him into the office. "But you, Sergeant Major Jones, do not have the authority to arrest an officer."

Sergeant Major Jones gave the slightest of looks towards me and sat down.

Looking as though he had won a victory, DeVere crowed. "I thought so. Now release my brother immediately!"

I gave a slight cough and an apologetic smile as I said, "Actually, Captain DeVere, it was me who ordered the arrest of your brother."

He turned on me and he had the look of a cobra about to strike. "And who gave you the authority?"

"I suppose the colonel did." I kept my voice deliberately calm and pleasant. DeVere had fallen into the trap I had set quite nicely.

"But the colonel isn't here and neither is the major. I am the senior captain in the regiment and so I am in command. I will order the release of my brother. So do it, Jones!"

"It is still, Sergeant Major Jones and Captain Matthews is quite correct." He threw a copy of the standing orders across the desk. "These are the standing orders which cover every eventuality should the colonel not be here. If you turn to page fourteen, you will see quite clearly that Captain Matthews has every right to arrest a fellow officer, if he has evidence. The only person who can countermand those orders is the colonel himself or the officers of a General Court-martial. Now on page eighteen it says that we can hold a court martial without the colonel. We have enough officers to form a court."

I could see that he suddenly saw a way out. "Then we can convene one and the charges will be dismissed."

I coughed again, "That is true but as a relative of the accused you, Captain DeVere, would not be able to sit and judge. That would be the three captains who are in this room. For myself I am quite happy for the three of us to sit in judgement on your brother. Especially as I have seen the evidence and, after all, we just need a majority verdict."

He could see then that David and I would both vote guilty. He formed his hands into fists and I could tell that he wanted to hit me. I was relaxed and I was ready should he be so foolish as to try that. I could see in his eyes that he hated me but there was something else. He was afraid of me. He was used to people caving in to his bullying. Poor Jackson had nearly lost his commission because of that bullying.

He unclenched his fists and took a couple of deep breaths. "What is this damned evidence then?"

I leaned forwards conspiratorially, "We shouldn't really tell you, you being the accused's brother and all that but we are all officers here aren't we? We are honourable men." If he detected the sarcasm in my voice he did not comment. "There is a wealth of evidence. Trooper Ramsden's statement that he was coerced by your brother and threatened."

"Coerced into what?"

"Blaming an innocent man, Captain Austen, of the recent thefts."

"He is merely a trooper. His word will not stand up to that of an officer, especially not a DeVere."

"Then there is the statement of Sergeant Sharp who overheard your brother coercing Ramsden."

He looked confused, "Sergeant Sharp, we haven't got a …you mean your servant. You can't promote him to sergeant."

I smiled, "I didn't. Colonel Selkirk of Horse Guards did."

"It is still circumstantial. You need more proof than that."

"Like someone seeing your brother handing over the stolen items to Ramsden?"

"And who saw that? Sharp again?"

Sergeant Major Jones' voice boomed, "No sir, that would be me…" he grinned, "and Captain Matthews and I would think that our word would be good enough. Wouldn't you sir?"

We had him beaten and he stormed out. The other two looked more embarrassed than anything and then they followed him out.

"Remind me never to play cards with you Robbie. You are the coolest customer I have ever met."

"A little tip David. Don't lose your temper. It gets you nowhere. Get angry but think and use your brain. The trouble with the DeVeres of this world is that they are used to riding roughshod over people and getting their own way. They have never had to think. Once they are baulked then they have nowhere left to go but shout, rant, rave and then leave with their tail between their legs."

"With respect sir, he is still a dangerous little bugger."

"I know and we are not out of the woods. Much depends upon what happens to the colonel."

An hour later we heard the sound of horses on the cobbles outside and our three brother officers returned. We would soon know the answer to our question.

Chapter 14

When they entered the office none of them seemed surprised to see me. Also they all looked quite happy. Sergeant Major Jones stood to attention. "Good to have you back sir." He hesitated, "Everything went well?"

Colonel Fenton gave us a broad smile. "It did. It seems we have friends there." He nodded to me. "Your Colonel Selkirk put in the odd good word or two and that young chap you and the major met, Von Doren? He was most eloquent. It was decided that no investigation was necessary as there was no evidence of any wrongdoing."

Major Hyde-Smith said, "So we can get back to normal now then."

I stood, "Not quite sir. We have had to arrest Lieutenant DeVere."

I thought I might have had a stronger reaction but the colonel just sat down and said, "Explain."

I spent the next half hour going through the events of the day. Percy looked first relieved and then I saw him colouring. He was becoming angry. I would need to speak with him later.

After I had finished Colonel Fenton asked, "What of Sharp and Ramsden? Where are they?"

"We sent them into Canterbury, they should be back soon."

"Captain Stafford, would you be so kind as to find them and bring them here. I need to speak with them and then make sure that they are safe. Major Hyde-Smith we need to hold a court-martial. We two and Captain Stafford can make up the members." He gave me an apologetic shrug, "You are a witness I am afraid."

"That is not a problem sir."

"Well, well this is an interesting set of circumstances. It is fortunate you came back when you did captain or poor Captain Austen here might have been what is the word...?"

Sergeant Major Jones said bluntly, "Stitched up sir."

"Quite, aptly put. Well major, we had better go and see the prisoner and then Captain DeVere. I realise it will spoil my appetite but this is the sort of thing we senior officers have to do. And thankfully, I am still a senior officer." He smiled, and as he left, patted me on the arm, "Well done Captain Matthews. You have behaved impeccably."

The dinner in the mess that evening was a frosty affair to say the least. The incident had created an even wider gulf between the officers. There was a clutch of officers seated at the far end of the table as far away from the colonel as they could get and then there were the rest of us. I was plagued by questions about our extended absence, Sharp's injury and his promotion. I was keenly aware of Colonel Selkirk's orders and I was vague. I talked of doing a service for Colonel Selkirk and how we had been attacked by robbers. The promotion was an easier one to field. I told the truth; Colonel Selkirk thought that he deserved it.

The court-martial was arranged for the following week. Whitehall was informed and, a couple of days later we received a visit from a general. He spent a long time in conference with Colonel Fenton. I suspect that Captain DeVere had had something to do with it for he walked around with a smug look while the two were behind closed doors. When the general left smiling Captain DeVere's smile turned to a scowl.

The colonel was too much of a gentleman to divulge the discussion which took place but Major Hyde-Smith let me know that the general had merely wanted to read the evidence for himself.

"Between you and me Robbie he was sent by DeVere's uncle. Luckily his star is on the wane. Even the old Duke is realising that he is a liability."

In the end the court-martial did not materialise. The two brothers resigned their commissions. Technically this was a disgrace, they were cashiered but as it was quite obvious that Lieutenant DeVere would have been found guilty. It was a way for him to leave with a modicum of dignity. They departed without a word to anyone but, as they mounted their crested, family carriage, they glared daggers at those they blamed, me, the Sergeant Major and the colonel. I do not think their looks bothered any of us.

The result was that we needed another lieutenant and another captain. Fortunately as some regiments had been disbanded and we now had a good reputation there were officers who wished to purchase a commission in the 11th. We were also able to recruit a couple of officers for the newly created E Squadron. I did not think that the two brothers would forget us. One day they would try to get their revenge. I would not put them from my mind and I would watch for their progress. We later heard that they had both bought commissions in the 7th Hussars. It amused me when I discovered that the elder, Charles, had tried to buy a majority and could not. He was still a captain. That would have rankled with him.

We were able to spend the rest of the summer and autumn drilling the new men and assimilating the officers. Although some of the new officers were a little distant it was a much less frosty atmosphere than when the influence of the DeVeres had been so apparent. Their coterie of friends also tried to assimilate more with the rest of us and the nights filled with debauchery at Mr. Popwell's inn, 'The George and the Dragon', were a thing of the past.

One morning I noticed that Sharp had some bruising on his face and his knuckles. "Trouble Sharp?"

His face remained impassive, "No sir."

At parade that day I saw that Seymour, Grant and many other of the sergeants also sported the evidence of a fight. None would tell me where they received the injuries. Eventually I went to Sergeant Major Jones. "All right Sergeant Major, give me the truth. What happened to Sharp and the others?"

He chuckled. "It seems some of the sergeants from A Squadron resented losing Mr. DeVere and the fact that Sharp was promoted for, in their eyes, no good reason. Well they began mocking Alan and then made the mistake of calling him an arse licker and making some suggestions about yourself, sir, and their relationship which he took to be offensive. It seems that the rest of D Squadron did. If I tell you that half of the sergeants from A Squadron did not make parade today then you know who won."

"It seems pathetic somehow."

"No sir, good for morale. A Squadron have always been top dogs in this regiment. Captain DeVere made it that way. Your lads have stood up to them. It will encourage a little competition and that is no bad thing." He saw my dubious look and said, "If there was anything to worry about sir, I would tell you."

We spent the next hard months preparing the men for an invasion which could still materialise despite the presence of the navy. The rains of autumn and the snows of winter did not stop us.

When spring finally emerged from the cocoon of winter the men were as drilled and trained as they ever would be. The regiment was a far cry from the disorganised and demoralised unit I had joined almost a year earlier. We were desperate for some diversion and we were given one.

The colonel addressed us all in the mess. "It has been decided, not by me I hasten to add, that we ought to be doing more than training." He held up his hands as he saw the looks on the faces of many of the officers. "We have, therefore, been asked to aid the Customs officers in the area and deter smugglers." He gestured at the map. "This coast is the closest part of England to France and that is where most of the smuggled items are coming from." I had seen the other side of the coin. We would be hurting Pierre and Jean. "We will each be allocated a section of the coast. Each troop will alternate with its brother troop. One night on and one night off. It will do the men good to be hunting men who do not wish to be found and, trying to be positive about it, this may well give the men good scouting skills. The Sergeant Major will issue each Squadron with its designated area."

Sergeant Sharp shared my misgivings. "I am not sure that I could shoot at Jean, sir."

"I know but it may not come to that. He is a wily old bird and he will be on his boat. We will cross that particular bridge when we come to it."

Our patrol area was Whitstable; famous for seafood and crabs it was not popular with smugglers. Our nights were dull and devoid of any action whatsoever. All of the other squadrons had some success during the first two weeks of our new operation. David and his squadron captured a boat load of brandy and wine. A few bottles found their way to the mess.

The colonel was right; it did hone the men's skills and my troop was desperate to emulate the rest of the regiment. All of them either chased away or captured smugglers. We had letters of commendation sent from London and the morale of the whole regiment, save D Squadron, was high. I could neither blame nor fault the men. They worked hard but, if there are no smugglers to be found, then you cannot create them. We rode each night to Herne Bay and then along the coast to Whitstable. The one positive element was that we were popular with the locals who found our presence reassuring. They still feared a French invasion. What we could have done to stop an armada I have no idea.

I was leading the troop with Lieutenant Jackson. He had come on tremendously since the DeVere's had departed. The men tended to view him as some baby faced mascot. Corporal Seymour had been promoted to sergeant and he looked after the lieutenant with all the attention of a mother wolf and her cub.

We halted that night, as we always did, at Whitstable. One of the locals, a crab fisherman with a gnarled face looking as though as he was carved from stone, approached us. "I seen a couple of ships out yonder sir. No lights."

""Fishing boats?"

He shook his head. "Didn't look like that to me sir."

I gathered the sergeants and Jackson around me. "Lieutenant Jackson, you keep half of the men here. Spread them out along the beach. Tell them to keep a good watch. We may have the chance to capture some smugglers tonight. It's our chance at last."

They all nodded their agreement,"We need something sir. Those arrogant bastards in A Squadron have been crowing about chasing off a couple of poxy fishing boats. We have to get a result tonight."

"We will get a result one night but it may not be tonight Sergeant Grant. We will lead our horses along the coast road. We will have a lower profile. Sergeant Emerson, you take ten men and ride the long way around and when you get to Herne Bay, come back along the road."

I was left with just thirty men. Sergeant Grant voiced his fears. "Leaving us a little thin aren't you, sir?"

I laughed, "If thirty of our men can't handle a few smugglers then I think we all ought to get a new profession don't you?"

He chuckled, "Aye sir, you are right but I do so want us to have some success. The lads deserve it. Their heads are going down a bit."

I knew what he meant but you could not manufacture a situation where you could get success. They would acquit themselves well once they had a foe; they had shown that in Pomerania, but they needed an opponent.

After half an hour of trudging through sand I was not sure that it was turning out to be such a good idea but we had to persevere. I had trained the men to be silent at night. I know it is hard to hide so many men and horses but it is slightly easier if they make no noise. I held up my hand for the regular half hourly halt and the sergeants and corporals raised theirs. I could hear the sea and then something else. I heard the sound of oars splashing in the water. I pumped my fist twice and, as it was repeated, every trooper took out their carbine. The designated horse holders grabbed the reins of their horses and the remaining twenty men squatted as they awaited my order. I waved the line forwards towards the sea, some hundred yards away. It was pitch black and I could see nothing but I was sure that something was out there. I held up my hand to halt the line and listened.

Sharp suddenly looked at me and mouthed, "French!" I nodded. I too had heard the language. I hoped it would not be Jean. I would not like him to end his days in a British prison.

I waved at the men to lie down. Peering into the dark I strained to see the boats. Suddenly I saw a shape and white foam marking the bows of a boat. Then there was another and another. There were three boats. Since when did smugglers bring in three boats? I raised my carbine and whispered to Sergeant Grant, "Prepare the men. This may be more than smugglers." I repeated the message to Sharp and heard the message as it hissed its way along the line of troopers.

The men wading into the water were still indistinct until I caught a glimpse of white trousers. These were not smugglers these were French soldiers. In an instant I took in the fact that this was not an invasion when I saw the small number of boats. The harbours had had hundreds of these barges. What worried me was that these three, no four, boats all contained French regulars. What was going on? "These are French regulars, be careful!"

Whoever had sent these soldiers to England would not have sent inexperienced novices. These soldiers would be good. I rolled on to my back. "Sergeant Sharp, send two riders from the horse holders to bring the rest of the men."

"Sir!"

He soon disappeared towards the horses. "Let them get closer. No one fires until I give the order." The whispered message was passed from trooper to trooper. This was now a serious matter. It was more than a game to see which squadron could capture the most smugglers. This was real soldiering.

With a sinking heart I realised that there were over a hundred men forming up on the beach. Even with the entire troop here we would be outnumbered. Until the rest arrived there were four Frenchmen for every one of my men. For all that I knew this could be part of a larger force. The French had done this before, in Ireland and in Cumberland. If we didn't stop them then the inhabitants of Herne Bay and Whitstable could be in peril.

I gauged that they were less than eighty yards away. I could have waited a little longer but I risked them seeing us. I knew that all that they would see would be the muzzle flashes of our guns and they would fire high when they returned fire; they would assume we were standing. It was now or never. As I shouted, "Fire!" Sharp rolled into the sand next to me. His nod told me he had done as I had asked.

Sergeant Grant yelled, "Reload!" The carbine, unlike the musket could be loaded from a prone position.

I knew, from their reaction, that the French troops were good. They all brought their muskets up, despite the dead and wounded and they fired a volley at us. I heard one cry of pain showing that we had not escaped injury.

I yelled, "Fire!" and the twenty odd guns barked.

Their leader must have realised how few we were for he suddenly ordered his men into a single line. Every gun could now be brought to bear and we would cause fewer casualties with our volleys.

"Reload!"

The French fired another volley and then I heard the order to fix bayonets. I yelled, "Fire!" just as their officers shouted, "Charge!"

Our balls took out some but they did not stop the charge. The only factor which was in our favour was the sand which slowed them up.

"Stand and fall back! Use your pistols." Unlike the French my men had pistols as well as carbines. I dropped my carbine which swung on its swivel. It made movement more difficult but freed up both hands. Holding my sword in my right hand I aimed my pistol at a huge sergeant who hurtled towards me. The ball smacked him in the shoulder and he spun round but the mountain of a man rose and lurched towards me. He was a brave man but I lunged forward beneath his jabbing bayonet and stabbed him in the neck. The soldier next to him tried to bayonet me in the side and I hit the end of the musket away with my pistol. I brought my sword around to slice across his neck.

I heard Grant shout, "Sir, fall back!"

I realised that I was isolated and I walked backwards. The French soldiers saw their chance and all tried to skewer me. A flurry of balls whizzed around me and men fell. I struck the ends of three bayonets away and then took a mighty step backwards. This was the dangerous part; I could trip over anything.

I heard Sergeant Grant shouting the commands to reload and then Sergeant Sharp yelled, "Sir, drop to the ground!"

I obeyed as Grant shouted, "Fire!" and the gaggle of men before me all fell.

I reached our lines and said, "Thanks. How many have we lost?"

"Six sir." Grant pointed down the beach, there were more men coming from that direction.

We needed more men and, until the rest of the troop arrived we were shorthanded. "Back to the horses. We will use the horse holders. We'll be Light Dragoons once more."

The order given we turned and ran. The French thought that we were fleeing and that they had won. They all cheered. Reaching the horses I ordered the men to mount. The men put their carbines away and drew their sabres. I took out my spare pistol as did Sergeant Sharp. "Ready! Walk! Trot! Jones, sound the charge!" The commands were given in quick succession and the bugle echoed in the night. We needed to hit the French while they were still disorganised.

I heard their officers ordering them to reload and to form lines. They were difficult manoeuvres to achieve at the same time and neither was done well. We struck the line before they had fired. The bayonets on the muskets formed a barrier but they made the muskets more unwieldy. Badger barged through two men and I skewered one of them. A face loomed up on my left and I fired my pistol blindly. We charged until we struck the water. I turned in my saddle and saw riderless horses. We had not escaped without losses. "Jones, sound recall."

The troopers quickly rallied. We were well outnumbered now. There was only one thing left to do and that was to go on the offensive. It would take them longer to organise than it would us. "Sound the charge!"

As we hurtled towards them all that I saw was a wall of fire as they opened fire on us. It was a ragged volley and, I suspect, they did not hit as many as they might have expected to. Then I heard a wail from their rear and saw horses. It was Sergeant Emerson and his men. There were only twelve in total but they had an effect far beyond their numbers. They fired as they rode and then their sabres slashed down on unprotected backs. It was more than enough and while some of the French survivors fled back to their boats, others lifted their arms in surrender.

"Keep them covered. Sergeant Grant, take some men and disarm them."

I heard the sound of horses behind me and saw Lieutenant Jackson and the rest of the troop. "I'm sorry, sir, we came as soon as we could."

"Don't apologise lieutenant, it was my orders which left you at Whitstable." I pointed to the boats, "See if you can capture some of those men fleeing or just shoot them. They are French regulars." I would have taken our men but the horses had charged too many times. It would have been a waste of energy.

"Sergeant Sharp, see to the wounded."

I turned to look for the bugler. "Jones, find someone with a fresh horse and send him back to the barracks. The colonel needs to be here."

"Sir."

I rode over to the disconsolate group of prisoners who were being watched by the eagle eyed Sergeant Grant. I could see the look of hatred on their faces. I saw that they were mainly the young soldiers. There was one lieutenant there and a wounded sergeant.

"Keep an eye on them while I go and check the dead officers for papers." I dismounted and walked through the bodies which lay scattered and bleeding in the surf and on the sand. I was looking for an officer. I hoped they might have some information which might help me to find out what their purpose was. I doubted that the lowly lieutenant would have had much of an idea.

I saw a captain with half his head blown off lying in the water. I opened his jacket and found a few soggy papers. I would have to dry them to read them. I could not find any others. I looked out to sea. The sun was just rising and I could see now that there were five boats in total and they were pulling away from shore. I wondered how they could have evaded the Royal Navy. They had certainly surprised us. The last thing I had expected to find on the Kentish beach was over a hundred French regulars.

Lieutenant Jackson rode towards me. Behind him his sergeant and a corporal had their carbines trained on the back of a major and a captain. This was more like it.

"Well done, James. A good haul."

I dismounted and approached them. I saw that they were from the 33rd Light Infantry; a good regiment. It was hard to read their feelings from their impassive faces but I assumed that they were less than happy.

I nodded to them. "Gentlemen, what did you hope to achieve by this attack?" I deliberately spoke in English. I suspected that they both spoke English, it would have been why they were chosen to come to England. Neither of them reacted to my words and I shrugged. "We will have to let someone else question them Lieutenant Jackson. Lead them over to the other prisoners."

The fact that they spoke English was confirmed when they both began to move before being prompted by Lieutenant Jackson. I smiled to myself. I led Badger across to the prisoners. James dismounted and walked next to me. "Why do you think they were here sir? Is it the invasion?"

I didn't think it was but I wanted to play dumb for the benefit of the two officers who walked before us. "It might have been. We will have to wait until the other squadrons report back from their patrols."

The two officers began to talk, not knowing that I understood their words. "The fool thinks we are the invasion. When General Bonaparte comes it will be more than a company of light infantry."

"I do not relish the thought of an English prison."

"Do not worry Captain Leblanc. We will not be spending any time in a prison. When we reach the men I will order them to attack their guards and you and I will steal a couple of horses. The frigate will have to wait down the coast for those barges. We will easily reach it before they do."

When they reached the other prisoners I summoned Sergeant Grant over. "Quietly move your men back, Sergeant Grant. In a moment that officer will make them attack our men. Shoot to wound."

"How do you... sorry sir. Yes sir." He turned to the twenty men he had guarding the prisoners. "Right men move away from the prisoners. Give them a little air eh? Just keep your carbines aimed at them."

"James, get your men to help Sergeant Grant. The prisoners will try to escape soon." He began to ask me something but I held my finger to my lips. "Sergeant Sharp, keep your carbine aimed at that captain if you please."

I had been reloading my carbine as we had walked and it was pointed at the major's knee. He was less than thirty yards from him and I would not miss. The two of them approached the lieutenant and spoke briefly. He stood to attention and then the three of them moved around the men. As soon as the two senior officers moved to the side I knew what was going to happen. I said quietly, "Get ready Sergeant Grant."

The lieutenant suddenly shouted to his men and they began to run at my troopers. There was the crack and pop of carbines followed by the screams of the soldiers. I watched only the two officers who both pulled small pistols from their coats and ran towards the tethered horses. Sharp and I fired at the same time. The two men screamed and went down clutching their knees.

I wandered over and tied a tourniquet around the major's leg. "That was foolish, major. Now you will have a limp for the rest of your life. Did you think we would not watch you?"

He tried to play dumb by shaking his head.

"I know you speak English."

Once again he played dumb. I had had enough. "Sergeant Sharp put a ball into the captain's head."

"No, no! You are right we do speak English."

"That's better. What is your name?"

"Major Vassili of the 33rd Light Infantry."

"And what were you doing here?"

"We were lost. We thought that we were close to the Batavian Republic."

I laughed, "Major Vassili, even a soldier knows east from west. Give me a better answer."

"I refuse to answer."

"A shame because the people who will take you away and interrogate you will not be as thoughtful as me."

"We are prisoners. Exchange us."

"Who for? All the prisoners you had from the conflict before were exchanged during the peace."

A slight smile spread across his face. "What about the civilians?"

"What civilians?"

"When you declared war there were some hundreds of civilians still in France." He pointed to the rising sun. "There are three hundred of them in Dunkerque alone."

That stunned me. "You may be right, major but it does not reflect on your people that you take civilians prisoner. War should be between soldiers and men of honour."

For the first time he had the good grace to look abashed. "You are correct sir but if it gets me home to my wife and family…"

"I understand."

We were interrupted by the colonel and the rest of the regiment. I saluted. "Sir, some of these men need a doctor. They tried to escape."

He looked at the corpse strewn beach. "Once again Captain Matthews, you have surprised me. Get your men back to the barracks and leave this to me."

"Sir, if I might have a word first." He dismounted and I told him what the major had said. "I am sure that if Colonel Selkirk knew this he would wish to do something about it."

"Like what?"

"Like try to rescue them."

He shook his head, "You again, Captain Matthews? You cannot win the war on your own."

"No sir, and this time I would need the help of some of our troopers and a captain that I happen to know."

"What do you want then?"

"I would like to ride to London and apprise the colonel of the situation."

He sighed, "I suppose so but get back here as soon as you can."

"Yes sir." I turned, "Lieutenant Jackson, take the men back to the barracks. Sharp, follow me."

Chapter 15

"But colonel we cannot leave the civilians in Bonaparte's hands!"

"It is very laudable of you Robbie but what you ask is impossible. Your colonel is correct, you cannot win the war on your own and you are too valuable to lose."

"I would not be risking much sir. Hear me out, I have a plan."

It had taken some time to actually get him to listen to me but he now nodded and said, "You have five minutes. Make the most if it."

"Sir, we control the Channel, is that correct?"

"Until those soldiers you captured arrived I thought so but I am less sure now."

"What I mean is that if I could get the prisoners from wherever they are being held then the navy would not have a problem getting them off would they?"

"No but how would you get them out. You don't know where they are."

"I know that three hundred of them are at Dunkerque. There cannot be many places where that number could be held. The only risky part would be when Sharp and I enter the town to find them. We could use some of our troopers and some marines. They cannot have that many guards; they are just civilians after all." I could see that he was weakening. "I promise you that I will not risk my life. I will only make the rescue if I think that I can get them out without loss of life."

He snorted, "That is a tall order in itself."

"Just think of the effect it would have both here and in France. The mighty Bonaparte would be seen as a leader who could not even keep civilians from the navy. He must be smarting over the loss of his soldiers at Whitstable."

"You are certain that it was just a practice for the real invasion?"

"Positive sir. He used me and my regiment for such attacks in the past. He likes to win. He finds out all the problems before he makes his attacks. He is very thorough. This way only he and his generals know what he tried." Colonel Selkirk nodded, "So sir, if I could have the 'Black Prince' to take twenty of us close to Dunkerque and you have a couple of bigger ships waiting for us we could do this."

He held up his hand. "Do not get ahead of yourself. I will put this to the powers that be. You return to Canterbury and I promise you that I will bring the news once way or another."

"Thank you sir."

By the time we had reached the barracks the prisoners had all been shipped off, under the guard of a line regiment, to a hulk on the Medway. There was a real buzz around the barracks as men talked of the incident. Even those soldiers from A Squadron were keen to speak to the heroes of 7th Troop who had thwarted the French attack. Sharp and I were cheered as we rode through the barracks.

"I'll see to Badger sir."

"Thank you, Sergeant Sharp, and I had better square this with the colonel."

Major Hyde-Smith was talking to Sergeant Major Jones in the office when I entered. They both smiled, "Well sir, you know how to fall on your feet and no mistake, isn't that right major?"

"It certainly is. You are not content with capturing a few smugglers. You stop an invasion."

"It wasn't an invasion sir. They were just practising."

"The same thing in my eyes, Robbie. When the survivors got home they would report that it was impossible to land in England as every beach is patrolled. Regardless of what happens in the future you have put doubt in their minds."

The colonel must have heard us and he came to the door. "You two had better come in here eh? Sergeant Major could you get us something to drink?"

"Yes sir."

We sat in the office and Colonel Fenton spread his arms. "Well Robbie, what did the colonel say?"

"He said he would speak to his superiors."

The major looked puzzled. The colonel elaborated, "The captain here wants to rescue the civilians held in Dunkerque."

He began to laugh, "Of course he does. Tell me Robbie, how will you do that?"

"Yes enlighten me too. I am intrigued."

I explained my plan. I was as honest as I could be and as realistic as possible. The Sergeant Major brought in the drinks and was about to leave when the colonel said, "Stay, Sergeant Major Jones and listen to this idea. I would value your opinion. Captain, please explain again."

When I had finished the old soldier nodded. "Well sir it seems a mad idea but then again a small group of men could sneak inside the town and find out where the prisoners were being held and then bring other soldiers to rescue them."

I smiled, "Thank you Sergeant Major."

"Would you be in uniform?"

"Not the ones who scouted out the town sir, no."

"Then what happens if you were stopped. You couldn't risk firing and you would put all your comrades in jeopardy."

"I would talk my way out it sir."

The major laughed. "How ridiculous! You would have to speak French fluently to get away with that."

In French I replied, "That would not be a problem sir as I can speak fluent French."

That was the first time that I saw the Sergeant Major stuck for words. The colonel was the first to regain his composure. "Then I suppose that the language would be the least of your problems."

"Indeed sir. And I have also been to Dunkerque before now." I did not mention that I had been there when I had been serving with the 17th Chasseurs."

"You are a constant surprise. Well Captain Matthews. Which men would you want?"

"I would think just twenty volunteers from my squadron. If I can get some marines from the ship as well then that would be perfect."

"And the colonel will be here when?"

"That I don't know major. He said he would come here in person."

"We will wait until he arrives before we jump the gun and ask for volunteers but we will not stand in your way, captain."

Sergeant Major Jones began to chuckle, "If I was just ten years younger sir I would be with you in a flash."

The colonel looked surprised. He seemed to see the old soldier in a completely new light. "You would Sergeant Major?"

"It would be the chance of a lifetime sir; to sail into an enemy land and steal prisoners from under their noses. Besides civilians shouldn't be involved in wars, it isn't right. I hope you pull this off Captain Matthews and that's no lie."

Colonel Selkirk arrived very early the next day and I was summoned, along with Colonel Fenton and Major Hyde-Smith, into the regimental office. The colonel was smiling, which was always an ominous sign.

"Well Robbie, it seems the gods of war favour you. Apparently the families of two ministers were in Dunkerque at the time war was declared. The two ministers have been hounding the Prime Minister for action to have them released. The diplomatic means have failed which means that your proposal was totally endorsed by the Cabinet. I was ordered to provide all the support that I could."

"Thank you sir."

"Now you still want to keep to your original plan?"

"Yes sir. I have been to Dunkerque and I have an idea where they might hold the hostages."

Colonel Selkirk's eyebrows came up a little, "You have divination as a skill now have you?"

I laughed, "No sir, but there is a monastery on the outskirts of the town, to the east, and the National Guard evicted the occupants ten years ago. They used it as a barracks for a while. It is in good condition and would be large enough to hold and guard the civilians. It is slightly outside of the town. I would take six men and scout it out and then bring the rest of my men to overcome the guards. The biggest problem we would have would be getting the people off the beaches and into the boats."

"Why not use the harbour?"

"The problem, major, is the guns which guard it. We would have to disable guns first which loses us the element of surprise."

Colonel Selkirk nodded his agreement, "The beach sounds better. A longboat can hold twenty people. That means fifteen boats. I will see that the ships which are sent to rescue you have that number of boats. I have the 'Black Prince' for you. Lieutenant Teer is looking forward to a reunion with you."

"When do we leave sir?"

"The sooner the better. Some of those prisoners you took the other day have been singing like birds. It seems that some of the hostages who were taken have been paraded around Paris as a demonstration of Bonaparte's power. We have no way of knowing if some of those were from Dunkerque. The ministers are keen to get their families back."

"I will choose the men this morning. If the 'Black Prince' can pick us up from Herne Bay then we can sail this afternoon. I assume you can arrange the transports to be off Dunkerque by morning?"

"Yes." He looked surprised. "You are confident that you can locate the prisoners and rescue them in that time?"

"No sir. But if we don't find them the first day then I will hide up with my men and find them the second day. That is why I want a small group of men. They are easier to hide. We control the sea and it will do no harm for the transports to lie off the coast until we arrive."

Colonel Fenton said, "You are a confident young man Robbie."

"I trust the men I will be taking."

"Well I will let you get on with it. The sloop will be at Herne Bay waiting for you."

After he had gone the major asked, "How will you choose your men?"

"I was going to ask for volunteers but that would only upset the men I didn't choose. I will approach the ones I wish to take. I need young soldiers who are quick thinking and fit. Sergeant Grant would be a good choice but for his age. I want ten marines as I will need men with the skills to load boats and who know harbours so that means I will be choosing nine men. I was hoping to take Percy Austen; I believe he has a smattering of French."

The two men exchanged a look and then the colonel said, "Very well I will leave it in your hands. Anything that we can do?"

"The men will need civilian clothes."

"I am sure that we have some somewhere. I will get the Sergeant Major to organise those."

"What I was going to say was, have we got the uniforms from the dead Frenchmen? They would fit the bill."

"I will get them for you. They may be bloody and dirty."

"More realistic then sir."

I went directly to Percy who was in the mess. I waved him over. He looked at me expectantly. "Now I am going to ask you something but you can refuse."

His face lit up, "Whatever it is I am game Robbie, you know that."

"Listen first and then answer. There are some English civilians held in Dunkerque I am going over there with some men to try to rescue them." He opened his mouth to speak. I held my hand up, "We will be going in civilian clothes and there is a good chance that we might not get back."

He shook his head, "It doesn't matter. I am still coming."

"Good say nothing to the others I will be selecting the men this afternoon. Brush up on your French."

"Bien sur!"

Sharp was also keen. He went with me when I approached the others. Sergeant Seymour grinned when I told him and Bugler Jones appeared surprised, "But sir, I am not the biggest trooper. Don't get me wrong, I would love to come but why me?"

"You have a quick mind and we may need someone who is small."

The other five were all obvious choices and they all agreed. I gathered them together under Sergeant Major Jones' watchful eye.

"You will not need your carbines but I want every man with his pistols and either a sap or a small cudgel."

"Swords sir?"

"No, I think not. They might get in the way. Knives would be better." I slid my Italian stiletto out of my boot. "Weapons like this."

Sergeant Major Jones tut tutted his mock disapproval, "Sir, that does not look like the weapon of a gentleman."

"Sergeant Major, where we are going we will not be behaving like gentlemen. Why do you think I picked this bunch of cut throats?"

The men took that as a compliment and began nudging each other.

"The Sergeant Major will issue you with French uniforms. Do not wear them yet. We will change on the boat. We meet in one hour at the parade ground."

Before I left I sought out, James. "Lieutenant, Percy and I will be off for a day or two. You are in charge of the squadron. Sergeant Grant will help you but keep the men drilled. Don't let them slack off."

He looked at me so seriously I almost burst out laughing, "Don't worry sir. I won't let you down and thank you for giving me this chance." He was turning into a promising officer.

They were all there early. Each man in full uniform but with a hessian sack slung over the rear of their mount. I led them out towards Herne Bay. We were escorted by Sergeant Grant and four troopers who would return with our mounts.

The sloop was tied up when we arrived. Colonel Selkirk must have had her nearby to have made such good time. We boarded quickly. Sergeant Grant saluted and said, "Make sure you get back sir; both of you. D Squadron is the best in the regiment now and I would hate to have to train up two new officers."

"Don't worry; we'll be back." Even as I said it I wondered if this was just bravado.

Lieutenant Teer was standing at the gangplank and I saw him grin and tap his shoulders. He had been promoted; he was now Lieutenant Commander. I shook his hand as I boarded. "Congratulations! I suppose they will give you a bigger ship now?"

"They keep trying but I like the Prince. Come along, get your men aboard."

"This is Percy Austen. He's another captain."

"Introductions later. Take her out, Jack."

I looked aft and saw a young lieutenant standing with the coxswain. "I see you have help these days."

"Yes, when I am happy enough he will become the new skipper." He laughed, "I am a perfectionist of course! It will be some time before I relinquish the prince. Bosun, see to these soldiers. They need to change out of these uniforms. If you two chaps will come with me we'll use my cabin." He shrugged apologetically to Percy, "As Robbie will tell you things are a little tight on the Prince but we like her."

Once in the cabin we began to change. Lieutenant Commander Teer chattered away as we did so. "Colonel Selkirk gave me the rough plan when he saw us yesterday but he was a little vague on the detail. As far as I can gather I am to take you and your chaps to Dunkerque, land you after dark and lend you a few of my men then lie offshore and wait for you to return with some civilians. Is that about it?"

I put my jacket on and said, "Roughly yes. There could be three hundred civilians."

"Three hundred? They won't fit on the Prince."

"I know. There should be some transports and bigger ships by the morning."

"Just one night eh? And where are these civilians?"

"We aren't too sure but I think they will be in the old monastery on the other side of town. The reason I need your chaps is that we will be loading longboats. My fellows can hold off any pursuit but they would be all fingers and thumbs when it comes to loading boats."

He rubbed his hands together. "Well I have the chaps already volunteered and the fellow to lead them."

"Who is that?"

"Why me, of course. If they give me a snotty to train then, by God, I will use him."

I felt better somehow. Lieutenant Commander Teer had already shown me that he was a capable naval officer and I knew he could speak French. The odds on our survival had just improved.

We closed slowly with the French coast so that we could land after dark. The sand dunes were extensive and meant that, although we would have a long walk to reach the road and the town, we would have plenty of cover while we did so. There was nowhere big enough for us to gather below decks and so I had the men crowd around me on the main deck. With swords weighing down the map I had drawn I explained my plan.

"I am giving all of you this information in case we are separated. There are four of us who speak French. Myself and Mr Teer can speak it well. Mr Austen has knowledge of the language and Sergeant Sharp can understand French and ask for simple things." He smiled self effacingly as they all stared at him. I want you all to learn a few phrases while we cross. 'Where is the bar?', 'Where is the port?' will be handy. Your accents will mark you as a foreigner but they may think you are Dutch. I am taking my men all the way to the monastery. Lieutenant Commander Teer and his men will wait a quarter of a mile from us."

Percy put up his hand and I smiled, he looked like a schoolboy asking to go to the toilet. "Why sir?"

"They are back up in case this goes wrong. If the monastery is the place where they are held then we will send for the sailors and affect a rescue. I want no noise so we use saps, cudgels, swords and knives. Hopefully we can do this without killing anyone. I do not think they will have many guards for civilians. There could be three hundred civilians. There will be women and children among them. They will not move quickly and we will need to keep them quiet. We will all carry rope. We can use it to tie up guards and to lead the civilians. We will head towards the dunes. The sailors and Lieutenant Commander Teer will escort the prisoners and we will be the rearguard. Once at the beach the transports should be there. When they see us they will launch longboats."

"Captain Matthews, would it not be better if the longboats were waiting in the surf?"

"It would indeed Lieutenant Commander but I have not spoken to the captains of those ships."

"Snotty! Come here."

The young lieutenant fairly raced to reach us. "When you see the transports coming to pick up the civilians I want you to close with them and ask them to launch their longboats and have them waiting in the surf. You will bring the Prince in close and support them."

He paled, "Me sir?"

"Don't worry Mr Redmayne, the bosun will do the steering; you just stand there and look determined." The sailors all laughed and Lieutenant Redmayne blushed.

"As soon as the last civilian is on board then signal the shore and we will join you."

"That sounds remarkably straightforward sir."

"It does, doesn't it Sergeant Seymour? The only problem is the French. They may decide not to play nicely and it could get a bit messy."

"When we land we move in small groups each led by a French speaker. That way we may escape notice for longer."

"French coast ahead!"

I looked at them all as I spoke. "This is it. Remember, talk as little as possible and if you meet someone, try smiling. They will just think you a bunch of sailors on a leave and you are lost."

One of the seaman laughed, "Why didn't you say so sir? We can all play that part to perfection!"

The reaction pleased me. They weren't nervous, just excited and that reflected how I felt. As we gathered at the bow I was pleased to see the sun setting behind us to the west. We had the maximum time to achieve our ends. Even if we arrived before the transports we could begin to ferry them out to the 'Black Prince'. Lieutenant Commander Teer had already given a recognition signal for his new lieutenant. We all looked like either pirates or smugglers. We had cudgels and were festooned with pistols. My men's French uniforms made them look like old soldiers and would not attract attention. The sailors had the ubiquitous clothes worn by sailors of both navies. The three officers had ignored my own orders and were wearing swords. I knew that we were used to them and would be less likely to trip up over them. The men were more familiar with cruder weapons and their fists.

I smiled as I heard them practising their French phrases. They had all taken it to heart. I think it did Sharp good to hear them massacring the language. It made his French sound much better.

Lieutenant Commander Teer was edging the ship as close to land as he could without grounding her. His new lieutenant would have to stand much further out. When he was satisfied he left his trusty bosun with the wheel and joined us at the side where the longboat was being lowered. This was the same sized boat as we would be using for the civilians. I was pleased that we all fitted in comfortably and there was no danger of water entering. I knew that civilians would be more likely to panic in such a situation.

We pushed off and the four seamen began to row us towards the beach. We were aided by the incoming tide, and soon the bottom ground on to the sand. The sailors left first and spread out in a defensive line and then the soldiers clambered, somewhat less skilfully over the side. The boat pulled off without a word and we were left on the beach in France.

Chapter 16

I led with two of my men, Seymour and Jones, and one of Teer's sailors. It was easy to find east as the sun was setting behind us. The dunes seemed to spread out forever. It reminded me of Egypt- without the heat of course. The sand sapped the power from your legs and I knew, that for cavalrymen used to riding, this would be exhausting. When we reached the end of the dunes I waved my hand to flatten the others to the ground. The road lay ahead. The green on either side showed where the sand ended. It was the main coast road but I hoped that, at night, it would be quiet.

As soon as Captain Austen joined me I left and headed south along the road. I had planned to leap frog all the way to Dunkerque. Each group would wait until the following group had arrived and then move on. It gave all of us added security. Within a mile or two we had reached the first houses and I halted behind the wall of a quiet looking farm. It was set slightly off the road and seemed deserted. It would make a good point of reference for our return.

Once again I left when Percy arrived. The four of us walked along the road even more cautiously. There would be more houses soon and, more people. Suddenly I heard the sound of a horse coming from the direction of the town. We dived into the ditch which ran alongside the road and lay there. I risked a glance upwards as the man rode by but he appeared not to have noticed us.

There had been some stagnant water in the ditch and when we emerged we were wet and rather aromatic. I saw the other three grinning in the dark; it was a lark to them. I now began to recognise buildings. I could see the tower of the town hall in the distance and knew where I was. There were no massive walls in the harbour but they did have guns there to prevent enemy ships entering. Lieutenant Commander Teer had been relieved that my plan did not require us to run that gauntlet. It did mean, however, that there would be some soldiers close to the harbour.

I turned to Sergeant Seymour. "Wait here. I need to get my bearings."

"What if someone comes?" I could hear the fear in the sailor's voice.

Seymour said drily, "Say you are lost!"

I slipped away and headed across the road to the port area. It was much busier than the quiet back street in which my men waited. I could see people sniffing as I went by. The ditch water had been pungent. It meant that people avoided me which was good. I kept my head down. If they thought that I was a down and out then so much the better.

Keeping my head down almost proved to be my undoing for a soldier suddenly thrust his musket across my chest. "Where are you going sunshine?" he stepped back as he got a whiff of my clothes. "Phew you don't half stink."

I played my indignant card. "I was looking for the prefect of police. A horseman ran me down as I was coming into the city. I wish to make a complaint."

The soldier laughed. He pointed down the street. "The police station is at the end of this road, just past the barracks for the gunners." He noticed my stained uniform, "Old soldier?" I nodded. "Just watch where you are going next time."

"Thank you sir and sorry."

I waited until he had entered the house and then I turned and retraced my steps. Percy was there along with his group.

"You had us worried."

"I just wanted to find out where the barracks were." I pointed behind me. "It is just down there. Wait until the sailors reach you and then follow us. We'll be going down there." I pointed and then took my men down an alley to the left. We were now heading away from the busy, populated areas and towards the monastery which was now less than a mile away. It was quiet as people were settling down to their evening meals behind closed doors and curtains.

The houses thinned out again and I had the men crouch down by a wall until the others joined us. It took about twenty minutes for Sergeant Sharp to finally arrive with his group, the last ones in the column. "A problem, Sergeant Sharp?"

"A couple of horsemen came behind us and so we hid in the ditch."

Seymour said, "So you'll stink the same as we do. If we get separated sir we can always smell each other out."

"Thank you, sergeant. Now we are less than a mile away. We will stay together until I can find somewhere for the sailors to wait."

I could not remember all the places along the way and I would have to decide if there was a suitable hiding place closer to the old monastery. In the end I found one which could not have been better. It was a barn next to a burnt out farm. I suspected the farm had been damaged by the French army when we had fought here and driven the English north. It was ironical really.

I gathered the others around me. Jonathan now had his sailors with him while the horsemen were back with their own officers. "I will send a runner back if I need you. If I fail to find them there then we will return and we will seek them elsewhere."

We had spent some time on the ship working out where else they could be held. I deduced that the only places where such a large number could be held would be in the hotels in the town and they were almost on top of the barracks. All of us were praying that my guess was correct and they would be here in the monastery.

As we left the barn I spread the men out. Jones and Seymour were with me while Sharp and Percy brought up the rear. I smelled wood smoke and stopped. The monastery was up ahead but, equally that could be a guard post. I waved everyone down and then slithered on my stomach along the ditch. Through the hedgerow I spied a small guard post and three National Guardsmen smoking their pipes around a small brazier. There was an entrance in the hedgerow. It looked like whatever gates they had had there had been taken away. They had probably been melted to make cannon. The guard post was just inside the hedge and the brazier in the middle of the road leading to the monastery. It formed a barrier which could be removed during the day. I snaked my way back to the others.

"I have a feeling this must be the place. There are guards there. "McEwen, go and fetch the sailors." When he had left I turned to the others. "There are just three guards. We need to take them without any noise."

Percy looked dubious, "That will be hard. How do we get close to them?"

He had a point and I was stumped. Sharp said, "We could always get them to come to us sir."

"Explain, sergeant."

"We are wearing old French uniforms. It is dark and they won't be able to see much. We could pretend to be two soldiers carrying a drunk back. I bet they have comrades not on duty who will be in the town tonight. If Seymour and me carry Jones as though he is rolling drunk and we are a little unsteady too it might fool them. We can make a noise and they will come out of their hut to investigate. If the rest of you are on either side of the entrance then you can overcome them."

Seymour grinned, "I like it sir, give it a try eh?"

"Very well. I'll go on the far side. Percy you have the rest of the men next to the hedge on this side."

We left quickly and I waited until I saw that the three men's attention was not on the entrance and I slipped across. I had made a sap out of a leather pouch and filled it with sand. I took it out. I saw Percy and the others on the far side and then I saw the three 'drunks' staggering along. They were playing the part well. Sharp was using the little French he knew and the others were tunelessly singing French nonsense they were making up. It sounded convincing. As they neared the entrance they all stumbled and fell face down giggling. It was a masterly performance for the guards could not see their faces merely the backs of their uniforms. All they would have seen was three off duty French soldiers who were drunk.

I heard the leader say, "What the…" and they stepped out towards the three laughing. "You three will be on a charge. Come on, get up!"

The three drunks continued to giggle and played at trying to rise, unsuccessfully. As soon as the three guards bent down to help them, we were upon them.

"Quick secure them and gag them. Tie their hands behind their backs and to their feet."

Lieutenant Commander Teer arrived, "Well done! This is the place then?"

"I can't see why else they would guard it. Have three of your men put the guard's hats on and sit with their guns."

"What if anyone comes?"

"Then the game is up. Let us hope that if anyone does come they just see three guards and don't look any closer."

As soon as the men were tied up, and the substitutes sat in their place, I led the rest towards the monastery which was just two hundred yards away. There were lights in the window. Someone was living there that was certain. Had the soldier I met not told me that the barracks were in the town I might have suspected they had used the old monastery for the gunners. The monastery gardens had been neglected and were overgrown. What had been the herb garden close by the kitchen was now a jungle. I headed in that direction as it afforded us some good cover.

Once we were hidden in the herbs I crept forwards to listen at the kitchen window above me. It was late at night but I assumed that there would still be someone there, if only clearing up. There was a light coming from the open door and the window. I was rewarded by the French cook talking to his assistant. "After you have mixed up the dough for the bread for tomorrow you can go to bed."

"Have the prisoners finished washing and drying the pots, boss?"

"Probably? They have gone back to their rooms anyway. Why do you ask?"

"I saw a tray outside the commandant's office. It was full of dishes and they had not been picked up."

"I'll have that Henri's bollocks tomorrow. He was supposed to collect them before he went off duty. Well they will have to wait. I'm not doing them. Besides, the commandant is probably giving that pretty young English woman one. Lock up when you have finished. I'm going into town tonight."

"All right chef but I am leaving that door open until then. It's hotter than Hades in here."

"I know but it makes the bread rise beautifully eh? See you in the morning, Charles."

"Night, boss."

I waited until I heard a door slam and then stood up. I pressed myself against the wall next to the door. I could hear the dough being pounded against the worktop and I risked a quick look inside. Charles had his back to me. I took out the sap and went quickly behind him. I smacked him on the back of the head and he fell, face down in the dough. I pulled him off. It wouldn't do to have the poor man suffocate in bread dough.

I ran to the door and waved the others in. I pointed at the cook and two men began to tie him up. I whispered, "There are English here. Our first task is to find and neutralise the guards. Split into groups of two. I'll take you Seymour. Start with this floor and then work your way up. I think most of them should be in bed by now. Sharp, leave two men here to guard our exit. Jonathan, take your men down the far corridor. Keep it quiet."

There were now five pairs to search the monastery; I hoped that would be enough. The monastery was a labyrinth of corridors. I took my half and we went along cautiously trying doors. We found that they were mainly store rooms. It was nervous work, slowly opening a door and not knowing if there were guards inside. We came to the first stair case. It was narrow. I took out my stiletto. I listened at the door at the top. I could hear nothing. I was aware that Percy and Jones were behind me. It meant we had four men should there be trouble ahead. I slowly opened the door and peered through. There was a guard at the end of the corridor on a chair. He looked to be asleep. I turned to Seymour and mimed creeping along the corridor and striking the man. He nodded. I stepped aside and Seymour slid slowly and silently along the wall of the corridor. He was a born assassin. He never took his eyes from his victim and he moved stealthily. He did not rush the last few steps, which might have alerted the guard, he just strode up to him and stuck him a blow on the side of the head. The only sign that he had done anything was a drop of blood from his forehead.

The three of us leapt from concealment. Seymour was already trussing the guard up and I looked along the corridor. There was a carpet and this looked to be the better part of the monastery. I spied a tray; it had to be the commandant's quarters. I pointed to Seymour and signalled him to watch. I took the other three to the room with the tray of food outside. Jones cheekily picked up a piece of sausage and began to eat it. I listened at the door. I could hear the sound of copulation. From the female sobs I gathered that it was not consensual. I slipped the door silently open and moved inside. The room was dimly lit by a candle. A huge bloated being was lying on top of, what looked like a young woman, who was struggling.

I stepped up behind him, pulled his head back and stuck the point of my stiletto into the side of his neck. "One word from you and I will kill you. Now get off the bed." I could see the terror on the face of the pretty young woman lying beneath him; she could have been no more than eighteen years old. I began to become angry. I jerked back on the man's head and heard the sound of water. He had wet himself. I pulled him upright. I wanted to pull my knife across his throat and end his life. I knew that I needed information from him first.

"Jones, tie his hands but don't gag him and leave him naked." I kept my knife on his neck. Percy had managed to gather the girl's dress and hand it to her whilst averting his eyes. "We are English and we are here to rescue you. How many of you are there?"

She had regained her composure and she stood close to me. She was tiny. She glared at the commandant and then pulled her hand back and slapped him so hard that I was certain they would hear the noise in Paris. "You can kill this pig now for me, sir." She turned to face me. "There are a hundred and fifty of us left. They moved a hundred yesterday."

"How many guards are there?"

She looked confused, "I don't know, they all look the same to me."

I put my mouth next to the commandant's ear. "How many guards? And before you lie if you do not tell me the truth then I will castrate you here and now!"

He was already white with fear and his eyes widened even more. "I will tell you; please don't hurt me. There are three men at the gate and ten more on the corridors. Two at each end." I was quickly calculating; we had taken out the three guards at the gate and one on this corridor. We had nine left to go.

"Jones, keep your dagger in this man's back. He is coming with us."

"But sir my clothes, my dignity."

"You lost all rights to dignity the moment you abused this young girl. Besides, I think it might keep you a little less likely to escape."

We picked up Seymour and climbed the stairs. We had a better idea now of where the guards were. It looked like there were two staircases with two guards at each end. Using the commandant as a shield we stepped out on to the next corridor. The two guards giggled and stared at the naked commandant; they did not seem to see the rest of us. Before they knew it, Seymour and Percy had leapt at them and knocked them out. They were soon trussed up.

"Where are the hostages?"

She pointed along the corridor. "This floor and the one above."

"Percy, you and the girl go and wake the civilians. Tell them to keep quiet and to take only what they can carry. Have them gather here in the corridor."

"How can we escape sir? There is a town and a garrison."

I smiled, "And I only have sixteen men but luckily for you one of them has a ship. Help the captain to keep the men quiet please."

She leaned up and kissed me, "I will and thank you."

"Jones, keep the commandant here. He may be useful again."

We slipped up the stairs. We had a little luck. The guards there were standing with their backs to the stairs playing a game of tossing coins at the wall. They both fell to our saps. It was going well and I hoped that Lieutenant Commander Teer and his group were having the same success. There was a worry niggling at the back of my mind about the cooks and the others in the monastery who would work there. I had to focus on the job in hand; so long as we didn't make too much noise we might escape.

When we had trussed them I went to the first door. It was locked, "Seymour, search the guards, they must have keys."

He came back jingling a set of keys. I saw that there were just three different keys. The first one opened the door. A lazy, laconic voice moaned, "What is it now? It's bad enough you serve us pigswill and give us rock hard beds without waking us at all hours of the morning."

I opened the door. "Sorry to disturb you sir. I am Captain Matthews of the 11th Light Dragoons and we are here to rescue you."

His wife's head popped out of the bed and gave a little squeal. I put my fingers to my lips. "If you could refrain from making any noise and pack just what you need we will try to get you to safety."

All the man said was, "'Pon my word."

The scene was repeated in all of the rooms. "Sergeant, take charge here, when they are all out make sure they can carry what they take and then bring them down to the next floor."

"Sir." He grinned. "Is this what you and Sharpie did before sir? Where he got his scar?"

"Something like that."

"Next time you go take me sir. This is good crack."

Downstairs there was a little more noise and Percy was struggling to keep them quiet. I shouted, "Quiet!" They all fell silent. "Ladies and gentlemen it will be extremely difficult to get you all safely back to England. If anyone wishes to stay as a guest of Bonaparte please return to your rooms. If not, then shut up and do exactly as I say!" No-one moved. "Good, then you all want to come. You have to carry what you take and we have to walk four miles or so to the sea and the beach. Look at what you carry and decide."

They all began to examine their luggage. "When they are all ready bring them down to the main hall."

"How did you do that Robbie?"Lieutenant Austen was shaking his head.

I shrugged, "I treated them all like recruits who know nothing. They are the spoiled rich, Percy, they aren't used to this. Shout at them a bit."

Jones nodded, "He's right sir. They probably need help to wipe their own arse and all."

I left them and descended to the main hall. It was silent. I began to worry where Lieutenant Commander Teer was. I decided that I would get this first group out and then worry about the rest. I went out of the main entrance. It was eerily quiet. I drew my sword I sensed that there was someone out there. Silently I took out my stiletto. Suddenly a bayonet flashed at my face from my left. I barely had time to deflect it with my stiletto. I stabbed upwards with my sword and the soldier fell to the ground with a surprised expression on his face. The second man was more cunning. He stabbed lower. I flicked my sword around and deflected the blade but it still sliced savagely into my thigh and I felt the warm trickle of blood. The moon had come out and it flashed on the blood on his bayonet. He almost shrieked with joy and pulled the musket back for the coup de grace. I lunged forward with my stiletto and ripped out his throat.

I grabbed the neck cloth he was wearing and tied it tightly around the top of my leg. The bleeding slowed but it still hurt. There appeared to be no others. I slipped back inside and saw that all of the prisoners had been brought down. The commandant was still naked and Jones' dagger still pricked his portly back. I leapt at him and put my sword on the tip of his nose.

"You lying fat bastard! There were two guards outside that you forgot about! Are there any others, answer me quickly or so help me I will geld you here and now."

He stuttered, "I forgot those two, please forgive me."

The young woman he had been raping came forwards. "You need all your men. Let me watch him."

I saw that she was right. I picked up the sword from the unconscious guard and gave it to her. She stuck the point in the small of the whale's back. "Jones, go and find the others and tell them that we are leaving." He nodded and ran off. The commandant looked less than pleased to be at the mercy of his young victim. "Percy, lead them off. Take them to the barn and wait there. Tell the guards at the gate to wait until I reach them. Seymour, give him a hand."

The civilians were all whispering, the noise would be heard once we left the building."Anyone who talks at all, stays here in France. We are in grave danger and I will tolerate no disobedience." I deliberately looked at some of the older men in turn and each one nodded.

Once they had all gone the place seemed quiet. I looked at the keys which I still had in my hand. I went to the front door and tried the keys in turn. One fitted. I waited to see if the others returned. I began to count in my head. I would give them a hundred. I had reached fifty when Jones appeared. He was out of breath. "They are coming sir. They had a bit of trouble."

"Right Jones, get to the barn, the others are there. Tell them to be ready to move when we arrive."

Lieutenant Teer, Sergeant Sharp and the other prisoners arrived a few minutes later. They were half carrying one of the sailors. "Sorry Robbie, Harris here was a bit slow. We had to kill one. "

"Never mind that now; the rest are at the barn. Get them there and wait for me."

As soon as they had left I locked the front door. It would not slow up any pursuit but there would be a delay and I was buying minutes. I hurled the keys into the brazier. The three guards were relieved to see me. "Ditch the hats but keep the muskets. Let's go."

The rescued civilians at the barn were now even more fearful. I ignored them. "My men and I will get to the main road and hold it. Count to fifty and then follow. No matter what happens get them back to the beach."

"Will do, Robbie." The naval officer suddenly saw that I was wounded, "You are hurt."

"I'll survive." I turned to my men. Get the muskets from those sailors and follow me."

We ran down the road. Perhaps it was Teer's words or reaction setting in, I don't know but my leg began to hurt like all hell was breaking loose. I would have to loosen the tourniquet soon. At the end of the road I sent Seymour to watch the other side.

"Right lads we are going to have to wait here and hold off anyone who decides to follow us. We only have five shots for each of the muskets so use them wisely. Keep hidden." As they took up positions I released the tourniquet. The warm blood both hurt and was a relief.

Sharp looked shocked. "Sir, you are wounded."

"I have had worse wounds before. Just keep a good watch eh Alan?"

"Yes sir."

It seemed to me that the noise of the one hundred and fifty civilians sounded like thunder but I suspect they were not. Even so I was pleased when they all turned the corner and walked down the road. I know they thought they were moving quickly but they were not and I could see the discarded luggage littering the road. It was like a trail for the French to follow. An idea struck me. "Percy, get the men to collect that discarded luggage and make a barrier across the road. It will slow down any pursuit."

"Yes Robbie." He turned, "This is fun you know."

He did not know how close we were to death. If the French caught us we would be shot. The trick was not to let that thought enter your consciousness, therein lay madness.

The barrier ended up, by the time we collected everything which had been discarded, a pile stretching across the road about five feet high. A horse could clear it easily but a man might stumble as he tried and all we needed was to buy time. I saw the first rays of the sun peeping through the streets behind me. The town would soon be waking up. Food would be delivered to the monastery. The people who worked there during the day or who had slept through the escape would be readying themselves for work. Some of those who lay trussed like chickens would be waking up. We couldn't leave until I was sure I had given them enough time. I prayed that the transports were waiting off the beach.

Our luck ran out when a column of soldiers marched from the town. I assume they were heading for the monastery. Perhaps they were the relief guards. I will never know. My men were all hidden but there were only ten of us. I could trust them all not to fire until ordered. I drew my two pistols and waited. The column reached the barricade and a conversation ensued. They were perplexed. The idiot in charge decided to merely climb over the barrier. It cost him his life. As the first eight soldiers in the French infantry column stepped over the barricade I yelled, "Fire".

They were caught unawares. I did not need to shout reload. My well-drilled men just did. A pall of smoke enveloped the scene and I could hear the moaning of dying and wounded men. I waited until we had fired five shots. The muskets were now empty and we had bought enough time. The sun was beginning to lighten the streets even more.

"Fall back!" I saw eight men move past me and I felt relieved. We had suffered no casualties. Perhaps I had been in the same position too long, I do not know, but my wounded leg gave way beneath me. One of the soldiers, more eager than the rest, had run across to our position. As I lay there like a helpless baby he raised his bayonet tipped musket to skewer me.

There was a flash of a pistol and the man's face disappeared. "Not so fast, sunshine." Seymour stood over me with Sharp by his side.

"Come along sir. It wouldn't do to leave you behind now would it?"

The two of them helped me to my feet and supported me. I found I could use my leg a little. "I am all right now. Let's go." They ran and I hobbled down the road with musket balls whizzing like mosquitoes around our heads. I saw that Percy and the men had formed a thin line. They made a gap for us.

"Keep going, Captain Matthews. We will slow them." Their seven pistols all cracked and then they were running next to us.

I saw the farm which marked the distance to our turn across the dunes. "Cut across the dunes. Run diagonally! We can slow them down. They will think we are lost!"

I noticed that, as I laboured across the dunes, my men all stayed close by me. Now that it was lighter I could see the dark stain which marked my wound. I knew that we were almost safe. Once we crested the next dune we would be able to see the sea.

To my horror, as I struggled to the top I saw a sea devoid of any ship save the 'Black Prince'. The civilians were milling around the beach with Lieutenant Commander Teer's men looking like sheepdogs.

"Percy, stay here with the men and form a skirmish line."

"What if there are too many?"

"Just keep them back right!" I knew I was being short with him but he needed to be more assertive and decisive. I half ran and half limped towards the sailors.

Jonathan made his way to meet me halfway. "What do we do Robbie? There are no transports."

"You need to get back on board your ship and bring her closer in. Ferry the civilians out in the longboat and any other boats you have."

"My ship can't take them all."

"I know but once the sloop is full we can put the rest in the boats and tow them!"

He nodded and grinned. "That will work." He glanced down at my leg. "How's leg?"

"What a stupid bloody question. It hurts like hell. Now give me all your pistols, powder and ball."

"Hooky, take the men's guns and ammunition with the captain and then get back here."

The two of us ran back to the dunes where I heard the popping of pistols. "Just drop them there and then get those people off!"

"Yes, sir!"

"Here lads, another pistol each. Where are they, Percy?"

He pointed to the east. I could see a line of hats bobbing above the sand about a hundred yards away. "Stop firing at them. You are wasting ammunition. Load the pistols and wait. Sharp, you put yourself on the right and Seymour on the left. Let me know if they try to outflank us."

I began to load the extra pistol I had just obtained. I found that my hands were shaking. I needed to calm down. The whole expedition was turning into a disaster. Percy rolled next to me. "I'm sorry that I am so wet Robbie."

"You aren't but you need to think for yourself and not wait for me to take all the decisions. I don't have the answers; if I did we wouldn't be in this mess, would we? I just make stuff up as I go along."

"But it always works out."

I laughed and spread my arm around. "This is working out?" I pointed to the sea. "If Jonathan can get them off the beach then we will have succeeded."

"And us?"

"Until they turn the key on that prison cell or say 'ready, aim, fire' then we have a chance to get out of this… somehow."

He smiled, "And that is good enough for me."

I heard Jones' voice. "Sir, they are coming again."

"Stand to! Wait until they are forty yards away, no more and when you fire keep firing and reloading. Keep low down, they may think we have gone. When I say fall back make your way back forty yards."

The chorus of assent was reassuring.

They had spread out and I saw a blue line some thirty men wide. They came along with muskets and bayonets in a determined fashion. I suppose they had worked out how poorly armed we were. They kept disappearing from view as they dipped into hollows and then rising as they crested the tops of the dunes. I had worked out which dune was forty yards away and as soon as I saw a soldier begin to appear I readied myself. When the skyline filled with blue I yelled, "Fire!"

A few men went down and they thought we had emptied our guns. I heard the officer yell charge and then our ten pistols all cracked again. Sharp and I had three pistols and there were two more shots after that. The blue line fell back leaving huddles of bodies littering the dunes.

I rolled on to my back to reload. I saw that there were fewer people on the beach and that the 'Black Prince' was much closer in. I had just reloaded when Sharp shouted. "Cavalry sir! About a mile away!"

"Fall back to the next position! Keep low so that they don't see us move."

Cavalry were a different matter to infantry. They could cover the ground quickly and negate our pistols. The game had changed. We would have to try to fool them by moving position. I sank into the sand and reloaded my last pistol. Looking over the dunes I saw that the blue line was longer. They had been reinforced. Of course, there would be a camp of soldiers destined for the invasion close to here. Then I saw the Chasseurs. They were moving quickly and would give the infantry courage. The blue line suddenly roared and ran to the dunes where we had been. I yelled, "Fire!" The surprised infantry were knocked from the dunes and took shelter behind the protection of the sand.

The cavalry were even closer. The sea was four hundred yards away and I could see that almost all of the civilians were off the beach. Just twenty remained.

"Right lads! Back to the boats. "Run!"

They needed no urging. We all knew what cavalry could do to infantry caught in the open. That day we were the infantry. My leg was really hurting and I had to grit my teeth to force my legs to move. I could feel blood trickling down my leg. I saw that I was falling behind the others. It could not be helped. I still had two guns unfired and, as I heard the hooves and the whoop of the horsemen I prepared to turn. The last of the civilians was being loaded aboard a small rowing boat and the surf was less than a hundred yards away.

I turned, just in time to see that three horsemen had outstripped the rest and they were thirty yards from me. I fired both pistols at the same time and then, throwing the pistols at the third I dived and rolled to my right. I felt a hoof scrape over my back. I quickly stood and drew my sword. Two Chasseurs lay dead or wounded but the third was wheeling his horse around and charging towards me. He leaned forward, eager to spear me with his sabre. The French sabre is not meant for stabbing; it is better for slashing and my sword was longer. I stood and waited. I lunged forward and flicked the end of his sabre away. I pushed hard and my sword went through his leg and pierced his horse. The horse reared in pain and threw the man to the ground. I ran to retrieve my sword and as I did so saw the rest of the Chasseurs. They were fifty yards away and the sea was a hundred from me. They would catch me before I reached it. I turned anyway and ran as fast as my injured leg would allow me. I could see the sloop ahead and then I saw four pricks of light. They were firing. I threw myself to the ground as four cannonballs whizzed just above my head.

I lay on the ground, dazed by the concussion of the shots and then felt four arms pick me up and haul me towards the sea. "That was bloody stupid sir, brave but stupid."

"Thank you, Sergeant Seymour, and for once I agree with you."

The cavalry kept a respectful distance as the guns of the 'Black Prince' sent enough balls towards them to prevent any heroics. Percy stood waiting for me on the beach. The civilians had all been taken off but the sloop looked low in the water and all of the boats appeared to be full. "Well, Captain Matthews. It looks like something of a stalemate. We cannot get off for the boats are full and the French cannot reach us because of the cannon."

"True Captain Austen, but if you notice the tide is receding and the 'Black Prince', will have to move offshore."

"Damn the Navy! Where are the transports!"

"It will do no good to berate them. We cannot do anything about that, can we? We know not what problems they might have encountered. Be happy knowing that we have completed our mission as ordered and the civilians are safe." A thought struck me. "By the by, what happened to the commandant?" Until then I had forgotten the fat naked rapist.

Percy pointed to the white, bloated body which floated in the surf. "The young lady decided he had served his purpose and she killed him. She seemed quite determined." He lowered his voice. "It seems he was fond of raping young women. She was not the first."

"But still, Percy; it takes a strong mind to stick a sword in someone." I hoped that she would not be haunted later by her deed.

"Ey up sir," Seymour's voice drew my eyes from the dead commandant. "It looks like they have decided to bring up their own artillery. And these aren't little pop guns either."

I saw that he was right. A Frenchtwelve-pounder had been brought up. She would pound the sloop and the small boats to pieces. Unless Jonathan sailed he would be left with matchwood.

"Sir, Lieutenant Commander Teer says he will have to pull out now sir." The young lieutenant in the small boat bobbed up and down with the eight crewmen. I recognised them as the ones who had been in the monastery with us.

"I know. Thank the commander for his valiant efforts."

"But sir, you can't stay."

I laughed. "I know that but until we learn to walk on water we will have to remain on the beach."

"No sir," He threw ten coils of the rope towards us, "grab the ropes and wade out. When you are deep enough the men will row us out of range and Prince will tow us."

It seemed a mad idea but then again the alternative was a prison. "Right lads, you heard the officer grab a rope and start walking."

I heard one of the men say, "I can't swim!"

One of the sailors laughed and said, "You don't have to swim son. Just hang on to a rope and kick your legs."

The salt in the water burned my wound but I knew it would also clean the wound and stop any infection. The men who were rowing strained as we began to float and kick our legs. Being the biggest I was the last to do so. Our progress seemed pathetically slow. I found I could only kick one leg. The water kicked up by Sharp was filling my mouth. I turned on to my back, still continuing to try to kick. I saw the gunners unlimbering the cannon. It would not be long now. As I rolled on to my front I saw that the sloop was closer now. Jonathan was preparing to sail. The sailors were swarming up the rigging ready to loose the sails. All of the other longboats, jolly boats and skiffs were secured and there was just us to go.

Suddenly I heard a boom as the twelve-pound cannon fired. The ball whistled overhead and travelled directly for the sloop. I heard the women onboard screaming. I waited for the crack which would signify that it had struck the small ship but, miraculously, the ball passed between the two masts. I heard the young lieutenant shout, "Come on you fellows row a little harder. The next one will take out the ship."

Then I saw the civilians in the little boat begin to move, "Shift over sailors we can give a hand."

As the extra arms pulled the boat began to move a little faster and I saw that we were less than fifty yards from the stern. That would be fifty yards too far for I was certain that they would fire again soon and the sloop was a static target. Then I saw the stern move so that the target became smaller. Jonathan had turned the sloop to present the smallest target possible. The commander was taking a risk as any hit would take out the rudder and leave the 'Black Prince' helpless.

The trick worked and I saw the cannonball skip along the side of the sloop and out to sea. A rope snaked out from the stern and fell just twenty yards from us. I wondered if the next shot would hit us. Suddenly I heard a sound like thunder as dozens of balls flew across the waves- they screamed towards the beach.

The young lieutenant whooped in a most wild manner, "It is the transports and a frigate!"

I rolled on to my back and saw the wrecked gun and dead bodies on the beach. That one broadside had saved our lives.

We were pulled next to the sloop while the other boats began to row towards the large transport lying half a mile off the 'Black Prince's' bows. More ropes were thrown down and the men were hauled one by one to the deck of the ship. I had been the furthest away and I was last to be hauled on board.

One of the civilians said, "I won't forget you, Captain Matthews. You showed bravery and courage today which makes me believe that we will defeat Bonaparte."

I was too exhausted to do more than nod. As I tumbled over the side the civilians all cheered me. The young lady I had rescued planted a kiss on my cheek."A true British hero!"

I smiled but inside I was picturing her killing the commandant. Clearly, she was not a woman to be crossed. "You are welcome."

As I tried to walk my injured leg gave way and the tourniquet snapped. Blood began to pour from my wound. The young woman ripped the end of her petticoat along its length and began to bandage the wound. "Move back and give him some air!" She was a forceful young woman. The man who married her would have his hands full.

The deck was so crowded that it was hard to see where the passengers could go. The two sergeants solved the problem by picking me up, "Thank you, miss. We'll take him below."

My arm was patted by all as they carried me through their ranks. I heard, "God bless you!" and "We will never forget you" coming from all around me. When we entered Lieutenant

Commander Teer's quarters it seemed strangely quiet. The two men gently laid me on the bed.

"I'll get something to bind it with. Joe, see if you can get some rum from the bosun. It will clean the wound."

I thought it almost poetical that it was Sergeant Sharp now ministering to me as I had ministered to him not so long ago. He must have had the same thought. He returned from the chest he had rummaged through with a cloth. "I will have to see if I can do as good a job on you sir."

"Don't worry about that Sharp. I am just glad to be alive."

When Seymour returned it was with a mug of rum and a small wizened man. "The commander sent Harry here, he's the ship's sailmaker and he sews up the men when they need it."

He smiled a toothless smile, "Aye sir and when they goes to Davy Jones I'm the one as sews 'em in their shroud with the last stitch through the nose." He chuckled, "Don't you worry sir, I'll use my smallest needle and the tiniest stitches. Why it will be neat enough to grace a tapestry." He nodded to Sergeant Seymour, "Give him a mouthful and then pour some on the needle. When your mate there takes off that bandage then pour the rest of it over the wound."

His authority spoke of confidence and skill. I swallowed the raw rum and lay back. "That's right sir, you relax. You'll just feel a couple of pricks." He laughed again, "And I don't mean these two sergeants either."

They both laughed and Joseph said, "Cheeky bugger!"

I closed my eyes and tried to relax. The rum burned a little but it worked for it numbed the pain and I genuinely felt nothing. I knew he was stitching but I felt little pain. After a while, he said, "There you are sir. I didn't bother signing it but I can do."

"That is all right Harry, and thank you."

For the first time, he became serious. "I think what you and the lads did was heroic sir. We showed these Frogs that they can't make war on our civilians. We are going to beat them. Mark my words."

After he had left I noticed the motion of the ship. "Are we underway then?"

Sharp looked out of the transom window. "It looks like it sir. I can see France getting smaller."

"Good. Check on the men. Make sure they are all safe."

Sergeant Sharp shook his head, "Let Captain Austen earn some pay eh sir? The lads are fine. Joe, here, will go and tell them you are all repaired."

When we were alone he shook his head. "We had no idea you had stayed behind sir. We thought you were running with us. Captain Austen played war with us for leaving you."

"Don't worry about it, Alan. It was my own fault and we came out of it well enough."

The door opened and Percy and the commander entered. Percy nodded at the commander, "I was just telling Jonathan here that you always cut things a little too fine for my liking."

"Actually Robbie I should apologise on behalf of the navy. There was no reason why they should have been late. Of course, as a lowly Lieutenant Commander, I cannot question our lords and masters but someone ought to. There were some really important people on board."

I nodded, "I know, one of them in the boat told me he would see that the event was mentioned back at home. Any idea who he is?"

"I think he is a brother of Spenser Perceval. He is an important politician. Some say he will be the next Prime Minister."

"Their rank doesn't concern me."

"And I see you had the lively young lady falling all over you."

"She was just a child. But she was interesting. Did you see her when she killed the commandant, Jonathan?"

"I did but I was too far away to stop it. He deserved to die but I didn't like the idea of Miss DeVere having that on her conscience." The sailor must have seen our expressions for he stared back at us. "You know her?"

"We served with her brothers. They both left the regiment under something of a cloud."

"Well I'll be blowed, small world eh? Anyway, you'll be pleased to know that, as we have offloaded the passengers we can sail back to Herne Bay at a decent speed and not the ponderous pace of a transport. Your men have changed into their uniforms." He pointed to a chest. "Your clothes are in there."

When we had both changed we went on deck. The coast of Kent was a welcome sight. We went to the rail and leaned over. I turned to speak with Percy. "A bit of a coincidence about the DeVere girl. Do you think it is the sister of the DeVeres?"

"It would make sense, Percy. All those people we rescued have money and she must be related in some shape or form. It is the name of a powerful family as we know. Her behaviour would lead me to believe that she must be their sister. It will be interesting if she is. I can't see either of them being very happy about what happened."

"Well they aren't our problem anymore, Robbie, they are in a different regiment."

"It is a small army, we will run into them again, of that I am certain."

Epilogue

It was some weeks before I was walking correctly again. Those weeks, however, had passed in a blur. Percy and I were whisked up to London where Colonel Selkirk was beside himself. "You two have surpassed yourselves."

"Sir, there were more than just us two. Commander Teer and all our men. Without them, we could have done nothing."

"Yes, yes," he waved the argument away impatiently with his hand. "I dare say they will get their reward but you, Robbie, are the talk of London. The story of a brave officer facing a regiment of cavalry on the beach and defending British women. Why the papers are filled with the story."

"Sir, it was a few horsemen, hardly a regiment."

"Modest as ever." He wagged an admonishing finger at me. "It will be your downfall. Anyway, the upshot is that the Cabinet is keen for us to come up with more ideas such as this. It is wonderful for morale. We are standing alone against Bonaparte this time but you fellows showed what can be done."

Percy shrugged as I gave him an exasperated look.

"Now we have to go to Westminster. The politicians whose families you rescued wish to thank you both." He saw my mouth ready to argue with him. "And there will be something for each of the men who went with you. And Commander Teer will be happy enough. He now has a frigate."

As we rode in a carriage towards the Palace of Westminster I reflected that they did not know Commander Teer. He would still yearn for the freedom of the 'Black Prince' but like me, his destiny was not in his own hands.

It was all very formal at the presentation, as one would expect. There was even a member of the Royal Family on hand. We were presented with engraved swords which expressed the gratitude of a nation. They had some gold on them and were far too fine to ever see combat. Still, they made a fine memento. For the men who went with us, there was a specially minted medal and, probably, more importantly, ten guineas for each of them. That would go down well, of tha, I had no doubt.

After the ceremony, Percy and I begged permission to return to our regiment. That was seen as a further example of our heroism. They all nodded approvingly. It was seen as the call of duty from brave officers. The truth was I preferred the company of my men to that of politicians.

As we stood, looking at Westminster Abbey and waiting for our carriage we saw, coming into the building, Charles DeVere and a man we later learned was his influential uncle. This was the first time we had seen him since his departure. I wondered if he had mellowed.

He stepped close to us and spoke so that only we two could hear him, "If you think that rescuing my sister made you acceptable in my eyes then you are wrong. The fact that you did not skewer her attacker when you saw what he was doing makes you just as culpable as he in my eyes. You will pay! And if any word of my sister's ordeal gets out then I hold you two responsible for that too."

With that, he stormed off. The older man tipped his hat and said, unaware of what his nephew had spoken, "Thank you, Captain Matthews. I am indebted to you for saving my niece. If I can ever be of service then let me know."

When we were in the carriage Percy put it into words, "Charles is unhinged. Thank God he is in a different regiment."

I remained silent. I had the feeling that our dealings with the DeVere family were not over. I closed my eyes. I could do little about his animosity. I knew I had done nothing wrong. I would just have to continue to do the best I could. I was still a Captain of the 11th Light Dragoons and for the first time in a long time, I felt at home. I had returned to France and witnessed the world of Bonaparte. I was now resigned to fighting the man I had once served. I could never go back to being a French soldier; I was now committed to the British army and my new regiment of British Light Dragoons.

The End

Glossary

Fictional characters are in italics

Trooper Alan Sharp- Robbie's servant

Captain Robbie (Macgregor) Matthews-illegitimate son of the *Count of Breteuil*

Colonel James Selkirk- War department

Colpack-fur hat worn by the guards and elite companies

Crack- from the Irish 'craich', good fun, enjoyable

Joe Seymour- Corporal and then Sergeant 11th Light Dragoons

Lieutenant Jonathan Teer- Commander of the Black Prince

musketoon- Cavalry musket

pichet- a small jug for wine in France

Pierre Boucher-Trooper/Brigadier 17th Chasseurs

Pompey- naval slang for Portsmouth

Paget Carbine- Light Cavalry weapon

Rooking- cheating a customer

Snotty- naval slang for a raw lieutenant

Tarleton Helmet- Headgear worn by Light cavalry until 1812

Maps

Maps courtesy of Wikipedia (William Robert Shepherd) *This image (or other media file) is in the **public domain** because its copyright has **expired**. This applies to Australia, the European Union and those countries with a copyright term of **life of the author plus 70 years**.*

Historical note

The 11th Light Dragoons were a real regiment. However I have used them in a fictitious manner. They act and fight as real Light Dragoons. The battles in which they fight were real battles with real Light Dragoons present- just not the 11th.

The books I used for reference were:

- Napoleon's Line Chasseurs- Bukhari/Macbride
- The Napoleonic Source Book- Philip Haythornthwaite,
- The History of the Napoleonic Wars-Richard Holmes,
- The Greenhill Napoleonic Wars Data book- Digby Smith,
- The Napoleonic Wars Vol 1 & 2- Liliane and Fred Funcken
- The Napoleonic Wars- Michael Glover
- Wellington's Regiments- Ian Fletcher.
- Wellington's Light Cavalry- Bryan Fosten
- Wellington's Heavy Cavalry- Bryan Fosten

A British force was sent to Swedish Pomerania in 1803 and in that year French troops overran Hanover. Many Hanoverians fled to England where they formed the King's German Legion. The KGL was the only force of Germans to oppose the French for the entire war. My use of the 11th is pure fiction.

Sophie Blanchard was consulted by Napoleon and there were plans to transport soldiers across the channel. My use of that element is pure fiction. Napoleon did begin a tunnel and you can still visit the workings. They are at Cape Gris Nez.

Although the French attack on Whitstable is fiction there are examples of French landings on the coast of England and Ireland during this time. The Royal Navy had such a tight stranglehold on the French ports that major invasion was unlikely however they did land troops. In 1804 Bonaparte was still thinking of invading and Nelson had not defeated the French at Trafalgar. I used this attack in the same way that Mountbatten used his attack on Dieppe in WW2 as a means of discovering problems with an amphibious landing.

The incident with the civilians is an interesting one. When the British declared war on France, there were some 3,000 civilians enjoying a visit to France. They were held by the army. Some of them were only repatriated in 1814. Others were repatriated earlier. I have created the scenario of a rescue by Captain Matthews. Others were obviously exchanged.

The buying and selling of commissions was, unless there was a war, the only way to gain promotion. It explains the quotation that 'the Battle of Waterloo was won on the playing fields of Eton'. The officers all came from a moneyed background. The expression cashiered meant that an officer had had to sell his commission. The promoted sergeants were rare and had to have to done something which in modern times would have resulted in a Victoria Cross or a grave!

Captain Matthews will continue to fight Napoleon and to serve Colonel Selkirk. The Napoleonic wars have barely begun and will only end on a ridge in Belgium in 1815. Robbie will be back to the same place he fought his first battles as a young trooper.

Griff Hosker February 2014

Other books
by
Griff Hosker

If you enjoyed reading this book, then why not read another one by the author?

Ancient History

The Sword of Cartimandua Series (Germania and Britannia 50 A.D. – 128 A.D.)
Ulpius Felix- Roman Warrior (prequel)
Book 1 The Sword of Cartimandua
Book 2 The Horse Warriors
Book 3 Invasion Caledonia
Book 4 Roman Retreat
Book 5 Revolt of the Red Witch
Book 6 Druid's Gold
Book 7 Trajan's Hunters
Book 8 The Last Frontier
Book 9 Hero of Rome
Book 10 Roman Hawk
Book 11 Roman Treachery
Book 12 Roman Wall
Book 13 Roman Courage

The Aelfraed Series
(Britain and Byzantium 1050 A.D. - 1085 A.D.)
Book 1 Housecarl
Book 2 Outlaw

Book 3 Varangian

The Wolf Warrior series
(Britain in the late 6th Century)
Book 1 Saxon Dawn
Book 2 Saxon Revenge
Book 3 Saxon England
Book 4 Saxon Blood
Book 5 Saxon Slayer
Book 6 Saxon Slaughter
Book 7 Saxon Bane
Book 8 Saxon Fall: Rise of the Warlord
Book 9 Saxon Throne
Book 10 Saxon Sword

The Dragon Heart Series
Book 1 Viking Slave
Book 2 Viking Warrior
Book 3 Viking Jarl
Book 4 Viking Kingdom
Book 5 Viking Wolf
Book 6 Viking War
Book 7 Viking Sword
Book 8 Viking Wrath
Book 9 Viking Raid
Book 10 Viking Legend
Book 11 Viking Vengeance
Book 12 Viking Dragon
Book 13 Viking Treasure
Book 14 Viking Enemy
Book 15 Viking Witch

Book 16 Viking Blood
Book 17 Viking Weregeld
Book 18 Viking Storm
Book 19 Viking Warband
Book 20 Viking Shadow
Book 21 Viking Legacy
Book 22 Viking Clan
Book 23 Viking Bravery

The Norman Genesis Series
Hrolf the Viking
Horseman
The Battle for a Home
Revenge of the Franks
The Land of the Northmen
Ragnvald Hrolfsson
Brothers in Blood
Lord of Rouen
Drekar in the Seine
Duke of Normandy
The Duke and the King

New World Series
Blood on the Blade
Across the Seas

The Anarchy Series England 1120-1180
English Knight
Knight of the Empress
Northern Knight

Baron of the North
Earl
King Henry's Champion
The King is Dead
Warlord of the North
Enemy at the Gate
The Fallen Crown
Warlord's War
Kingmaker
Henry II
Crusader
The Welsh Marches
Irish War
Poisonous Plots
The Princes' Revolt
Earl Marshal

Border Knight
1182-1300
Sword for Hire
Return of the Knight
Baron's War
Magna Carta
Welsh Wars
Henry III
The Bloody Border

Lord Edward's Archer
Lord Edward's Archer

Struggle for a Crown

1360- 1485
Blood on the Crown
To Murder A King
The Throne
King HenryIV

Modern History

The Napoleonic Horseman Series
Book 1 Chasseur a Cheval
Book 2 Napoleon's Guard
Book 3 British Light Dragoon
Book 4 Soldier Spy
Book 5 1808: The Road to Coruña
Book 6 Talavera
Waterloo

The Lucky Jack American Civil War series
Rebel Raiders
Confederate Rangers
The Road to Gettysburg

The British Ace Series
1914
1915 Fokker Scourge
1916 Angels over the Somme
1917 Eagles Fall
1918 We will remember them
From Arctic Snow to Desert Sand
Wings over Persia

Combined Operations series
1940-1945
Commando
Raider
Behind Enemy Lines
Dieppe
Toehold in Europe
Sword Beach
Breakout
The Battle for Antwerp
King Tiger
Beyond the Rhine
Korea
Korean Winter

Other Books
Carnage at Cannes (a thriller)
Great Granny's Ghost (Aimed at 9-14-year-old young people)
Adventure at 63-Backpacking to Istanbul

For more information on all of the books then please visit the author's web site at www.griffhosker.com where there is a link to contact him.

Printed in Great Britain
by Amazon